Silver-Tongued Temptress

by

Sara Ackerman

The Westby Sisters, Book 3

Silver-Tongued Temptress

Cover Art by *Debbie Taylor*

The Wild Rose Press, Inc.
PO Box 708
Adams Basin, NY 14410-0708
Visit us at www.thewildrosepress.com

Publishing History
First Tea Rose Edition, 2018
Print ISBN 978-1-5092-2015-1
Digital ISBN 978-1-5092-2016-8

The Westby Sisters, Book 3
Published in the United States of America

His forehead rested on hers, and he sighed.

"Of course I loved you. How could I not?" Silken heat caressed her cheek, and she looked into his dark eyes, almost obsidian in the dim loft light. "You were funny and fierce and loyal. I lived on your smiles until I saw you again. There was no one else but you."

There *was* no one else but her. Tension coiled in her stomach, but she refused to allow fear to prevent her from knowing. "Four years is a long time. Is there someone now? Have you found another?"

He groaned and gathered her in his arms, nuzzling his nose against her neck. "God help me, but no. There has been no one but you." Luka kissed her, a gentle meeting of lips which sent tingles skittering along her spine. She wiggled her arms out of his embrace and wrapped herself around him like clinging ivy on a tree.

"Take me with you."

"Don't be foolish. You're the daughter of an earl, and I'm—"

"You're Luka, clan chief and the man whom I love."

He stood and strode the short distance to the small, dirty window. Leaning his arm against the wall, he sighed. "It won't work. My life has beauty, but there are trials I would not wish upon you."

An idea so delicious and wicked as to make her blush from her ears to her toes intruded in their conversation. There might be a way to change his mind after all.

Dedication

To R—
My past, present and future

Prologue

The Atlantic, June 1810

She was dying. Consciousness, when it came, was riddled with fuzzy memories of searing heat, fear, and pain. Though sweltering flames no longer plagued her, she never wished to be as hot again, though she'd be lying if she said she wouldn't welcome some warmth. Shivers wracked her body, and her teeth chattered in her head. The Atlantic at night was frigid, and her charred captain's uniform did little to stave off the biting cold. At first the cool, lapping waves had been soothing and had helped take the edge off the worst of her discomfort, but now the water's chilling embrace cloaked her, urging her to concede to its greater power. A stubborn part of her refused to give in to the pull of its waiting, dark depths, yet soon even that small resistance would disappear.

Fear had abandoned her, too. For a woman who had spent years dodging death, she had never entertained the possibility she could die. How wrong she was. Yet with her own demise near, she no longer feared. Instead, she welcomed her release as one would an old friend, even imagining Death's shadowy figure slipping its arms around her body to cradle her, biding its time as she bobbed in the ocean atop a ragged plank.

Pain alone remained to remind her she yet lived.

Though an ache pounded in her side, it had long since ceased to throb. A dull twinge resided there, right under her heart, and with each passing moment, the ache lessened. The searing agony which had sent a trail of fire down her left leg had long since been silenced. Soon, all suffering would cease.

Sandbags descended on her lids, making it nearly impossible to stay awake. It would all be over soon, and she could rest for an eternity. Exhaustion numbed her to all else save her own pitiful plight. Her duty to her country, her life in London, her family—all were meaningless compared to the beckoning haven which awaited her beyond. Lights illuminated the distant horizon, though darkness veiled the sun, and she extended a shaking hand to touch the dancing orbs. They were beautiful. Her sisters would love to see them.

My sisters. They must know what happened to me.

The reminder of her sisters roused her from the inevitable descent to death, and she forced her tired lids to open. Gritting her teeth against a fresh assault of pain, she pulled out the dagger she kept within her boot's leathery folds. Her hands shook as much from the cold as from the effort, but she grasped onto the wooden hilt and held it in her hands. With painstaking care, she dragged the knife's sharp tip over the charred wood, every letter firm and precise. When she finished, she traced each word with her finger, reminding herself who she was.

Her job done, she rolled to her back and stared at the circling orbs, their light brighter and more intense than before. Consciousness was fading, and swirling darkness claimed her. Death, which had remained with her to the end, tightened its grasp, and she smiled, mouthing the words she had etched on the plank: "I am Bea Westby." Her lids closed on her final sigh, and the circling lights came closer. Distant shouts echoed, and rough hands grasped her arms, but she ignored them.

What did it matter? She was dead already.

****

An explosion rocketed the night sky, sending columns of red and orange flaring across the horizon. Luka Stefano watched the flames from the small island of Herm, some three miles off Guernsey's main archipelago, and swore.

"*Merde*! Fortier, Andres!" he yelled to his two companions. "Get the boat. Maybe there will be something to salvage, if we hurry." The ship had been compromised, and along with it, so too had her cargo.

His men hustled to the single-masted sailboat which had taken them from France to Herm earlier in the afternoon. He leapt into the boat, digging the oars in the sand beneath to dislodge it while his two men pushed the wooden vessel off the shore. Once she caught the tide, they vaulted into their seats and rowed. Sore shoulder muscles from a too-recent crossing screamed with each stroke he took, but he pushed through his discomfort. They had to reach the ship. He needed the money this run would provide him.

"Faster," he urged. The men grunted and pulled through the water, each stroke taking them closer to the floundering ship.

Acrid smoke enveloped them as they approached the burning ship, and he tore off a length of his shirt to wrap around his nose and mouth. His eyes watered and burned, and he gritted his teeth against the painful sting.

"Stefano, we can't see. How are we to find anything in this smoke?" Fortier asked.

"We're close enough. Use your oars to sift through the water. Whatever you find, bring it aboard."

Oar in hand, he poked the blunt edge into the dark waters. His men hauled in several smallish crates, and the small boat listed to one side. When the vessel righted itself, it bumped something floating on the water. He recoiled when his hand met with clammy human skin. Hefting his lantern overboard, he peered through the thinning smoke. A body floated nearby, draped across a sizable wooden plank. "I've found someone. Help me haul him over."

The three men tugged the unconscious man's sodden, scarred hide into the ship. They let him drop with a thud to the hull. "Is he alive?" Fortier asked, poking the seemingly lifeless man with his toe.

Luka pressed his ear to the man's chest and heard a faint thumping. "He's alive, though barely."

"What about the rest of the cargo?" Andres resumed his seat and grabbed his oar. "The smoke's too thick to find anything. Our lanterns do nothing in this haze."

"Leave the rest. Let's get out of this smoke and back to shore. We can come back at dawn, when the air has cleared. If not, the general shall be pleased we returned with a prisoner."

They took up their oars and rowed to shore. "Who is it?" Andres asked, jerking his head to their unconscious prisoner.

Luka grunted and pulled a clean stroke. "From what I saw of him, I'd say the captain, though judging by his size and the peach fuzz he calls a beard, he's a

4

sorry excuse for one."

"What will General Reynard do when we return without those supplies?"

"You worry about rowing this boat to shore and leave the general to me. Enough talking. Save your breath for your exertions." For the next half hour, they rowed in silence, the lapping of waves against the side of the sailboat being the one sound in the otherwise still night. As they neared the shore, the smoke thinned and cleared and moonlight glinted off something metallic on the injured captain's hand. A worn bracelet made with strips of old cloth tied to a copper face adorned the man's slender wrist.

It can't be. He ignored the unsettling sensation taking residence in his gut and concentrated on guiding the ship to shore. His two men jumped into the water and dragged the vessel onto the sand. Once on shore, he rolled the man over and stared hard, trying to see past the soot and singed facial hair. The smaller man's eyes fluttered open, and he was struck by their icy blue intensity. They held his own for endless moments before slumping closed again. Luka sucked in a breath. *But it is.*

"Stefano, we have the rest of our supplies. We are ready to sail."

He took one more look at the inert prisoner, lying near-lifeless and injured in the hull, and came to a decision. "Take the rest back to France." He hefted the captain's slight weight in his arms, ignoring the familiarity of the curves nestling against his chest. "This one is mine."

"You'll hang if they find you," Fortier argued. "The general will want to question this English *capitaine,* and he will see to it you are punished for withholding his prisoner."

"I took no oaths, nor do I hold allegiance to the French and their cause. The general will be pleased he no longer needs to pay for my services. Deliver the goods we managed to salvage, and tell the general I died in the fire getting his supplies. My death will be of little consequence to him, and there are many more to take my place. Take the clan and leave. Return to Russia. The wars remain far from there yet. You'll be safe."

"But, Stefano," Andres hedged, "what of you?"

"You forget I know this island well. When I am done with my own interrogation and have dispatched the captain, I'll make my way to Russia."

He held up his hand to stem any further arguments. "Go. Until I return, you are now the leaders of our clan. I entrust you with the safety of our people." Both men slapped him on the back before they hopped aboard, pushed off, and rowed away, leaving him standing on the beach with the captain in his arms. Though it pained him to leave his clan, he had more pressing and personal business to attend to.

The bundle in his arms moaned, and he studied his pressing and personal business. He ripped off the ridiculous tricorn and wig and confirmed his suspicions. When blonde curls spilled over his arm, a grim satisfaction replaced his earlier bewilderment.

It was she, and he had her right where he wanted her.

Part I

"The past has a way of sneaking up behind a person and biting him on the arse. But I'm sneakier and always bite first."

~Luka Stefano

Chapter 1

Herm, Channel Islands, July 1810

A bloodcurdling scream ripped through the tranquil night, jolting Luka from a sound sleep. He sat upright and grabbed the knife he'd stashed under his pillow. As he leaped from bed, his chest heaved and his heart pounded a sharp staccato in his ears as he surveyed the cottage's darkened corners.

"Put your knife away, you fool. It is her."

His grandmother shuffled out from the shadows, holding a candle, her long white nightdress enfolding her frail figure in its voluminous folds. The firelight's flickering dance illuminated her weathered face and accentuated the deep circles underneath her wizened eyes. "She suffers." She cast a glance over her shoulder to the opened door of the small room where she had been sleeping next to her patient. Every night for the last month she had slept there, tending to the woman's wounds and bringing her through the worst of her injuries.

Through the open door, he saw the woman's pale head thrashing on the white linen pillow, the moonlight illuminating her wan pallor and clenched jaw. Her hands fisted around the sheets, and she moaned. He shuddered, thankful she didn't scream again.

Mingled pain and fear made for a distinct and

chilling sound. Many times he had heard such a scream from men on the battlefield who knew their time had come, men who had been rent from their homes, thrust into alien situations, and forced to commit unspeakable acts against other humans. He was familiar with those screams, though familiarity did not breed indifference. They never failed to raise his hackles. Yet when he had first heard her panicked yells shattering the night's peace, a primal part of his being had reared up and protested. He had desired to protect her and slay whatever demons plagued her, but the best he could manage was to pin her to the bed while his grandmother tended to her injured leg's scorched flesh. She had thrashed, and he had been forced to employ more force, until his fingers had dug into her shoulders to restrain her. The next morning, angry bruises stood out against her bleached skin like mud on a canvas of white snow. The sight had sickened him. It was the first time he had ever marked a woman.

Even now, with the echo of her howl cradled within the shelter of these modest four walls, the restless beast prowled, eager to take on whatever torments haunted her, to thrash them to submission and allow her some measure of peace. "But why does she suffer? The stab wound has closed and mended without infection. Your own remedy has ensured she will not lose her leg. New skin is growing." He ran a frustrated hand through his tousled raven locks. "What ails her?"

"Not all pain is physical, Luka."

"I know, Grandmother, but her body is healing. Why won't she awaken?"

"Her mind is unwilling to accept all that has occurred. She will awaken when she is ready. Give her

9

time."

"I have given her a month. Already the summer grows long. If she sleeps much longer, travel will be near impossible. I must return to the mainland before the first ice." His people awaited him, and as their leader it was his duty to see them settled, fed, and protected. Absence from them made him uneasy.

"You are the one who brought her here. You will stay until she is well."

"I should never have fished her out of the water."

"Why did you?"

Grandmother had never asked why he had brought the woman to her cottage. She had taken one look at her injuries and beckoned them in, already rushing about the interior as she gathered herbs and other supplies to tend her wounds. Of course she had recognized her. All in his clan knew her. Lady Beatrice Westby, the wealthy daughter of an earl. She was the last person he should have fallen in love with, yet she had almost become one of them. At the age of eighteen, she'd been willing to run away and be his wife, to leave her world behind for his nomadic lifestyle. On the eve of their elopement, he had left her without a word, knowing his way of life was unsuited for a lady. He wanted better for her, though he suspected his motives were less altruistic and more governed by fear. Unable to comprehend a life attached to a woman who would have grown to despise him, he had run away, a callow boy unfit to love a woman of quality such as his lady.

Nothing had changed between them. He was a nomad and she a lady, but this time he stayed. Tonight was not the first time he had questioned whether he had done the right thing in bringing her with him. After all these years, doubts assailed him, and the apprehensive youth he had been returned to torment him.

"I need to know, Grandmother. She must know."

"You'd risk everything—your clan, your livelihood, your freedom—to keep her here?"

"If there is even a small chance, I have to find out."

"What if she is unwilling to cooperate?"

"I will make her see reason."

"I did not nurse her back to health to have you torture the poor woman. Once I perpetuated a horrible hoax on her and her sisters, and I vowed if ever I could do her a good turn, I would. She was brought to me so I could heal her and fulfill my vow. You will not harm her."

"I have no intention of causing her harm, but if she refuses to answer my questions, I will do what I must."

"Haven't we hurt her enough? It is evident she has not had an easy life since you two last met."

"Her struggles and her pain are of little importance to me. There are other, more pressing matters I wish to discuss with her."

"Better she had died in the water than be brought here to be treated with such cold indifference from a man she once loved."

"I promise you this—No harm will come to her as long as she cooperates."

"And if she doesn't?"

He remained silent, refusing to voice what he had been planning to do to her since finding her floating in the ocean.

"God help her."

"Maybe you're right. I should have left her. While you're praying for her soul, tell your God this—I will

11

discover what she has hidden, and nothing short of divine intervention will save her if she lies."

He flopped back on his cot and flung an arm over his face, a clear act of dismissal. She had no right to question his motives. His rights, denied for almost ten years, were important, not the pale, injured woman who had once stolen his heart.

His muscles tensed, and he resisted the urge to lash out. His grandmother didn't deserve his ire, no matter if she was protecting his former lover. Gnashing his teeth, he pushed aside all tender memories of their brief time together and focused his energy on his growing rage. It suited him, for in anger there was clarity, and one fact remained clear. She would pay for the damage she had caused him.

It was quiet for so long he thought his grandmother must have returned to the sick room and her post by her patient's side. He removed his arm from his face and jumped, surprised to find her standing by his bed, her small hands fisted and trembling. Surprise had him sitting back in alarm, but it was her voice, full of censure and sorrow, which pierced the black cloud of anger and shamed him into submission. He lowered his head.

"You should have left her alone, Luka, but we both know you never could." Turning on her heels, she retreated to the far side of the cottage and to the room holding the one woman he had never forgotten.

Chapter 2

York, England, June 1793

Lady Beatrice Westby, aged eleven, was the apple of her father's eye, the queen of the nursery, and the most popular young lady in the neighborhood. With her golden hair, piercing blue eyes, and heart-shaped face, she was beautiful, or so everyone told her. However, being eleven and in possession of her own mirror, she had looked in the glass enough to know it to be true. Beauty, though, faded, and Beatrice had long accepted she must have more to rely on than her pretty face and pleasing disposition. Aside from possessing one large, old-looking mirror, Lady Beatrice also possessed a keen sense of society's constructs and the obligations required therein. These rules held no interest for her, and it was with some impending dread she looked to the future and her own eventual presentation to her peers' midst. When opportunity to cause mischief availed itself to her, she accepted with alacrity. Having no wish to hurry along her childhood, Beatrice often found herself in unpredictable situations, and as her younger sisters followed where she led, her father's stern hand was not an uncommon occurrence on her backside as he meted out punishment for whatever her latest escapade had been. Her sisters, who were too scared to create mischief without her, adored her *joie de vivre*, as did all

13

the little girls in the vicinity. She was the undisputed leader, and Beatrice found she enjoyed the admiration of her peers. Thus, she had lived eleven years with unfettered adoration from all who knew her. Few could resist her patented blend of coy innocence, striking beauty, and unquenchable zest for life.

"Except this boy," she muttered. Peeking from behind an oak tree on the eastern edge of her father's property, she spied on the young fellow who stood in a clearing some fifty feet away, talking to an older woman.

The gypsies had arrived for the summer. Her father, the Earl of Westby, had long been hospitable with the Rom, who came each summer to York to camp in her father's eastern woods. In exchange, the Rom's chief gifted her father with one of their prized horses, bred for speed and stamina. Her father adored his stallion. In fact, she suspected he doted on it more than he did her mother. She suspected her mother knew that, as well, though she'd never be so impertinent as to ask. For several years, she had heard her father wax eloquent about his horse and the superior horseflesh the Rom bred. Beatrice, whose curiosity had been piqued, wished to meet them, and so she had snuck out of the nursery and made for the eastern woods. For the last half an hour, she had been trying to gain the attention of the young black-haired boy who had come to the clearing to assist an older woman with the washing. He failed to take notice of her. Beatrice did not like the word "failure."

It was a hot day, the air stale and oppressive, and she wiggled as the sweat pooled on her back. Failing on a hot day was so much worse than failing on a cool day.

At least if it had been cool, she would have been able to retreat in some comfort. Now, if she fled, the sultry June day and her pooling sweat would serve to further her dissatisfaction. She scowled at the boy, angry he had forced her to even contemplate fleeing.

The boy, several years older than she, noticed her and grimaced. He pointed.

"Who's the girl staring at me?" the boy asked, his voice carrying on the slight breeze to her curious ears.

He had noticed her! Bea stared at the boy and watched the older woman pull her curly raven tresses off her neck and tie it back with a purple scarf.

The woman jerked her head to the small copse of trees where Bea was hiding. "Her?"

"Yes. There is a girl not much younger than me hiding behind the oak tree. Who is she?" the boy asked.

Bea ducked behind the trunk and pulled herself farther into the tree's great shadow. A hot breeze whistled through the tall grasses, lifted her blonde curls, and whipped them about her head, betraying her hiding spot. With curls flying about her head, she was like a ruffled chicken and imagined how ridiculous she must look hidden behind a tree but with her hair visible to the world. Leaving the relative anonymity of the tree trunk, she stepped from behind it and watched the boy.

He tugged his linen shirt away from his skin and shifted on his feet. He fidgeted and squirmed, casting impatient glances to the older woman in the brilliant purple scarf, who, for all intents and purposes, was content hanging out her washing to dry.

The boy furrowed his brow and scowled at her. Never one to be cowed by an irritated male, Bea lifted her hand and waved, a grin wreathing her face.

If possible, the boy graced her with an even more derisive scowl before he swung his foot and kicked a rock. He picked it up and measured its size and heft. When his fingers folded around the solid projectile and he raised his arm behind his head, anger was swift to rise in her breast. Before she could storm over there and give the cretin a piece of her mind, a voice whispered in her head, *You'll attract more flies with honey than with vinegar.*

Her ire abated, if only for the moment, so Bea decided to put into practice what she had seen the ladies at her mother's card parties employ when they wanted to gain the attention of a young man. She bit her lower lip and looked at him from underneath her eyelashes before resting her cheek against the trunk to gaze at him with wide, blue eyes. Even though this flirting business made her feel like a ridiculous pigeon, she sighed loudly. *How boys are so stupid to fall for a simple sigh is beyond me.*

But the longer she gazed at him, the more agitated he became. In growing astonishment, and with some self-congratulatory praise for having mastered so many feminine wiles at such a young age, she watched the boy tug the hem of his shirt from his trousers and yank it over his head. He had the shirt halfway over his head when the older woman intervened.

"Luka!" the raven-haired woman scolded. "Keep your shirt on. There is a lady present."

Luka. Too fine a name for such a prickly, unpleasant boy.

"What lady? You mean her?" He jerked his arms toward Beatrice, but trussed up as he was, trapped in his own shirt, he resembled a puppet more than a young man. Bea stifled a giggle.

The woman helped him right his shirt before grabbing another wet garment, snapping it in the breeze and hanging it with the rest of the colorful clothes flapping in the hot wind. "She's the earl's daughter. Lady Beatrice. She's most likely curious and wants to be friends. Put your shirt back on and go talk to her."

He scowled and scuffed the dirt, his reluctance obvious even from where she stood.

"Do I have to, Grandmother?"

His grandmother grabbed him by the ear and twisted. "Go, boy, and put the rock down. There will be no throwing stones today."

Bea waited while he dropped the rock and skulked over to where she stood. Once there, he opened his mouth, then closed it shut, having said nothing. He kicked the tree instead.

"Aren't you going to say something?" Bea asked. "It's rude to stare. You do know that, don't you?"

"I…ah…"

She cocked her head to one side. "Are you slow?" She exaggerated each word to aid in his comprehension.

"I am not!"

"Of course you're not," she said, hoping her tone had captured her mother's blend of sweet condescension. "But if you were slow, I imagine that is what you would say, hmm?"

"Girl, do not speak to me in such a rude way! I am to be chief one day."

"You may call me Lady Beatrice, *boy.*"

"I am Luka Stefano, the chief's son. Do not call me 'boy.' "

The chief's son? Here I'd prepared myself for a boring day. "If you are the chief's son, you will know which horses are the best racers."

He squared his shoulders and raised his chin. "Of course I do. I know all the best racers because my father and I trained them."

"Show me." She peered up at him from beneath her lashes. "Unless you lie and are not the chief's son."

He pulled himself to his full height and puffed out his chest, though it was little more than bony ribs. "I am who I say I am. Come. I will show you."

She curtsied, and the great chief took her hand in his and led the way.

"You don't know it yet, Luka Stefano, but you are mine."

"What?"

She gifted him with a sweet smile. "Nothing."

Chapter 3

Herm, Channel Islands, August 1810

Luka awoke, sat upright, and panted, staring wildly about him. The lingering echo of Bea's sweet smile refused to fade, and for a moment, he was caught between past and present. *Where am I?* He searched for a familiar landmark to orient himself and dispel the lingering pull of his dream until his vision grew accustomed to the pre-dawn darkness. A crash and a roar penetrated the rapid flow of blood in his ears, and the familiar salty sea tang returned him to the present. He was in Herm. In his grandmother's cottage on Herm, to be precise.

He had dreamt about her again.

Raking his hands through his tangled mass of black hair, he leapt from bed and pulled on his trousers and boots. Last night's dream was vivid, more vivid than any other he'd had about Beatrice since fishing her from the cold Channel six weeks ago.

He fed the fire and sifted through the fading dream images as consciousness cleared sleep's fog and chased his nighttime visions away. This dream in particular, their first meeting, brought a reluctant smile to his face. At age eleven, she was every inch the warrior lady. Impetuous. Commanding. Brave. He remembered her daring as she sat on the paddock fence, watching the horses race about the enclosure. Though years and misunderstandings had separated them, he had never forgotten the simple pleasure she found from watching the horses run. It was what he'd admired most about her. No, this dream resurrected something new, something he had buried long ago.

At age thirteen, when he had been more boy than man, he had fallen for her, captivated by her beauty and enchanted by her wit and bravery. He had fallen in love with her the day they met, and he was afraid he had never stopped.

"*Merde*! This complicates everything."

The fire flickered in the stone hearth, its welcome flames dispelling the morning darkness. It did little to ease his frustration. He stormed outside to the small freshwater stream behind his grandmother's cottage, bent and scooped a pitcher full. Stomping back to the cottage, he poured the water into the teapot and put the kettle on to boil. He lumbered to the sideboard and removed the bread, cheese, and fruit from last night's meal, then slammed the food onto the table and sank onto his chair, stuffing a piece of bread into his mouth with considerable force.

"What foulness infects you this morning?" his grandmother asked. She tightened her shawl about her shoulders and removed the kettle from the fire. Angry as he was, he had missed its incessant whistling. His grandmother had heard and had awakened to tend to it. She didn't scold but took two cups from the sideboard and poured each one of them a cup of tea. He grabbed the sturdy china handle and gulped the hot liquid, scalding his tongue.

"*Merde*! Ouch!" He grabbed his ear where his

grandmother had twisted it. "What was that for?"

"Watch your tongue, Luka." She stood over him, anger darkening her features. "You may be chief, but I am your grandmother. You disrespect me with such language."

"My apologies, Aba. I had a rough night."

"More dreams?"

He shouldn't be surprised she knew about his dreams. Though he had not spoken of them, Aba knew all. "About Bea. Last night I dreamt of our first meeting."

"Hmm."

Aba. As inscrutable as the grave. When she was ready, she'd tell him her interpretations of his dreams. In the meantime, he was hungry. He pared an apple and popped a slice into his mouth before offering her one.

They chewed in companionable silence, which gave him the time he needed to rein in his temper.

"When is the last time you bedded a woman?"

The apple stuck in his throat, and he choked, coughing until the offending piece dislodged. He grabbed his tea to ease his cough and burned his tongue yet again. This time, he limited his swearing to an internal string of profanity which would have made a hardened sailor blush. When he had calmed himself and was certain he would not tell his grandmother to mind her own damned business, he said, "I'm not comfortable discussing this with you."

"It's been at least six weeks. Did you bed Widow Badi before sailing to Herm? She is an eager one."

The fat, greasy widow who traded her services for food and shelter came to mind, and he shuddered. "She may be eager, but I am not."

Aba refilled his teacup. "You need a woman. Sail to Guernsey today. Find yourself a woman or two. Stay a couple of days. When you return, you will be refreshed."

"I am fine."

She snorted. "Sure, you are fine. You have chopped enough wood to see me through two winters."

"Someone needed to clean the downed tree. I have nothing else to do while I wait."

"Luka, she has not awoken for more than minutes at a time. Maybe when you return she will. You can take her to bed if the women of Guernsey do not tempt you."

"I am not sailing to Guernsey, and I am not bedding a whore."

"Beatrice is not a whore."

"No, but I do not harbor any romantic love for her. It would be wrong to bed her when once I did."

"Why not go to Guernsey? The women there do not expect love."

He pushed his chair back and slammed his fist on the table, rattling the teacups in their saucers. Aba looked on with cool indifference.

"Because I do not need a woman! Now stay out of my affairs, you nosey old woman!" He stalked to his bed and pulled on his shirt. He grabbed his haversack, shoved some food into it, and stormed to the door.

She stopped him before he made his escape. "Do you want to know why she haunts your nights, or why you won't bed another woman while she lingers in the other room?"

He counted to ten and reminded himself strangling his grandmother would accomplish nothing save to release some of his tension. He smiled through clenched teeth. "No, but I'm sure you're going to tell me."

"You love her, and your conscience objects to what you have planned for her if she awakens."

"I do not love her. Not after what she did." He shuddered and suppressed the urge to bound into the sick room and shake the woman awake. "Any hope of us loving each other died nine years ago."

"Believe what you will, Luka. We both know it's a lie."

He grabbed his hat from the peg by the door and squashed it onto his head. "I'm leaving. I'll be back by dinner."

She shouted to his retreating back, "If you're not going to Guernsey, at least take your ax. You need something to do to burn through your foul mood!"

Chapter 4

York, England, July 1795

Beatrice was full of energy, the excitement of the day humming through her fourteen-year-old body. "I've never been to a fair before," she said, her eyes agape as she took in the bustling small town. Villagers milled about the town center, stopping here and there to peruse the merchants' tables along the main road into town. Behind the church, a makeshift ring had been created, and horses with their riders riding bareback were demonstrating their archery skills. A small band played in the town center, and couples danced to the lively tunes picked out on weathered fiddles.

"Never?" Luka asked. She shook her head and ducked her chin. Luka had changed in the nine months his clan had been in France, and she was not accustomed to his altered appearance. Taller now, he stood at least a head above her, nor was he skin and bones, either. Broad-shouldered and long-limbed, he had gained muscle in his legs and arms, testament to the hours of hard work he spent breeding and training his family's horses. He had let his raven hair grow out, too, and now clubbed it in back with a leather thong.

"We have a harvest festival every October, and my sisters and I are allowed to participate in some of the activities my mother plans for the tenants."

"Let me guess. You favored the dancing."

"Hardly. My favorite are the games, but Father will not let me participate anymore since I have become a young woman."

She stopped at a merchant booth selling decorated paper fans. "He insists I learn to curb my wild impulses and become a lady." Opening the fan, she fluttered it in front of her face, concealing all but her eyes. "Am I hopeless?"

His cheeks flushed, and he swallowed. "Hardly," he rasped, the deeper timbre of his changing voice causing a foreign fluttering to catch her by surprise.

Flicking her skirts, she dropped a shallow curtsy and waved her fan, ignoring the unease his response had created. "I thank you for your confidence. I shall try not to disappoint."

"It'll take more than a curtsy and some fancy fan movements for you to become a lady, Tris," he said, using his nickname for her.

"Pray, tell me, my roaming nomad, what is required to become a lady?"

"For one, a lady doesn't sneak off to a fair with an unrelated man." He raised his eyebrows, and she flushed.

"Oh, bother. No one cares where I go as long as I am home for meals. Besides, Papa likes you. He told me so himself."

"Did he tell you this before you snuck out the servant's entrance to meet me here?"

"You worry too much, Luka. No one will care." She stopped to sniff a cart with roasted almonds and ceded to impulse. Digging out a coin from her reticule, she paid the man and received a small bag. As she chewed her nuts, she prepared herself for a lecture. Luka gifted her with *the look*, which meant one of two things. Either he disapproved of something she was planning to do, or he was going to impart his wisdom, as was his right as the older of the two.

"I am an unrelated man, and you are a female in desperate need of a chaperone. People might talk."

"I brought Harriet." Bea pointed behind her to where her maid sat talking to a friend.

He snorted. "A fine chaperone she makes."

She grabbed his arm and linked hers through it. "I agree. If she were more attentive, we couldn't walk like this."

He extracted his arm from her entwining. "A lady is never forward with a gentleman. She never forces herself on a man or demands his attention."

"Gentleman? No ladies and lords or English and Rom here, remember? You're Luka and I'm Bea. Where we come from, who our people are"—she waved her hand in dismissal—"it doesn't matter. None of it does, at least not to me."

He said nothing but stopped in his tracks. They had walked the length of the village and now stood on the far side of the church, resting in the shadow of the great spire with the music and the vibrant noises of the fair muted and distant.

"I suppose you're going to tell me a lady cannot have an opinion, let alone voice it?"

"I would never presume to tell you what you can or can't say. My advice is intended as a caution. Other gentlemen with whom you will be expected to meet and interact might not be as tolerant as I am. I don't want to see you hurt."

"My debut is several years in the future. We can meet and carry on as we have."

He shook his head. "I'm sixteen now, which in my clan makes me a man. I have responsibilities to my family and my people. One day I will lead my clan, and my father wants me to be prepared."

"What are you saying? Can we not be friends?" How had everything changed between them? They had never lacked for conversation, yet their difference in class was one subject they had avoided. Now awkwardness hung between them. *Luka believes he speaks the truth. Our class differences will make continued interactions difficult, if not impossible.* The earth shifted and a gap opened between them where none had existed before. The separation cut as keen as a knife's edge.

"If it is possible, I wish for us to remain friends." But she heard the note of caution underlying his words.

She knew what he was saying, or at least what he was trying to say. Being a lady, or a clan leader, came with responsibilities, and neither could ignore them any longer. They were growing up, and in the twilight of their childhood, Luka was warning her they could not continue as they had in the past. Though she was nowhere near ready to abandon the halcyon days of her youth, she did not wish to interfere with Luka's responsibilities and duties to his clan. They both had roles to play, and in his own way, he was encouraging her to play hers.

Weariness wrapped around her soul as she contemplated a life of pretend, of fitting in with her peers, of spending nights upon nights in crowded dance rooms, seeing the same people over and over again.

How am I to bear it? Looking at Luka, the boy she had claimed as her own two years ago, she knew her answer. She would play her part until she was free to do otherwise. They both would.

A stone bench beckoned, and she walked the several paces to the trees that sheltered it. Sitting, she placed her reticule and unfinished bag of nuts by the bench's leg. "You have given me a list of what a lady must not do, Luka. Tell me, what *can* a lady do?"

He joined her on the bench and smiled, as if he guessed her purpose in changing the subject. It was not an unlikely scenario. Luka seemed to know her own mind even before she did.

"A lady must be sweet, kind, and considerate of others."

"Are you sure brainless and weak aren't on this list of yours?" She batted her eyes at him and attempted an insipid smile.

"Don't be impertinent. I wasn't done."

"Please, do go on."

"Above all, a lady must be observant and cunning, for through careful study of her opponents, she can control a room with a cool smile or a well-timed word or two. Never underestimate the power of your intelligence, Tris."

Their conversation played in her head, and though she was loath to admit he was right, he did speak sense. They could not continue as they had forever. One day soon they would go their separate ways, but it wasn't today. Plus, there were a few things she wished to discover before it happened. "Have you become clan leader yet?"

"Not yet. When we return to France for the winter,

I will assume more of my father's duties."

"Even if you are technically a man, you have yet to assume your place as a man in your clan?"

"Well, yes, but I don't see what relevance any of this has to do with—"

"If you are not yet a man, you are a boy, and as I have not yet been presented to society, I am not a lady."

Suspicion clouded his features, and he scooted farther away from her on the bench. "I suppose."

"Which means right now we're a boy and a girl. Friends."

"Friends."

"As friends, I could, oh, hold your hand." She grabbed his hand in hers.

"A lady does not—"

"We have established I am not yet a lady." She had to resist gloating when a look, not all dissimilar to panic, crossed his face. Panic faded, and he smiled, conceding her this one victory in a day fraught with change and disappointment.

He relaxed and squeezed her hand. "You are too cunning by half, Bea. You'll make an excellent lady one day."

"Since I am not, I could ask for a kiss, and you might agree to give it to me."

"I might?"

"Because I am your friend, and we're Bea and Luka." Her eyes drifted closed and a featherlight touch caressed her cheek.

She moved her head and their lips met. It was a soft kiss and lasted no more than a moment, but she was content.

"Thank you. I shall treasure your gift always."

"As will I." Removing his handkerchief from his pocket, he opened it and took out a small object.

"This is for you. While I was waiting for you, I found it at one of the merchant stalls and knew at once where it belonged."

He held the trinket and tied it around her wrist. Delicate bands of purple, black, and red cloth crisscrossed her wrist, attaching to a copper face etched with the letter *B.*

"It's beautiful. Thank you."

Raising their entwined hands, he pressed a kiss to her knuckles.

"My lady?" Her maid Harriet had found her. "It's time to go home."

Bea cursed her maid's unfortunate timing but conceded to her demands. The hour grew late, and she did not wish to land in her father's bad graces. "Goodbye, Luka. I will see you tomorrow."

"Tris, I don't know if it's a good idea."

"Nevertheless, I will be there when the sun comes around again," she said, using their familiar farewell in hopes it would soften his stance on their continued friendship. She waited with nervous expectancy for the remainder of their farewell, a tradition they had established when they both were children.

He arose from the bench and took her hand in his. "As God wills it, so let it be."

Tension eased from her shoulders as he closed out their ritual, and she smiled before waving and leaving the church, her inattentive maid in tow.

****

"Did you enjoy the fair, my lady?" Harriet asked as they walked past the church and to the town center.

"It was wonderful." She had wrapped her hands around her middle, reliving every detail of her first kiss, when she stopped and clutched her maid's arm. "Harriet, my reticule! I left it by the church. If I leave it there, the rector will find it and Papa will know where I've been today."

"I'll wait here, my lady, but hurry."

Though she couldn't run, she did speed along the road, past the musicians, and around the church. Luka had gone, but her reticule remained where she'd left it against the bench's leg. Thankful she had remembered, she ran toward it but stopped short.

In a recessed alcove, Luka was pressed against the stone building. His lips, the same ones which had kissed hers moments ago, were engaged in kissing another girl.

"Luka!" she screamed. "I'll never forgive you!"

"Bea!" he gasped and jumped away from the other girl, a busty, round-faced wench with fat, black ringlets. Her lips were red and swollen from too much kissing. His eyes darted back and forth, guilt rolling off him in waves. "It's not what it looks like."

"It's exactly what it looks like. You'll pay for this, Luka Stefano! Mark my words, you'll regret the day you met me." On a sob, she clutched her reticule to her middle and ran away from the shadows and their heartbreaking secrets.

Chapter 5

Herm, Channel Islands, August 1810

Herm's westernmost beaches were all but deserted this late in the afternoon, shadows hugging the coast as the sun sank further on the horizon. The fishermen had returned from their day's labors hours previous, and the men constructing the new hotel had retired an hour ago, and the muted hammering ceased. Only the miners continued their toil, and they were below the earth, unable to see Luka and what had transformed into his daily obsession.

The waves crested high today, the white foamy peaks churning their restless dance. He might have some luck and retrieve more than broken small pieces of driftwood. Ever since the night of the explosion, he'd combed the beaches for traces of *The Stallion* and her cargo. Early on, waves and the sharp current had deposited sizeable detritus along miles of sandy beaches. He'd collected most of it, dragged it to a secluded bay, and burned it. He wanted no one, neither the British nor the French, to suspect the islanders of conspiring to bring down the vessel.

He picked up a piece of driftwood and threw it on his small pile. "As if either side gives more than a passing notice to what happens here."

While the British controlled Herm, only Guernsey

and Jersey, the two largest of the Channel Islands, were well fortified with British soldiers, garrisons, and formidable gun batteries. Herm, an island of farmers and some fishermen, received protection from Guernsey and had held no real interest to the French for much of the war. With Napoleon's forces concentrated on the peninsula, a renewed interest in Herm's strategic location had prompted some French naval vessels to arrive in Herm's port, testing the British defenses. For this reason, Luka wanted all traces of *The Stallion* removed.

There was another, less noble rationale motivating the removal and destruction of any remains from *The Stallion.* He didn't want to be found by either the French or the British. Should either government investigate the explosion and search for salvage on the lesser islands, his life was forfeit. The British hunted him, and his recent defection from the French military ensured they searched for him, too. Had Fortier or Andres comprehended the peril in which Luka had placed his life when he urged them to leave, they'd not have gone, and he'd needed them to go. Yet his refusal to return to France and the regiment with which he was associated signed his death notice. Even though he'd promised his two clansmen General Reynard would not mourn his loss should he not return, the man was ruthless, greedy, and possessive. After all, Luka was the famed French Wolf, a mercenary who'd reputedly steal his own grandmother's bedclothes while she lay sleeping.

"As if the old woman doesn't sleep with one eye open. She'd cut off my fingers before I could lift her quilt's corner." He chuckled, half-suspecting his grandmother of starting the rumor in the first place, but his amusement was short-lived, for he faced a serious threat to his life. The knot of tension in his chest tightened, and he laid a hand against it, rubbing the corded flesh in hopes of easing some of his burden. It never worked, and the knot grew each year, burdening his conscience the longer he played this dangerous game.

When the war broke out, Napoleon had conscripted the horses of Luka's family, depriving his clan of their livelihood and consigning them to near death, for without the livestock, buyers disappeared, taking with them their much-valued coin. By the end of the first winter, his family was starving. The elders had experienced hardship before, and had assured him they'd survive on their limited rations, but it was the children, their tiny pinched faces and feeble cries, that prompted him to steal for profit.

His skills as a horse trainer transferred into a life of thievery with surprising ease. Patience, stealth, and persistence, three qualities valued by any horseman, guided him well as he contracted his first small jobs. Those early days he remained local, raiding nearby British encampments or stealing from supply carts on the road. His reputation for covert speed and discretion spread until he'd attracted the attention of General Reynard, a short-statured, beady-eyed man. The general had hired him for his exclusive use, joking Luka was much like a dog sent to fetch for him. Luka had pinned the shorter man to the ground, pressing his foot against the man's throat, and growled. After some tense negotiations, in which the general pled for his life while threatening to take Luka's, Luka had earned the nickname the French Wolf, a vast improvement over being called a dog.

With a steady income, his people flourished, and no one questioned their good fortune. Much like a wolf, Luka guarded his secret, only sharing his plans with Aba, unwilling to risk any lives save his own. When the general contracted him to steal from *The Stallion*, Luka deviated from his usual solo recovery tasks and invited two of his clansmen to accompany him. He'd made the decision *The Stallion* was to be his last job. Extra help would allow him to steal more, which meant a higher commission to see to his people's security.

The explosion ruined his plans for long-term security, though it proved providential in other ways. The general couldn't have known about the explosion; therefore, he would have no way to confirm whether Luka was dead, relying on Andres and Fortier's tale of what happened on the ship. Luka, who had grown to question who he was as a man, had found a way to escape the life of a thief and retire the French Wolf forever.

He stacked the last of the driftwood onto his growing pile and returned home. Tomorrow he'd return to the beach to search again. Each day he found less and less, but the repetitive task filled his days and occupied his mind. It gave him something to do while he waited for Tris to awaken.

Luka spied Aba standing in the doorway of the cottage, and his mouth dried.

"Maybe today is the day after all." Breaking into a jog, he flew across the sand, his chest light after months of worry and waiting.

"She is awake," Aba said as a way of greeting.

He tried to push past his grandmother, but she did not budge. A slight breeze could carry her away, yet he, a towering oak tree of a man, could not move her. "Move out of the way. I want to see her."

"Luka, there is something you should know."

"What? Has the accident addled her? Is she dumb?" He licked his lips and peered over his grandmother's shoulder, but it was too dark for him to see much.

"Not exactly, my boy."

He grabbed her by the shoulders and set her aside. "Let me see her. This is what I have been waiting for. I must talk to her."

"There is much you do not know." He ignored her, intent on the noises coming from within the sickroom.

"Luka?" His name on her lips was music to his ears, a sweet melody he'd resigned to never hear again.

He rushed to the dim room, the fading light of day doing little to penetrate the shadowy corners, yet her pale face, a stark contrast in the darkened room, was visible.

Taking the candle from beside the bed, he held it over her to better see her face. The small flame outlined the terrible ravages her illness had taken. A wan, sunken face with dull, pain-raddled eyes stared back at him, and he was hard pressed to find a trace of the Beatrice he had once loved. Her smile, when it came, chased some of the illness away, and he was reminded of the young woman she had been.

His brows wrinkled, and he cleared his throat. *How will she greet me?* Their last meeting had been passionate and filled with expectations. His note and craven departure had destroyed those hopes. She might demand an accounting for his actions, and though he dreaded the impending confrontation, he owed her an explanation.

Yet she smiled and used her meager strength to pat the bed in invitation. He'd wanted to remain aloof, standing in case she regained her sharp tongue and railed at him for his previous shabby treatment. Despite the clenched warning his stomach gave him, he sat on the end of her bed, a cautious distance away from her, and waited.

"Luka, I am so happy to see you. I was afraid." Her voice choked, and tears slid on her cheeks.

"What were you afraid of?" Conscious of her fragile health and tender emotions, he used the voice he reserved for skittish horses and uncooperative mares.

"I feared you had perished in the accident. When Grandmother told me I was the only survivor, a part of me died, and I wished I had not woken, not if you were gone from this world."

Confusion replaced concern. She did not seem angry at him. In fact, she had scooted nearer and rested her head on his shoulder. He had not expected affection or forgiveness, though he had wished for both.

"Explain to me how my absence would cause you such pain."

She cocked her head and frowned, her gaze having gone cloudy. "Don't you see? I would have died had you also not lived, but you are here, Husband, and I have never been so happy. You have eased my heart and filled it with gladness. We are together again." Her small arms wrapped about his middle, and she nestled her head on his shoulder.

Some pieces of this puzzle had gone missing, for

he was more confused now than when he had entered the sick room. His grandmother walked into the room, and he pinned her with a hard stare. Demanding answers from her had never worked; Aba revealed what she wished to when it was convenient for her.

"Aba, is there something I should know?" His command as clan leader, though, was unmistakable, and he would permit no evasion from her today.

"Had you stopped to listen, I could have told you your wife was confused and scared you had been harmed, but now she sees you are well. She is overwrought from the fright your absence caused her."

"But we're not—"

Aba cut him off with a firm shake of her head. "See to your wife, and when she sleeps, we'll talk." She left the room.

More confused than ever, Luka was left to comfort a wife he had abandoned years ago.

Chapter 6

York, England, April 1800

"There you are, you stubborn girl," Luka said, his head popping over the edge of the stable's hayloft where she had retreated after finding Luka in her father's front hall. He had been away for four years, and Bea had been ecstatic upon spying him. Luka had been less so and had dismissed her with a raised eyebrow and a cool, formal bow. She had asked him if they could speak after his business had concluded, but he had ignored her and followed the butler to her father's study.

She raised her head from the piles of fragrant hay, her secret hiding spot when she wished to be alone. "Go away," she said, horrified to hear her voice wobble and crack. "I never want to see you again!"

He ascended the ladder and stood over her, his shoulders and head hunched to avoid contact with the sturdy barn beams.

"You'll soon get your wish. After six long years, I have concluded the last of my business with your father and my other English buyers. There is nothing here to keep me, and I no longer have to fear for my life every time I enter the country. The one bright spot of this wretched war is that, with soldiers coming and going, no one pays much attention to one man ferrying horses.

Regardless, I leave tomorrow for the Continent and have no plans to ever return. This is goodbye." He turned to leave, kneeling to better gain a foothold on the ladder.

"What? No, you can't leave."

"Now you want me? Make up your mind, Tris."

"I never meant for any of this to happen."

"What did you expect would happen? You accused me of theft of an expensive animal. I had no other option. It was either extradition or hanging. Neither suited, so we left."

"Why didn't you write?" She grasped his upper arms and forced him to look at her.

"To say what? 'Sorry things didn't end well, but don't worry. I didn't take it personally when you slandered my name and accused me of stealing your father's prized stallion'? Not likely." He laughed, a short derisive bark. "It was better we cut ties altogether."

"Why did you seek me out today?"

He turned away to avoid looking at her, and hope pounded like a relentless staccato behind her ribs. "You care for me, don't you?"

"Beatrice, it's not as simple as you imagine. It's been four years, for God's sake!"

"I have never stopped loving you," she said.

"We were children. What did either of us know about love?"

"When you left, there was a gaping hole in my chest where you had been. I had lost my best friend and confidant. I nearly expired the month following your departure, but your return was the constant hope which kept grief from consuming me. The summer you left, I went to your campsite every day. For two weeks I waited, rain or shine, before I understood you'd not be returning."

"Tris—"

"With your absence permanent, I told myself I'd never love another. You are the only man for me. What we had was love. Maybe because of our age we were able to recognize it for what it truly was and not pass it off as some other emotion, so don't sit there and tell me my love was not real because we were children."

His forehead rested on hers, and he sighed. "Of course I loved you. How could I not?" Silken heat caressed her cheek, and she looked into his dark eyes, almost obsidian in the dim loft light. "You were funny and fierce and loyal. I lived on your smiles until I saw you again. There was no one else but you."

There *was* no one else but her. Tension coiled in her stomach, but she refused to allow fear to prevent her from knowing. "Four years is a long time. Is there someone now? Have you found another?"

He groaned and gathered her in his arms, nuzzling his nose against her neck. "God help me, but no. There has been no one but you." Luka kissed her, a gentle meeting of lips which sent tingles skittering along her spine. She wiggled her arms out of his embrace and wrapped herself around him like clinging ivy on a tree.

"Take me with you."

"Don't be foolish. You're the daughter of an earl, and I'm—"

"You're Luka, clan chief and the man whom I love."

He stood and strode the short distance to the small, dirty window. Leaning his arm against the wall as he looked out, he sighed. "It won't work. My life has beauty, but there are trials I would not wish upon you."

An idea so delicious and wicked as to make her blush from her ears to her toes intruded in their conversation. There might be a way to change his mind after all. She removed her slippers and, with trembling fingers, unbuttoned her dress. "You said it yourself. I'm fierce. Maturation hasn't altered much of my personality. I will come with you as your wife if you are willing or as your woman if you are not." In one silent swoop, she pulled the garment over her head and placed it on the hay. Next she unrolled her stockings and put them in a neat pile by her shoes.

"I will not damage your reputation by sullying your name with illicit behavior."

Shimmying out of her chemise, she padded over to him and wrapped her arms about his waist, resting her head on his broad, muscled back.

"Illicit only if it is not approved by the Church. Make an honest woman of me, Luka, and let us never be parted, from this day hence."

He shifted, the powerful twisting of his torso muscles bunching and smoothing as he turned to face her. Steel bands clamped about her waist. "What are you doing?" he asked, his voice a harsh rasp.

"I'm making it impossible for you to say no." She took him by the hand and led him to the makeshift pallet she had constructed from her cast-off clothing. Lying back on the hay, she held out her arms to him, refusing to be embarrassed by how she wished to express her love.

He swallowed, an audible gulp in the otherwise quiet stable. Shaking his head, he said, "You haven't changed a bit. You remain the most stubborn, headstrong female of my acquaintance."

She ran her bare toes along his calf and thigh. "Marry me, and I can torment you for the rest of your life." Her hand brushed the tense muscles of his thighs, inching higher and higher until he grabbed her wayward hand and growled.

He ripped off his jacket and shirt, fumbling with the buttons on his trousers. Pulling them to his knees, his boots halted their progression. For several minutes he struggled to rid himself of his footwear. "You're a menace. An hour in your company and you've got me tangled in knots again."

Her foot caressed his smooth leather boots. "Leave them on. I find it…stimulating."

With a muffled curse, he fell to his knees. She wrapped her legs about his waist and pulled him closer. "Was that a no? Or a yes?"

In one smooth stroke, he entered her. She arched her back and cried out from mingled pleasure and pain. He moved within her, his strokes hard and powerful. An unfamiliar ache took hold of her, a blooming warmth mingled with a sharp edge of passion. She moved with him, frantic to ease the terrible ache when he surged and stilled within her. He slumped atop her and she purred, stroking his slick black hair and back. Sunlight poured through the small hayloft window and shone off Luka's bronzed skin. He was beautiful, and he was all hers.

"It's a yes. I'll take you with me on the morrow."

Chapter 7

Herm, Channel Islands, August 1810

"Take me to Guernsey, boy," Aba said.

He whipped his head around and yelped. Aba stood on a platform above the docks.

"How did you find me?" With Bea's recovery coming in slow stages, he'd taken to hiding at port during the morning to escape Aba and his wife. Home was intolerable, especially as her head wound and subsequent memory loss had concocted this ridiculous marriage. Yet to her it was as real as the pounding waves outside the window. She adored him, and purred affection any time he was near. His conscience pricked for the deception, but to avoid causing her a more severe mental lapse, he played along and tried to be a dutiful husband.

A dutiful husband did not plot revenge on his spouse. This realization had soured his mood for days and only worsened when he abandoned his plan for good. Years of plotting had been destroyed by one of Tris's sweet smiles. He'd have to employ other methods to find the answers he sought.

"There isn't much on this island I don't know. Figured out where you were going weeks ago. You can't stop it."

"Stop what?"

"Don't play dumb with me. You've been up to mischief for years. As a grown man, you've a right to do what you will, but as a clan leader what you had planned for your woman was dishonorable, and you know it, too."

"Maybe I did. Nothing has changed. I will find out what I desire, but this time I'll use gentle persuasion."

"You're going to take advantage of a sick woman who has no memory?" She curled her lip and spit on the dock. "Years of stealing have hardened you and turned you into a reckless, callous man."

"I've done what was necessary to ensure our family's safety. Besides, Tris believes we're married. I'll be doing nothing more than asserting my rights."

"Rights you lied to have? Rights you stole? Your father would roll over in his grave if he were here to see the man you are now."

"Father is dead, and it's because of him I'm in this situation in the first place. I was too young to be chief, but there was no other choice. He's the one who died and left us. I did my best to carry on."

"Do you even consider the danger you place everyone in, should you be captured?"

"Their safety is my main priority. Why else would I take such risks?"

"There must have been another option. Stealing is never justified."

"We had to eat. You'd have us starve and be grateful for the privilege, but at least I'd have my honor." He and Aba had argued for years about his method of feeding the clan. She'd never stopped him, though her silence was censure enough. Even now, after having provided so well for his family, she judged him and found him wanting. He ran his fingers through his hair and bit the inside of his cheeks to stop a scream. She willfully misunderstood.

He missed her approach and flinched when her weathered hand cupped his cheek. "I'd have you remember how you were raised. You are not this man."

"Yes, I am, Aba. I'm whatever type of man our people need. I won't be a thief forever. I've told you before you needn't worry. I'm done with that life."

"Your heart is good, Luka, but as long as your intentions are dishonorable, you will remain a man divided."

"I'm trying to find my way."

"For your sake, I hope you find it soon. Beatrice is recovering and will want to return home. Whether you accompany her is not even your biggest concern. Two countries hunt you, my Wolf. What will you do then? Hide? Or accept responsibility for your actions?"

His head reeled, the implications of his defection sinking in. "I want to do what is best for me and our family."

"What's best is not always right, and until you see the difference, I can't stay. Please, take me to Guernsey."

Once her mind was decided, there was no dissuading her, so he took her carpetbag and loaded it into the hull before helping his grandmother into the boat. Taking his place at the oars, he stroked, the physical exertion doing much to clear his head. Once clear, he panicked, for in his haste to do his grandmother's bidding, he'd forgotten his wife.

"What of Tris? Who is tending her today?"

"I cast a spell and put her in a deep sleep. She'll

awaken tomorrow morning."

His rhythmic stroking faltered. "You're jesting with me."

She rolled her eyes. "Of course I am. I asked a village friend to come up around noon to check on her and bring her lunch. She'll leave dinner on the sideboard for you for when you return."

The issue of Tris's comfort solved, and given Aba's ornery constitution, he anticipated a quiet journey full of loud, uncomfortable silence. He was right, and with nothing but the measured slapping of oars on water, he had all the time in the world to stew on his grandmother's reprimands. By the time they arrived in Guernsey, his jaw ached from constant clenching, and a small tic vibrated under his left eye. How soon guilt had turned to anger. All the while Aba had played the injured party, it was he who'd been slandered and abused. He was a man grown as well as a clan leader, and in no way did he need his grandmother's advice.

When he had helped his grandmother to shore, he waited for an apology or at least an admission he was somewhat right, but the old woman was ever contrary, and experience had warned him to avoid anything but cautious optimism. He was right to be wary. She turned to walk away, so he stopped her. "Aren't you going to apologize?"

"I've done nothing of which I am ashamed. I leave those recriminations to you. I don't want to see you again for another couple of months. Fact is, I might winter here, and you can get me in spring." She hugged him, a tight embrace which contradicted her harsh words, and walked away. Not once did she look back.

There was nothing left but to row home.

****

Moonlight glistened off the black water as Luka pulled into port, weary and depressed. He trudged home and hesitated when he reached the cottage, bypassing the comfort of the cozy home in favor of the warm August winds and crashing waves.

"Maybe the answers I seek are out here," he said and settled against a large tree. Though he doubted enlightenment was within his grasp this late at night after a full day of rowing, he had nothing but time to try.

"There you are."

"Tris?" He whipped his head around to stare at her labored progress across the beach. "Why aren't you in bed?"

She shuffled across the sand, careful to navigate around the debris of broken sticks and rocks the waves had brought with it to deposit on the shore. Panting, she sagged onto the ground, avoiding a serious bruising when he grasped her about the waist and pulled her to him.

"You shouldn't be out of bed. It's late, and you're still recovering."

Heaven help him, she snuggled closer in his embrace and nuzzled his neck with her nose. "I awoke, and you had not yet returned. Aba said she was leaving but told me you would be home in time for supper. Supper was hours ago, so I came to find you."

Even as he steeled himself against the warm temptation of her feminine curves nestled against his body, his arms encircled her waist, and he rested his head on her crown. "I don't wish you to hurt yourself."

He recognized the truth as he said it. He didn't want her to injure herself. She was too important to him. When she placed a chaste kiss on his neck and licked where her lips had been, he groaned. *Which means I don't want to hurt her either, so seducing her is not an option.* With one dilemma solved, another presented itself. *How am I to steer our relationship toward platonic waters when she is convinced we are wed?*

She laughed, a throaty-pitched murmur wrapping him in its heady familiarity. "Impossible. You and Aba watch me like hawks. I can't get away with anything, even if I wished to."

"Aba's gone now, visiting her sister in Guernsey. It's me you have to worry about, and if I have my way, you'll be chained to the bed most of the time she's gone."

If possible, she melted further in his embrace and purred. "Why, Luka, you'll undo all of Aba's hard work if you keep me in bed day and night. Most likely, though, I'll expire from all the pleasure you'll give me instead of any pain you might cause to my injuries. In any case, what a way to go."

The image of her naked and sprawled on the bed, her arms raised above her head, had him regretting his rash words, yet having said them the image remained. A tightening in his groin prompted him to shift her weight on his lap so she rested between his legs, her rounded bottom cradled on the sand. "Patience. You have been sick far too long and must regain your strength."

"Being a clan chief has made you too serious by half and has curbed your appetite for a little fun." He heard the pout in her voice. "We are married, and there is no harm to indulging in some marital exercise."

"Not until you are well." Convincing her of her continued weakness had possibilities for success. If he could keep her in bed convalescing, she'd not insist on any marital activities. *If I coddle and pamper her enough, she'll be too content to protest.* It was a solid plan and eased his conscience, yet the more his body became reacquainted with hers, the desire to drag her back to the cottage and exercise those marital rights became an incessant clamor, heating his blood and whipping it to a frenzied riot of need and lust.

He needed to get away from her, but trapped as he was, a tree behind him and her warm body in front of him, he had few options. He latched onto the first topic which came to mind. "What caused you to awaken?"

"I had a bad dream." As if sensing his retreat, she snuggled deeper in his arms and hid her head in his shirt.

"Do you wish to tell me about it?" Distracted by the fresh scent of her hair, now silver in the full moon's light, he played with the silken masses of her curls, disgusted with himself when the sensual pleasure of her silky hair caused his hands to shake.

"I remembered the day I found you kissing the village girl behind the church and how angry I was."

"Ah. What an unforgettable day."

She slapped him on the chest. "You mistake my meaning on purpose."

"I know."

"I was so horrible to you afterwards, when I…when I…"

"You were young. It's forgotten."

"Not by me. You could have been deported or

hanged. I should never have lied. I put you and my sisters in danger."

"Your father put your sisters in danger when he asked Aba to curse you." He snorted. "Ridiculous man. As if the Rom have magical powers. We are mortal the same as he."

"Yes, but we were unaware. As far as my sisters or I were concerned, your grandmother was capable of great and terrible magic." She shuddered. "Had you seen her as I did, you'd have believed as well."

"She told me about it, later, after we had left and were on our way back to France. She said the sky darkened and the wind whipped around the clearing. It almost had her believing she was magical."

"What a horrible child I was."

"Forgive yourself. Young girls in love do funny things."

"I'm glad you came back to me."

The night breeze swirled across the ocean, bringing with it the smell of fall and a foretaste of the winter to come.

"Luka? What's wrong? Do you regret coming for me?"

"Why do you ask?"

She twisted in his arms to look at him, her eyes wide and wary. "Everything has changed since the accident. I have, to be sure, but so have you. You're altered as am I. There are my dreams with such disturbing images. Sometimes I see—"

"What do you see?" he asked, his voice calm and gentle. *Maybe this is it. Maybe she has seen images of what I need to know.*

"Nothing makes sense. The images are jumbled

and of unfamiliar people and places. *Something* happened before the accident, but my memory has as many holes as Mother's Belgian lace. I'm confused and scared, and I worry you no longer care for me or with my injuries you don't find me attractive. I worry my injuries frighten you, and for this reason you have decided to remain distant."

"There is more to the story than this one narrative. Much has happened of which you remain unaware."

"You don't have to explain. Much has transpired between us. When you're ready you'll tell me."

"Do you ever wish I hadn't returned?"

"Why would I? Your return restored a semblance of normality. It gave me a reason to hope when there had been none for years."

"You would have gotten over me eventually and in time seen the curse was a fake. My return did nothing but resurrect anger and resentment for your father. You never were the same after I told you what had happened."

"He had lied to us. All three of us believed we had been cursed. Evie couldn't speak. Amelia spoke the most awful truths, and no one believed a word I said. If anything, your return brought back my sanity. You had died, or at least so the rumors said, my lie having killed you. For years, I mourned your passing and blamed myself for your death."

"My actions little deserved such devoted mourning. I compromised you, jeopardized your security, and endangered your welfare. Pleasurable as our joining was, I was older, and it was my duty to guard you against scandal. My God, even now you could be married to a man of your station, not injured and outcast from your family."

"My family? For years, my family perpetrated a cruel hoax, making my sisters and me believe God had smote us for our lie, while it was my father who had decided to punish us. In spite of my sisters' refusal to believe the curse had been false, at least I knew. With you there, I had a safe place and strong arms to run to. Even had you not returned, I was preparing to run away and find your family, to seek forgiveness and beg to stay with them."

"To what end?"

"To whatever end they needed me. I know I could never have replaced you, but I was willing to offer myself in service to your family. I loved them, Luka, like my own. I always have."

"I had no idea."

"But I told you. Don't you remember?"

He remembered all right. It had been midsummer of her thirteenth year, and she had snuck out of the nursery to meet him by the great bonfire. All night he and his family had laughed, danced, and sung. Tris had too, her cheeks flushed and rosy from the flames' heat and the exertions of dancing around the burning wood. Her smile had rivaled even the fire's brilliance, and he had fallen all the way in love with her. As dawn's early light streaked the sky and birds' calls echoed across the trees, he had walked her home. Before slipping in the servant's entrance, she whispered her secret in his ear. She loved him and his family.

But I didn't believe her. He had judged her too harshly and had dismissed her sentiment because a love between nobility and nomad was as rare as a rose in winter. In how many more ways could he hurt her?

"I regret nothing, Husband. Do you?"

Yes, there are so many regrets, most of which involve you, my heart, but I have caused you enough pain for a lifetime. I shall spare you my guilty conscience's confession. "You're right. It was for the best."

"Besides, if you hadn't returned, we'd never have come to an understanding, and I'd be rotting away on my father's estate, a lonely social pariah."

Unable to resist, he repositioned her in his lap, chuckled, and brushed his lips over her hair. "I doubt it. You were too vibrant and too tempting to simply waste away, alone and unnoticed."

Her body sagged and her head drooped. Sleep was not far from claiming her. "Hmm?"

"Go to sleep. I've got you."

And, God help me, I don't know how I am going to leave you again.

Chapter 8

London, England, May 1800

He had left her. Irritated, Beatrice scanned the crowded ballroom for a glimpse of her betrothed, Marquis the Lord George Darimple. The orchestra launched into a lilting melody signaling the supper waltz, yet her partner with his charming smiles was nowhere to be found.

Amused titters cut through the noise of the ballroom, and she turned to glare at the group of debutantes laughing at her predicament. They had undoubtedly seen her indiscreet search and found delight in her seeming unease. She turned her frosty stare on them, arched an eyebrow, and glared. One by one, the other girls blushed and studied the floor. There was a reason Beatrice was the Incomparable. Setting aside her golden good looks, svelte feminine form, and handsome dowry, she also had snagged the most eligible bachelor of the season after one meeting.

"Which is why it is so irksome he has decided to abandon me," she muttered.

Beatrice was accustomed to receiving what she wanted, and it was a rare occurrence when she experienced disappointment.

There was one notable exception to this rule. She hadn't been able to keep Luka, no matter how much she had loved him. She pushed aside the unpleasant combination of anger and grief and schooled her features to its usual mask of calm, cool hauteur. Since Luka's defection almost a month ago, it was a useful look to hide her emotions, which were too raw and exposed to bring out and examine. Hence the look. It spoke of confidence and bored disdain, and though neither lurked inside, it had served its purpose of reminding those silly, simpering debs who controlled this ballroom.

"There you are, my lady."

Bea controlled her anger and resisted the urge to spin and chide her betrothed for his ill-timed withdrawal from her side. "I didn't know I was missing," she said, placing her gloved hand upon his superfine navy-blue coat and gifting him with a placid smile.

His blue eyes twinkled, though a hint of a challenge lurked in their steely depths. "You did," he whispered. "You noticed and worried I'd leave you standing here without a partner."

"Maybe, though the loss of a dance is of little consequence when compared to the absence of your company." The sweet smile she forced to her lips about gagged her, but she had a role to play, and appeasing her betrothed was of utmost importance.

"So you missed me, my lady, did you?" He took her in his arms and spun her onto the ballroom floor, and she gave herself over to the lilting rhythm of the waltz.

"Perhaps I did. Perhaps I didn't," she said, teasing, and winced when his hand tightened around hers. He twirled her to the exterior of the ballroom and out onto a balcony which led to a walkway through their host's fragrant gardens.

"What are we doing out here?" A nervous tremor laced her question. She fluttered her hands away from his, smoothed her skirts, and smothered the instinctive urge to run. For even if he were her betrothed and a respected peer, she bristled whenever he was near. In time, she'd grow accustomed to him, and this unsettling suspicion he was more beast than man would fade.

At least I hope it will.

"I left to arrange a surprise for you."

"A surprise? How delightful. Will you show me?" Her response had pleased Lord Darimple, for he smiled at her delight and took her hand with more consideration than he had on the ballroom floor.

"Come, I'll show you." He led her to the balcony steps and through the garden. They stopped upon reaching a small gazebo tucked behind a grove of trees on the far edge of their host's property. Someone had taken the time to light the sconces, and the warm firelight cast a cheery glow on the small building.

"It's lovely." They entered the gazebo, and Bea took in the scene—Champagne on ice, two glasses, and a blanket adorned the floor.

"What's all this?" True nervousness beset her. Even though this was what she had hoped would happen, the imminence of the event's arrival did little to ease her fears.

He pulled her onto the blanket, and they sat. "Our betrothal was contracted with such haste, we haven't had much time to acquaint ourselves. Let's remedy our situation, shall we?"

"Won't people notice our absence?"

"We are betrothed. The other guests will expect us to sneak off for a little romance. Don't worry. I'll not do anything you don't want."

She took the proffered glass of Champagne and drank. "I can't see any harm in getting to know each other."

"What a good girl." He refilled her glass. "Let's make you more comfortable." Lord Darimple removed her gloves one by one and tossed them aside. Holding her hand in his, he returned her half-empty glass to her other hand. "Better?"

She swallowed the rest of her Champagne and resisted the urge to respond how she wished. When she placed the glass on the blanket, he loomed over her, his intent obvious even to a green girl of eighteen. He examined the modest neckline of her ivory gown and slipped a hand under the fabric to cup her breast. She hissed out a warning. "This isn't a good idea," she whispered as he kissed her neck, all the while fondling her sensitive flesh.

"Relax, Tris." She shuddered at hearing Luka's nickname for her on his lips. "It'll be over before you know it."

For good measure, she feigned a struggle, but he subdued her with his powerful body, pushed her back to the blanket, lifted her skirts, and entered her with one swift surge. Something inside of her ripped, and she bit her lip to keep from crying out in pain. When she would have thrashed and bucked, she forced herself to remain motionless until her betrothed was done. She didn't have to wait too long, for he gave a final push and collapsed on top of her. His retreat was almost immediate, and it brought swift relief to her limbs, which had been trapped beneath him while he rutted. As he straightened himself out, she rearranged her skirts, gathered her gloves, and stood, hands clasped in front of her, and he finished the repairs to his costume.

"There was hardly any blood." He straightened his cravat in a more respectable position. "Are you sure you were a virgin?"

She flicked an imaginary dirt speck off her bodice and raised her chin. "Of course I was, but I'm also an active female who likes riding. Mother told me there might not be much blood because of it." She lifted a delicate shoulder. "You may cancel our betrothal if you wish, but I speak the truth when I say I was a virgin until tonight in your arms."

She waited for him to probe further, but instead of anger or censure, he leered at her. "You like to ride, do you?" He slapped her on the rump and took her hand in his. "Once we're married, I'll make sure you have plenty of practice." Lord Darimple laughed at his own joke, though she didn't find it to be of particular amusement. "Come on. I'll send word to your mother you've taken ill and I'm escorting you home."

She allowed her betrothed to escort her to his carriage. She allowed him to fondle her breasts once they were in the carriage, and she allowed him to stick his tongue in her mouth before she exited his carriage. She even allowed him to linger at her door for far longer than was decent while he reminded her again to whom she would soon belong.

For someone who never allowed anything to be done to her, she knew herself to be acting with uncharacteristic passivity, yet she cared not. Lord Darimple was free to take whatever liberties he wished with her body; it no longer mattered. Her body was a simple shell which sheltered her wounded heart and battered soul. To those, she would never grant him access, and though her pride demanded she reassert herself and send Darimple home with a flea in his ear, there was another who was far more precious to her than her wounded pride or broken heart. If her body was the price for its safety, she would exchange her power and will to this man.

Once Lord Darimple had left, Bea climbed the stairs and dismissed her maid. Undressing with haste, she washed away the night's activities, pulled on her nightgown, and slipped under the covers.

No, she didn't love Lord Darimple, but at least his name would protect her child. God protect *her* if he ever found out it wasn't his.

Though exhaustion left her cold and weak, sleep, much like her sense of peace, eluded her.

Chapter 9

Herm, Channel Islands, September 1810

Sleepless, lust-filled nights, enforced inactivity as Beatrice's nursemaid, and constant worry her memories were forever lost had destroyed all but a small pocket of Luka's remaining vestiges of good humor. His irritation, though, had been honed to a knife's edge. Concern for Bea's welfare and the secrets she possessed had produced a brief tempering to the steely brunt of his displeasure, and for now, his frustrations remained sheathed.

This morning's walk to Herm's small port on the western side of the island had served to whet his anger until it was a fine-edged weapon he was eager to wield.

The walk itself was in no way upsetting. He journeyed the short distance to the port daily to talk to the fishermen before they left for the morning's catch and to see if a supply run from the main island had delivered news from his grandmother stating she was ready to return to Herm. In almost two months of daily walks, he had received nothing aside from the occasional tip of where fish were biting. Today, a letter awaited him. Not from Aba requesting he fetch her but from Fortier.

His people were in danger.

As soon as he spied the letter with his name written

in Fortier's unmistakable hand, dread had taken root in his chest. A letter was one omen his people did not ignore. While his clan was literate and could write, there was little need to do so when everyone lived and traveled together. On the rare occurrences when family was parted, the written word was used to convey situations of extreme distress.

"And where am I?" he asked the silent cottage kitchen as he hacked through an apple, the force of his slicing blow rendering much of the fruit to mush. "Thousands of miles away playing nursemaid to my childhood sweetheart."

When he had bid Fortier and Andres to take the clan to Russia, their safety was his primary concern, yet his instincts had failed him. He'd sent them to the heart of danger.

He cleaned off the remains of the mutilated apple and grabbed another, ensuring this time he did not destroy it in his anger. "All of them are trapped because I insisted on exacting my revenge to appease my pride."

His stupid pride. Had he set aside his vengeance, left Tris with Aba, and gone with Andres and Fortier to lead his people to Russia… "I'd have taken the same route and be as trapped as they are now." Hanging his head, he clenched the knife handle until his knuckles hurt. There was nothing he could have done to save them. Nothing his presence would have altered. Yet it was his duty to see to his family's safety. For this reason alone, he had failed.

Fortier cautioned him not to blame himself, stating it had been a matter of time for the war plaguing much of Europe to spread to eastern Europe and Russia. It was their ill-fortune to arrive at the peninsula in late

July when Russia was marching against the Turks. While circumstances looked dire, they had not been injured. They were, however, immobile and trapped between the two battling armies, seeking shelter in the hills and mountains cradling the region. He took comfort in knowing his family were safe in Fortier's and Andres' capable hands.

"Maybe Andres' hands," he said. Fortier had taken a great risk leaving the mountains to find his way to a supply ship heading west to Great Britain. "Who knows if Fortier ever returned to Turkey. Are my people safe three months later?"

In his letter, Fortier told him the family would leave for Russia when fighting ceased and one side had been declared the victor. For their sakes, he prayed it was Russia. They all knew the language and the customs, and if Russia won, there'd be regiments staying to defend the newly acquired territory and regiments returning home. If his clan attached themselves to one of those returning, they'd be assured of safe passage. Fortier urged Luka not to worry for their safety and to assure him they'd be waiting in their wintering grounds in southern Russia.

He pulled the porridge off the fire and stirred it one last time, thumping it into a wooden bowl with a grimace of disgust. He detested porridge, but it was one of the foods his "wife's" stomach could handle. "Yet even if she regains her memory today and I leave tomorrow, I'll not make it there before the first snow flies." Plus there was the added threat of warring armies across the continent.

"Passage on a supply ship would take too long. Fall storms, too, make travel by water more difficult." No matter how he examined the problem, he was stuck on Herm until the fighting ceased or spring arrived.

Though nowhere near resigned to this delayed timeline, he comforted himself with the knowledge Fortier and Andres were strong leaders who'd not endanger their people. Grabbing a tray from the sideboard, he arranged the porridge bowl and the plate of apples on it, poured Beatrice a cup of tea, and carried the tray in her room.

She was awake and sitting against the headboard, her blonde curls tousled from her night's sleep. Flushed cheeks and a sleepy smile declared she'd not been awake for long.

He put the tray across her lap, opened the curtain to let in the morning light, and sat at the end of the bed.

"I heard you talking to yourself, Luka. Is everything all right?"

"Nothing for you to worry about."

"I'm your wife. I want to share your problems."

White teeth worried her bottom lip, and her brows furrowed. She wished to help. His head acknowledged her desire to assist him, but his heart remembered her deceit. Sharing anything remained difficult while her memories remained missing and his were not.

"Please."

He sighed and gave in, never able to resist granting her desires, as long as they were within his means to give. This he could give her. "News from Fortier and Andres. They encountered some trouble when heading to Russia Seems the fighting has erupted there, too."

"Oh, Luka. You blame yourself for not being there with them. Despite your desire to protect them, you're only one man."

He'd feign indignity for her aspersions against his ability to protect had she not unerringly sussed out the heart of the problem—guilt over his absence and the knowledge his presence would have changed nothing. A decade's separation and a considerable head wound had not diminished her capacity to understand him and the inner workings of his mind. No one else had ever known him as Bea did. He'd all but forgotten how close they were, his anger over her deceit blocking all the blessings of friendship they'd shared.

"I wish to be there with them, but…" *I'm stuck caring for you because we have unfinished business.* Her uncanny perception, and his revelation that little had changed between them, loosened his tongue, and he spoke with uncharacteristic abandon. She remained ignorant of events past age eighteen. He dared not speak of those events, else he'd run the risk of causing further confusion and pain. For many reasons, hurting her was no longer an option. The time they shared as children was too meaningful to sully with anger or revenge. Besides, she'd not forced him to leave his family. *It was my choice.* He let the significance of this statement settle about him, yet he had remained quiet too long; she had guessed his meaning.

"But you're here nursing me. If I hadn't been injured, would you have been with them already?" Unable to bear the pain he had caused, he stood and looked out the window. "I can tell you would be. I'm sorry, Luka. I'm sorry I've taken you away from your family."

"You're part of my family, too, Tris. Your welfare is as important to me as theirs."

The smile she gifted him was almost worth the

time spent nursing her back to health, and a comfortable warmth eased away much of his anger. "Thank you, Luka." She spooned some porridge into her mouth. "You've been taking such good care of me. I'm much better." She swirled her spoon around in her bowl before setting it aside. A gusty sigh escaped her lips, riffling his hair and inducing a general uneasiness in the region of his stomach. Since the day they'd met, her sighs boded ill for his sanity and peace of mind. He'd best proceed with caution.

"What's wrong? Is the food not to your liking?"

"Oh, no. Everything is fine, but why haven't we…? Never mind."

"Why haven't we what?"

"Could I have a bath today? Aba allowed me a bath if my leg stays pink and the wound remains closed."

"A bath?" Her mind switched topics with alarming speed. Perhaps her scattered and often disjointed conversations had resulted from the injury.

"If it's not too much trouble."

"It'll take some time to heat all the water and haul it in."

"Never mind. I can take a sponge bath with water from the basin."

He was reminded of a discovery he had made several weeks ago on his daily walk, a small, warm pool, tucked in the surrounding woods. It was a short walk from the cottage. "You know what? I can promise you a bath today. Gather your dressing gown and a towel, slip on your shoes, and I shall escort milady there."

Though curiosity brightened her eyes, she obeyed and finished her meal in a trice. While Luka left her to gather her things, he tidied the kitchen and disposed of the scraps. Within moments of leaving the room, she was by his side, and the two set off across the island.

****

She sighed and rested her head against a natural rock ledge in the small, pooling spring. "This is lovely. However did you find it?"

"A happy accident," he said over his shoulder and whipped his head around to return his stare at the patch of wilderness sheltering the water. After arriving, he had helped her sit at the edge of the pool and had turned his back while she disrobed. Even now he remained turned away from her to afford her some measure of privacy. This was the lie he told himself to carry on the farce he remained unaffected and indifferent to Bea's presence. The reality of his forced isolation was much more basic. If he looked at her bare, golden skin and lush feminine curves, he might not be able to stop himself from falling for her seductive trap.

"Won't you join me? I won't bite."

You may not, but I will. He hazarded another glance over his shoulder and gritted his teeth. Water droplets glistened on creamy shoulders. Her head was thrown back, exposing the slender column of her neck. Honey blonde curls spilled over the tender skin and onto the tempting swells of her breasts. She stretched her arms over her head, baring those heavy mounds to his greedy eyes. The dampened curls wrapped around the plump flesh, and he shuddered. With her head thrown back, water droplets glistening on her bared neck and shoulders, she looked every inch the goddess temptress. "I'll stay here and keep watch." He congratulated himself, happy to note his voice did not crack or betray his intense longing.

She feigned a moue, or at least he imagined it was one. When he pushed the red haze of lust to the background, he noted she was not faking indignation. She was distressed, and unhappiness rolled off her tense shoulders in waves. "You no longer find me attractive."

Damn and *merde*. "I'm sorry, Bea." He moved from his watchful position nearer to the pool. Squatting on his knees beside her, he lifted her chin and wiped away the tears which had escaped to streak her face. "You are recovering. I do not wish to unduly tax you."

"It's not because of my scars? They are hideous, I know. I look a fright."

He remembered this side to her. Appearance had been of the utmost importance to her. She wanted to be the most attractive woman in the room, and any who dared to approach her brilliant, shining beauty was seen as competition, an enemy to be subverted and destroyed. It wasn't enough to be called beautiful. She had to be the shining example, the exemplar, the Incomparable.

"Your scars are not hideous, nor could you ever be."

"Why won't you get in the water with me?"

"I—"

"And why won't you touch me or sleep in the same bed as me? Why haven't you once kissed me or told me you love me? Am I so altered, or are you? Do you regret our marriage?"

Her questions came all at once like a rush of hot air from a blazing fire, but like fast-burning fire, her righteous indignation lacked substance, and she deflated. Sullen and sulky, she crossed her arms over her chest and turned her head away. "This was a mistake. I want to go back home."

"You've soaked for less than a quarter hour. Stay a little longer, relax your muscles, and I'll take you back home."

"No, I want to go home to my mother and sisters. You don't love me anymore. Maybe you never did."

How much of what she is saying would have been true had we eloped ten years ago? He'd left to prevent the possibility of resentment and eventual loathing, though in her current state of mind he couldn't be too sure it wasn't the loss of memory altering her personality. It was difficult to believe Beatrice, a spy and master manipulator, had ever pouted. She'd been too busy fighting for her life to worry about such trivial matters as courtship and marriage. He had to remind himself she was unwell and had regressed to a much younger time in her life. To her eighteen-year-old self, to be precise. She had ever been headstrong and spoiled, and he had adored her in spite of her challenges. Whatever had transformed her to a cool, calm intelligencer had happened after they parted ways. It was to this time he wished she had returned, yet without confusing her more or damaging her fragile health further, he had to convince the woman she currently was. It didn't matter if she had the body of a woman much older, her mind was telling her she was a fresh debutante from the schoolroom. This Beatrice was the one he had to appease.

"But of course I want you, my heart. Why would I marry you and whisk you away to an island honeymoon if I didn't? You are the one for me. My worry for your health and for the undue stress you have experienced in our haste to be away from England concerns me. Not a day passes in which I don't castigate myself for placing you in such a dangerous situation. Had I known the vessel we took from England was not seaworthy, I never would have arranged passage on it. As it is, the captain of our ship is lucky to have died in the explosion, because if he were alive, I'd give him reason to wish he were dead."

"Do you mean it?"

"With all my heart."

"This is the reason why you have avoided more intimate forms of affection? You are ashamed of your actions?"

Sure, why not. He had waved *adieu* to reality and common sense the moment he dragged her from the water. What was one more lie? "I am fearful of causing you more harm."

She sat there and seemed to be considering his words. A familiar determined purpose wreathed her face, and an inkling of dread took root in his stomach. Her determination had never boded well for him in the past. The last time he had seen it, he was trying to convince her why they should wait until they were married the next day before consummating their relationship again. He didn't have to dig too deep to recall who emerged victorious, and it wasn't him. She'd had him flat on his back in the meadow, her skirts rucked around her hips, riding him to completion, in less time than it took him to saddle his horse. He needed to proceed with caution.

"What's going on in your pretty little head, Tris?"

"Hmm? Oh, nothing." She smiled a secret, witchy smile, and his stomach flipped. "I am tired, though,

Luka. I am ready to return to the cottage. My limbs have gone all limp. I'm so relaxed. Help me rise?" She asked the final question while peering at him from beneath her lashes. A becoming flush crept over her neck and cheeks, and he bit back a curse. She was planning something, but without appearing churlish, he had no other recourse than to comply. He offered his hand and helped her from the hot pool, wishing he could blind himself upon spying her in all her slippery nakedness. Her expression remained innocent and blank as she stood there in the clearing, water dripping over the swells and curves of her full breasts and wide hips. He suppressed a twitch and bent to retrieve her towel and wrapper. When he stood and helped her don her wrapper, the innocent mask remained, though he swore he caught a glimpse of a wicked smile curling her plump, red lips as she watched him bend before her.

As if it were preordained, the sun broke through the clouds, and the slanting light filtered through the trees to ring her golden hair in a misty circle of light. Luka wasn't a praying man, but he'd taken up the practice after she'd awakened and their broken engagement had transformed into a marriage. Desperation had never entered into his conversations with God until the last several weeks, when her amorous advances had increased. For a man who was apathetic at most about a higher power's existence, he'd fallen to his knees countless times, begging for a sign, any sign, that his torment neared the end. God, it seemed, had a sense of humor, for instead of an angel of mercy to end his misery, He'd sent him a devil. A feisty, sly she-devil.

Through narrowed eyes, he glared, hoping to see

beyond her innocent mask to the mischief lurking behind. Angelic innocence stared back.

Oh, she's up to something, all right.

He'd best be wary, for if he weren't mistaken, his days of pushing her away were over. Luka's time was running out.

Chapter 10

London, England, January 1801

Bea was out of time. Though she could pretend the contractions which had heralded her child's birth early this morning were nothing more than indigestion, the popping noise and subsequent gush of water from between her legs she could not pretend away. Bemused, she watched the water pool on the rug in her bedchamber and for a moment didn't comprehend what it truly meant. Another contraction tightened her abdomen, dispelling any notion she had about disguising her child's imminent expulsion into this world.

She was in labor. "Right on time," she grunted as the sharp edges of pain spread out through her back and disappeared. "Let's hope for both our sakes, little one, this is the sole aspect in which you mirror your father." Luka valued punctuality, one of his more endearing traits. His punctuality meant more time in his company, an event she anticipated with eagerness each summer morning when she had slipped out of the house and awaited him in the stables. His ready smile and impatience for adventure had matched her own, and she greeted his timeliness with excited ardor.

Until now. This child's punctuality might be what condemned them both, for her husband, Lord Darimple,

73

wasn't expecting his presumed heir for another four weeks.

"Argh!" She clutched her belly and willed the contractions to stop, but another one followed on the heels of the last. Crying out, she fell to her knees.

"My lady, is it time?" asked her maid, Harriet, as she rushed into her bedchamber.

"The pains have been coming off and on all morning. I prayed to be wrong, but my water has broken. It won't be long."

Harriet knelt by her side and offered her hand. "Let's get you in bed and call for the doctor."

"Nay," Bea said. She pointed to the chair she had vacated before baptizing the rug and said, "Push the chair over." She rent one of her stockings and hit her shin with a sharp downward slap of her palm. Again and again she hit herself until her skin reddened and broke.

Harriet fluttered around like a ruffled chicken, and pushed Bea's hands away from her legs. "You must stop, my lady. You'll hurt yourself."

"That's the general idea. Push the blasted chair!"

Though Harriet's pursed lips declared her displeasure, she did as her mistress had bade her.

"Help me to my side." Bea bent her leg a bit behind her, the effort of so much movement causing sweat to bead on her forehead in spite of the chilly room. Raking her hands through her hair, she dislodged several pins and wispy blonde strands floated around her face. She screamed.

"Help! George, help me! I've fallen!"

Comprehension was swift to dawn, and the maid yelled. "My lady? Are you well?"

"Run out of the door and find George. Scream down the house if you must, but get him here," Bea hissed.

Harriet hadn't been gone for a minute before Bea's husband burst into the room, saw her lying on the floor, and rushed to her side.

"What happened, Beatrice?"

She grimaced as another contraction ripped through her lower abdomen. "George, I tripped on the damned chair and fell."

"Can you rise?" He helped her to a sitting position even as she shook her head.

"The baby is coming."

"It's too early."

A sharp pain doubled her over, and she screamed. "I am aware! Get the doctor!"

George helped her rise and get into bed before leaving for the doctor. Harriet had just stripped her out of her wet and soiled clothing when Bea grasped her maid's hand, desperation causing her to grip with more strength than was warranted. "There's not enough time," she panted. "The baby is coming now."

Her maid paled. "What are we going to do? I've never delivered a baby."

"Get the cook. She delivered the scullery maid's baby last month."

The next thirty minutes were a blur of screaming pain and mind-numbing exhaustion, but the cook had competent hands and a commanding voice, cutting through Bea's pain and giving her the strength to continue.

"One more push," the cook said.

Harriet held Bea's shoulders, and she bore down as

enormous pressure flooded her lower abdomen, followed by blessed relief.

A feeble wail pierced the room, and Bea sagged back against Harriet's arms.

"It's a boy, my lady," the cook said. She had already cleaned and wrapped him, placing him in Bea's arms. "And he looks like his father."

Bea stared at the dark haired, golden-skinned child and sent her cook a panicked look.

"Or at least I imagine he does, having never met the man."

"You need to get rid of the child, my lady," Harriet said, fear creeping in to color her words. "The master will kill you when he finds out."

Clutching her babe tighter to her chest, she said, "No. I can't send him away. He's all I have left of Luka."

"Give him to me, my lady," the cook said. "I can find him a good home. We'll tell the master he was stillborn and you instructed me to send him away."

"Never. He's mine. I'll leave if I have to, but I'm not getting rid of him."

"It's your funeral, my lady, but don't say I didn't warn you. The master is not a forgiving sort." The cook gathered the soiled linens and left, her parting words tainting the joy of her son's birth.

Bea slept, and when she did, her dreams were filled with secrets, forbidden love, and foreboding whispers of disaster yet to come.

Chapter 11

Herm, Channel Islands, September 1810

Sensual whispers caressed Luka in his sleep, and he shifted, flinging a muscled arm over his head. Soft, warm hands caressed his bare torso, trailing hot fire across his stomach to the straining flesh standing at attention below. When smooth fingers encircled his girth, he writhed, a groan trapped in his throat.

"You're so warm," his dream whispered. "And so hard." Nimble hands caressed his muscled arms and silky tresses tantalized his chest, increasing his pleasure until it bordered on pain. Hot breath fanned over his naked skin as liquid heat traveled over his face and neck and onto his chest. The fiery trail progressed to his torso. Decadent, moist kisses pressed on the taut planes of his stomach. He was going to burst. As he had for the last two months, his dreams left him hard and wanting. Luka surfaced from his dream, his hands encountering silky soft skin, and pinned his dream-temptress to the mattress.

"What are you doing?" he asked. Moonlight played over her heart-shaped face, and her teeth flashed brilliant in the darkness.

"Good. You're awake," she said and wriggled underneath him.

He lowered more of his weight atop of her, and she

stilled, unable to move under his coiled, lean hips. "I'll ask you again. What are you doing?"

"It's obvious, my husband. I failed to find sleep by myself. I came to seek your comfort."

"You are naked."

"As are you."

"I don't want you in my bed."

She squirmed, and triumph flashed across her face as she encountered hard resistance, the traitorous evidence of how much he did want her in his bed.

"Liar."

God would reward him when he died for his iron will and saint-like patience. Though if she kept wiggling underneath him, her pretty blue eyes soft with expectant passion, he was not going to be able to stop himself. He deserved a damned medal for what he was about to do. "You shouldn't be here."

She traced lazy figure eights over the warm skin at the small of his back. "Tell me you want me to leave, and I will." His muscles tightened and shimmied as her roving hands traced lower onto the taut globes of his buttocks. "See? You don't wish for me to go?" She bit the corded muscles of his neck.

He trembled above her and reminded himself of all the reasons bedding her was a bad idea. She was ill. She wasn't in her right mind. She had breasts like a goddess and silky thighs he wanted to part and explore. His head lowered and bridged the small space between them. Her breasts were upturned and beaded, waiting to be tasted. *A small taste will—*

Reality intruded when a soft sough escaped between her lips. *What am I doing?* With a forceful shove, he pushed away from her, jumped from the small bed, and rushed across the room. One hand was on the door latch while the other yanked up his breeches with surprising haste.

"Don't go," she pleaded, a slight tremble in her sweet voice. "At least tell me what I have done to turn you from me. I...I promise I'll do anything. Let me be your wife."

Her plaintive plea had stopped his departure, though he remained turned away from her, his shoulders stiff and unyielding. He bowed his head. "You don't know what you're asking." A warm, naked woman pressed against his back, and he stiffened. His endurance for her sweet charms was almost to the breaking point. He needed to leave. Maybe if he rowed to Guernsey, he'd bed one of those whores his grandmother had urged him to find. Maybe he'd jump off a cliff and dash his head against some rocks. Maybe—

She rubbed against him like a cat. "I want you. I know what I agreed to when we married. Don't you want the same? Ever since I've awakened, you have shown me no affection, given me no embraces aside from those I've had to beg for. I wish to be with you, to have your warmth by me as I fall to sleep and your arms around me when I awaken."

He shuddered in her arms, defeat resting heavy upon his shoulders. In his haste to save her from herself, he had wounded her pride and damaged her confidence. Once he had promised to never hurt her, and he had done nothing else since rescuing her. Exhaustion, guilt, and arousal created a potent, and albeit confusing, turmoil within himself. Resigned to capitulation by his own conscience, he turned and wrapped his arms about her, resting his head on her crown. She melted in his embrace, and tears dampened his chest. His arms tightened. "Shh. I'm sorry, Tris," he murmured. "Ever since your accident I've been consumed with worry for you and your health. Your strength is returning, true, but I don't wish to tax you with any unwanted attentions."

"They wouldn't be unwanted, Luka."

"Maybe not, but hurting you is unacceptable. Until I know you are one hundred percent better, we will abstain."

Thus having delivered his final say on the matter, he scooped her up in his arms and carried her to her room. He placed her in the bed and pulled the covers over her body.

"Stay." Tiredness slurred her words. "I shall sleep better with your arms around me."

"We talked about this. Not until you are well."

She held out her arms to him. "I promise I won't ask for more than to have your arms around me. Please."

He sighed and ran his hands through his hair, his shaky hands, but he slid under the covers with her. She snuggled in his embrace and purred a sigh of satisfaction.

"I trust you to keep your word. No more sneaking in my bed naked, and no more trying to seduce me."

"I wouldn't dream of it."

****

She had been asleep for hours, curled next to him like a cat in the sunshine. How she could sleep was beyond him. He could not. She had trapped him neatly in bed with her after all. Now, with her warm body, *her warm, naked body,* next to him, he was right where he didn't want to be. Trying to be noble hadn't worked. She took offense to his distance. What else could he do?

When she nestled closer to him, his body stiffened and throbbed against the rounded temptation of her bared bottom. He groaned and rolled to his back, hoping she stayed put, but she rolled with him and turned so her full breasts rubbed against his chest.

Lord, this is going to be an endless night. She flung a slender calf over his legs, and he swore he heard her purr.

If he didn't disentangle himself soon, things were going to get a lot worse before they got better. She'd regain her memories soon and remember they weren't married. If he made love to her before that time, to allow her to do her "wifely duties," she'd hate him forever and take her secrets to the grave.

She had no idea what it meant to be a wife. He'd heard she'd married after he left and broken their engagement, but also that it hadn't lasted more than two years. Bea's brief society marriage had not prepared her to be a wife, let alone the wife of a clan leader. *Maybe if she has to be a wife, I'll finally get some sleep.* A chieftain's wife had a difficult job. Full days of tending to various familial needs would sap anyone's strength, let alone someone recovering from a serious illness. While his family was not here, he was. *She will be my wife. More importantly, it is my duty to show her exactly what being a wife entails.*

Bea wrapped an arm about his waist, and he kissed her head. "Tomorrow, my dear, you shall find out what it means to be married to me."

Chapter 12

London, England, January 1801

Bea jerked awake, disoriented from labor's exhausting toll. Her husband loomed near the bed, expressionless save for the tight lines about his mouth.

"The baby," she whispered. "Where's my baby?" She pawed through the covers hoping to find his little dark head.

"Your baby is gone."

"George?" She scanned the dim room until finding him seated in a chair near the window. "Where's the baby?"

"The baby? You mean *my heir*?"

"What's going on, George? You're scaring me."

He stalked to where she sat in the bed and paced beside her. "Imagine my elation when I returned with the doctor to find you had delivered our child. Imagine how my elation turned to surprise when I spied a thatch of dark hair and golden skin."

"I can explain."

"How you tried to foist your bastard off on me?"

"Where is he? What did you do to him?" She clutched at his hands, but he pushed her away.

"Dead," he spat.

"Did you kill him?"

He uttered a harsh laugh. "As if I'd stoop to

sullying my hands with mongrel blood. He was dead in your arms when I found you asleep."

"You're lying."

"Consider yourself lucky I'm not, for if he'd lived, I'd have shown him no mercy."

Bea wrapped her empty arms around her middle and rocked, hoping the movement would help ease the sharp edge of pain and grief. "And now?" she whispered, her head bowed.

"You'll receive none from me. The life you've enjoyed as my wife? It's over."

Chapter 13

Herm, Channel Islands, September 1810

Today Bea's invalid status ended and she learned what it meant to be his wife. Luka entered her bedchamber, snapped open the curtains at the ungodly hour of dawn, and rocked the mattress with his foot until Bea stirred. "Good. You're awake."

Bea moaned. "What time is it, Luka?"

"Time for you to make my breakfast."

She rolled over and pulled the sheets over her head. "Go away. I'm tired."

He ripped the covers away from her and slapped her rear.

She squealed.

"Get out of bed! You've lain abed long enough. It's already nearing seven o'clock, and there's much to do today."

She scrambled to find the sheets and clutched them to her bosom. Pushing her riotous curls away from her face, she leveled him a hot glare.

"Luka! What are you doing?"

"I've told you it's time to get up."

"Get up?"

"To make my breakfast?"

"I'm sorry. Your breakfast?"

"Are you going to repeat everything I say? Yes, my

breakfast. I'm famished."

She scooted closer to the headboard. "What's changed? Last night you were incensed with me. Today, you are annoyed but no longer angry. Your moods change faster than a summer storm, and my head aches from trying to stay abreast of your current frame of mind. What has whipped you into a foamy lather today, my nomad lord?"

He folded his large arms over his chest and stood with legs apart, using his power and size to intimidate her. "I'm hungry."

Bea blinked, doing an admirable impression of an owl, yet she remained in bed.

"Well?"

She licked her lips. "I—but of course, Luka. I shall cook your breakfast. You've cared for me all these weeks. Please have patience with me. I have had little experience in the domestic arts."

"Even you can slice bread and fruit and put on a pot to boil."

"Thank you for the encouragement. I will try not to disappoint you."

He tossed her a garment, a simple, satin frock of sapphire blue.

"How kind, Luka. Wherever did you find such a gown? This can't be Aba's."

"Aba had this saved in a trunk for my sister. She won't mind if you wear it, especially as you won't be able to tend your duties in your night rail."

"My duties?"

"Cooking, washing, cleaning, mending. Your wifely duties."

She forced a cheery smile that did nothing to mask

her irritation. "Sounds like there is much to do. I should dress."

He didn't budge. She gave him a pointed look which he ignored, so she let the sheet fall to the bed. Sitting on its edge, she raised her arms over her head and stretched. He growled at her blatant machinations and shifted his stance to ease some of his burgeoning discomfort. "I will leave you to get ready. Don't be too long."

Striding through the door, he latched it behind him and repaired to the kitchen, doing his best to hold back his laughter at her muffled curse behind the closed door. He'd given her much to mull over. Now it was time to wait and see who came out the door: his dutiful wife or a spitting hellcat.

****

"Oh, God. What have I done?" It was dark, the sun not even a faint promise of day on the horizon. Luka crept about the small cottage like a thief in the night, anxious to be out of the house and away from Bea. His plan had backfired horribly, and now he wished himself on the opposite side of the island. He gathered the last slices of bread from the loaf his grandmother had made before she left, took several apples from the sideboard, and hurried to the door.

"Luka? Where are you going?" *Merde.* Tris had caught him. She set her candle on the table, scrubbed her face with her hands, and yawned. "It's not even light."

"Ah, well, I was going to talk a walk, see if I could catch a rabbit or two for dinner tonight."

"The sun's not even out," she said, and shuffled to his side. Laying a heavy head on his chest, she wrapped her arms about him. "And the bed is so cold without you."

"I'm not tired."

"Liar. You haven't slept a night through in over a week, thrashing to and fro. It's almost enough to make me lose sleep."

"I beg your pardon. I have no wish to disturb your slumber. You go back to bed, and I'll set out to find us some fresh game for dinner. I'll be back later this afternoon."

"This afternoon?" She raised her head from his chest to look at him in alarm. "But you haven't eaten. I can't send you out without a full stomach. I'll go change and—"

"Don't put on that dress." If he had to live through one more day of seeing her flit about in her infernal dress, he was going to go mad. The fabric hugged her like a second skin, all her luscious curves accentuated for his perusal. As she attended to her duties, the soft fall of skirts swishing about her legs and swaying over the rounded swell of her buttocks drove him mad. Creamy shoulders bared to his ravenous gaze day after day and the lush swell of her breasts spilling over her bodice had prompted more than one late-night swim. Better she stay in her night rail, her plain, virginal night rail, than for him to suffer through one more minute of seeing her in her damned dress.

"What? Do I look hideous in it?"

He cleared his throat. "No, you look lovely."

"Why can't I wear it? You gave it to me to wear when I perform my duties. Cooking is one of my wifely duties, isn't it, Husband?"

She had boxed him in there. "What I mean is, if

you are determined to cook me breakfast, don't bother getting dressed at such an early hour. You can cook as well in your night rail as you can in your dress."

Not exactly a lie. A change of attire won't alter her horrible cooking one way or the other.

He smiled under her sudden scrutiny and resisted the strong urge to squirm. Here he was, a grown man of one and thirty, squirming because a woman, not even a woman he was related to or tied to by marriage, leveled him with a no-nonsense look. Tris, though, had the knack of cutting through his posturing to find the heart of the matter. He imagined her shrewd intelligence was part of what made her such a good intelligencer in the first place. Sweat beaded on his forehead while he held her glare. Her lips pursed, and he resisted the urge to fidget. *She's on to me. Lord, this woman is too cunning by half. Maybe if I kiss her she'll forget about all else, and I can make my leave.* A sunny smile wreathed her heart-shaped face, which was clear of all former suspicion.

"All right. As long as I can feed you before you go, I shall refrain from pouting. I do so love my dress, but you speak sense. If you are eager to be off, I shall have to do without."

She turned and walked to the fireplace, her actions swift and sure as she laid logs in the hearth and lit a flame. A warm blaze soon crackled.

"Clever. You've learned the important skill of building a fire."

"I am as surprised as you." She bustled about the room, gathering the tea kettle and cups, her movements graceful in their efficiency. The ewer on the sideboard contained water from the night before. She grabbed the porcelain container and poured water into the kettle, her movements fluid and graceful. "Perhaps my father taught me when I was younger. However, it might be pure conjecture. If he had, though, it was the one time he deviated from his indifferent approach to raising children. His tutelage is the most likely scenario, for how else would I know how to light a fire? Not from my mother. She was of the firm position my sisters and I should master other, more important skills."

Her back was turned toward him, yet he heard the smile in her voice and tempered one of his own. She was always a wild one, shunning the more delicate arts in favor of untraditional pursuits like horseback racing, climbing trees, and running. Bea was a hoyden at heart. Even when he'd been thirteen he had known she was trouble. He doubted she had outgrown those tendencies, lost memory or no.

"It is a most useful skill. I never understood why you English insist on sheltering your young women. Everyone should know how to care for himself, whether it's setting a fire or cooking a meal. Needlepoint and how to wave a fan about is hardly useful."

"The next time I see my old governess, Miss Potts, I'll be sure to pass on your complaints, even if she is sure to disagree." She put her nose in the air and in a nasal voice said, "A lady must never do for herself what she can pay others to do for her."

"Miss Potts?"

"The one and only. Though perhaps after a week of eating my cooking you'd like a chance to tell her yourself what a lady needs to learn." She was stirring his porridge, a becoming rosy flush on her cheeks.

He shuddered, more from the reminder of her cooking than the banked fires stirring in his gut. If this week had taught him anything, it was to be careful what he wished for. He'd wanted to keep her occupied tending to household chores. If she were busy cooking or cleaning, she'd have no time to concoct new ways to get into bed with him. His plan had backfired, though he didn't know how. Even anticipating unmitigated disaster, he'd not foreseen her unabashed glee which occurred with every mishap.

All week he'd been served barely edible food; it was undercooked, too salty, or burnt. She served it all with a smile and a sassy wiggle of her hips, and he was helpless to do anything but eat or else risk hurting her.

There were times when he imagined a glimpse of his former Beatrice, a young woman who wouldn't have blinked twice at doing a task poorly in order to avoid doing it. In fact, on more than one occasion he suspected she deliberately sabotaged his food. Yesterday morning's porridge had been served too soon, swimming in milky-white water. The oats were chewy and, to add insult to injury, she had substituted salt for sugar. He almost choked to death on the first bite. After spying her trembling mouth and tear-filled eyes, he had spooned the offending mixture into his mouth with forced gusto, doing his best not to asphyxiate himself or upend the contents of his stomach onto the table.

He dreaded what she'd serve him today. "No, no, my dear. You cook well for someone who is learning."

She continued to stir his porridge and smirked. "Perhaps you take displeasure with my sewing skills."

After a disastrous breakfast several mornings past,

he had handed her several worn garments needing to be mended. She had taken the garments without complaint, and he'd left the cottage, satisfied she'd learned her place. When he returned later in the afternoon, she presented him with his mended clothing. A hole in the sleeve of his shirt had been sewn together with pink thread—and in a heart pattern, no less. His hose, having turned out a large, toe-size hole, had been darned to within in an inch of the heel. His little toe didn't even fit in the opening. Anger blossomed like a summer rose, and he'd opened his mouth to yell, but he saw those red lips of hers quiver and glistening tears dampen her cheeks. As anticipated, his anger wilted, and he had snapped his jaw closed, his outraged pride silenced. Now here she was baiting him with her deceit. *Oh, she is good. I see why she's called the silver-tongued temptress.*

"Why, Tris, your sewing skills are innovative and clever, but I suspect you already knew that, hmm?"

He held her gaze with his own, but she neither darted her eyes nor squirmed under his intense scrutiny. She had never retreated from a direct challenge, and she didn't look as if she was going to now.

"So you enjoyed the dainty heart-shaped lips I stitched on the rear of your small clothes, too?" Devilry had possessed her, for she no longer bothered hiding her triumphant smirk.

Why the sneaky little… He hadn't known about *that* particular surprise, as he hadn't bothered with his smallclothes for days. It had been too hot, and he'd been too eager to leave the confines of the small cottage. Most mornings he was lucky to have his boots thrown on before he escaped to other parts of the island.

"Your innovation knows no end. It's a shame they will be hidden under my breeches, for I wish the world to see how much my wife loves me. So much, in fact, she is too happy to kiss my—"

"Luka! You're impossible!" Dangerous fury contorted her features, and she advanced, brandishing the porridge-laden spoon in her hand. She shook it in his face, and he watched fascinated as a glob of hot meal dribbled from the handle to land in his lap. He removed the warmed food from his pants and popped it in his mouth, barely avoiding gagging as the saline porridge slide like hot, rubbery oysters down his throat.

"I'm not the one who has been deliberately making life miserable this past week."

"I told you I was not adept at domestic duties," she said, her lips quivering anew. "I've done my best." She lowered her head, blonde curls falling in a riotous tangle over her shoulders.

"Oh, stuff it." He pushed back from his chair and grabbed her by the chin, forcing her to look at him and face the havoc she had wrought. Defiance stared back. She wasn't sorry, not one bit. "Don't you shed fake tears again. I know you've been intent on botching every task I set you."

She wrenched her chin free and stomped to the kettle. Grabbing a bowl, she ladled out a heaping spoonful of the salty mush and slammed it into the container. She stomped back to the table and threw the dish and his meal onto it. "There. Are you happy? I have done my wifely duty this morning."

"Where are you going?"

She stopped and turned, fury contorting her gentle features to one of feral savagery. She was an avenging angel. With her blonde hair, she was a Valkyrie. A warrior. His girl had never been meek and biddable. He'd been daft to even imagine she'd accept his demands with anything less than ferocious noncompliance. Her muscles coiled and trembled, and her eyes darted to the butcher knife hanging by the fire. For a moment, he feared she might do him harm.

"To my room until you leave. I've had enough of you and your husbandly demands. If this is what marriage is, I want nothing to do with it. You could have hired a servant girl and saved yourself the trouble of providing for a wife."

"I didn't want a damned serving girl."

"No, you got yourself a wife to do the work for free. What a fool I was, believing you cared for me."

"I do care—"

She advanced and grabbed his shirt front and shook it. "Why won't you touch me? Even now you shy away from me. Am I so repugnant? Do I disgust you?"

"Stop being dramatic. There are circumstances of which you are unaware."

"Tell me why you won't love me!" she shouted. "We are man and wife. I want to be more than your maid. I want to share your bed and your life, but every time I show you any affection, you shun me. Why won't you let me be your wife?"

"Because you're not my wife! You never were and you never will be."

Her face blanched, and she flinched as though struck. "What?" Confusion clouded her features, and she shook her head. "Why would you say something so hurtful?"

"It's true. It's the first true thing I've said to you

since you've awakened. We are not married. The night before our elopement, I sent you a letter to break off our engagement. I left your father's estate before dawn and sailed to France from Portsmouth. I have not been back since."

She dropped the fabric of his shirt and backed away until her feet hit the wall. Her curls swayed with the force of her denial as she shook her head over and over again, her hands covering her face as if their barrier alone could spare her the awful truth.

"No, you're lying to me. We are married. I remember it."

"We were never married. I was too scared you'd grow to hate the lifestyle I led and your hate would one day turn on me, so I ran away. I'm sorry, but I left you almost ten years ago."

"You're punishing me. I-I'm sorry I wasn't better at cooking your breakfast. It was wrong of me to challenge your orders." She rushed to the fire and dumped out the hot porridge to the wooden floor. In a flurry of movements, she rushed about the cottage gathering supplies. She dumped water and oats in the hot kettle and stirred. "You're my husband, and I must do as you say."

"What is going on?"

"You are my husband, and it is my duty to care for you, as you cared for me. If I hadn't been so disobedient, you wouldn't be saying any of these things. I have to make it right."

She stirred the pot, her frantic movements causing liquid to dribble over the sides into the fire below. A sizzle and hiss filled the empty space following her rushed apology. This cringing, cowering, quiet woman was not his Tris.

What the devil is going on? She crouched her shoulders and knelt by the fire, stirring the mixture and rocking side to side. When a low keening came from between her lips, he rushed to her side, to fix the anguish his truth had caused.

He approached her as he would a spooked mare. "Beatrice, come away from the fire. You will hurt yourself." He placed a hand on her shoulder, and she flinched, cowering away from his light touch.

"D-don't hurt me, George. Please don't hit me. I won't do it again. I promise I'll be a good wife."

Alarm bells sounded. She was more disoriented than he had known. "I'm Luka. There is no George here. I won't hurt you. I won't let anyone else hurt you, either."

Her tear-stained face turned to look at him. "Luka?" she asked, her voice small and trembling. She moaned and dropped her head in her hands. "My head is going to break in two."

"Let me help you to bed. A nice nap will clear away some of those cobwebs. I'll have breakfast waiting for you when you awaken, and we'll talk."

She clung to him, waves of terror emanating from her small, trembling body. "Oooh, the fire. It's too close." Her hands clawed at the fabric around her neck, pulling, ripping the cloth away from her skin. "I'm choking. Why can't I breathe?" She gasped for air and tugged until the fabric ripped and draped about her shoulders.

"Are you remembering what happened to you? Tell me what you see."

But her eyes had gone blank, and she swayed like a

new tree in a stiff breeze. "I'm going to get your shawl and take you to bed." He seated her in the chair and raced to the room to retrieve her shawl, but when he returned the front door was ajar. She was gone.

Biting back a curse, he took off after her in hot pursuit.

Chapter 14

London, England, May 1801

Bea had known better than to run. George had told her every time he caught her she was not to run. Her avoidance made him angrier. Look at the trouble running had gotten her in this time.

She surveyed the kitchen floor at the two bodies lying lifeless in jagged pools of their own blood.

"My lady? What has happened here?"

As if she was a separate entity from her body, Bea watched herself turn and stare at the man in the kitchen doorway. He was tall, taller than George had been, and had brown hair. His steel-gray eyes regarded her with worry and a hint of fear.

"I-I don't know," she admitted, the man's voice sparking faint recognition and jolting her out of her stupor.

He approached her as one would a wounded animal, and she shrank against the wall, hiding in the shadowy corner by the fireplace. "Are you hurt?"

Bea looked at her hands and at her body. Blood covered her skin and had soaked through her dress. "There's blood on me." She looked at the knife clutched in her bloodied hands and dropped it, the metallic clang echoing on the stone floor. "Why do I have a knife? What did I do?"

"First tell me if you are hurt," he said. "We'll figure it out together."

"My head. I hit my head after George struck me."

His mouth tightened. "Was this the first time?"

She shook her head. "No," she whispered. "Since we've been married, he's punished me, to shape me into a more dutiful wife. After the b-baby died, it worsened."

"What happened today?"

Images played behind her closed lids—George's angry face, her fear he'd finally kill her. "I ran. I know I'm not supposed to run, but I was scared, and so tired."

He had approached her hiding spot in the corner when shock sent trembles through her arms and legs, and she sank to the floor.

"What happened?" he asked, crouching to her level so their gazes collided.

"He took Harriet, my maid, and punished her because I had run to hide in the kitchen."

"Harriet?"

"She's over there," Bea said, and pointed around the fireplace to the crumpled form of a young woman. "He raped her. She wasn't fast enough, and he must have caught her in my room after I left. I could hear her screams from all the way here, until they stopped. He brought her to the kitchen to show me what my disobedience had caused. He d-dropped her body like she was a piece of r-rubbish." Bea brought her knees to her chest and wrapped her arms around them, rocking and keening through her grief. "Harriet," she moaned. "Oh, Harriet. She was my one friend."

A large, warm hand enveloped her smaller ones, and she flinched.

"I'm not going to hurt you, my lady," he said. "Can you tell me how your husband died?"

"He came after me with such rage, and he pushed me against the wall..." She freed a hand and touched the back of her head, wincing when she discovered a large, raised bump. "I fell, and—"

"He beat you," he said.

"He turned his back on me, certain I was dead. Then something snapped. I saw Harriet's body, and I saw the knife..." She remembered the rage coursing through her body at the moment when she had decided he must die.

"He'd have killed me eventually," she said. "It was only a matter of time before he went too far. I had to do it."

"I know. It'll be all right."

"How?" She wrung her hands as the implications of what she had done became clear. "I killed my husband. I'll hang, for sure."

"You won't. I promise."

Her eyes, which had been swimming out of focus after the blow to her head, narrowed to study the man before her. It took all her energy to concentrate on his face, to remember from where she recognized him. Weariness robbed her of thought, and she ceased tormenting her overtired brain. "Who are you?"

"My name is Thomas Wickes."

Sara Ackerman

Part II

"A man's past is simply that: his past. It's what a man does in the present which decides whether he's worthy to be one."

~Thomas Wickes

Sara Ackerman

Chapter 15

Guernsey, Channel Islands, September 1810

Thomas Wickes pushed his hands through his tawny hair and nearly screamed in frustration as he watched the crew of the supply ship bustle on the Guernsey dock reloading the ship in preparation for her evening departure. Aside from much-needed supplies from the mainland, the ship had brought him news from England and orders from his superior at the War Office to stop his search for Lady Beatrice Westby.

He was not ready to abandon his search. To do so was to admit she was gone, and losing her was not an option. Yet a part of him knew his efforts were futile, for the more he searched, the more the certainty she was gone intensified. Crumpling the missive containing his new orders, he turned on his heels and marched away from the harbor to town.

Guernsey's cobblestoned streets were deserted, as most inhabitants either were working or enjoying their midday meal. Neither option appealed, for his head pounded and his concentration had disappeared upon reading his letter. He was restless and regretted the day's missed opportunity to continue his search for Beatrice. Since the night she'd gone missing, he'd not stopped moving, using his considerable resources to investigate Guernsey and her surrounding islets.

Tedious, backbreaking labor aside, at least in productive activity he found a measure of peace. To do nothing was inconceivable, for the harmless whispers he was able to ignore while working mutated to discontented ravings when idle. Already a persistent buzz droned in his ears. He needed a cast iron pan to smash against his skull. Painful oblivion was preferable to this constant worry.

"What I need is another person to talk to," he said as he turned down a side street off the main thoroughfare. A woman going about her day's errands heard his mumbled request, for she tugged her shawl about her shoulders, ducked her head, and scurried past him. He didn't care. There were few people he trusted enough to unburden himself, and none lived in Guernsey. Had Alfred Coombes and his wife, Evelyn, not returned to England several weeks ago, he'd go home and seek out the quiet solicitor. Alfred was steady and often possessed valuable insights, but he was gone, and Thomas's modest two-story brick home sat empty.

Unable to bear his own company, he made his way to a small pub, needing a drink to drown out the discordant mutterings of his mind. At the Gilded Peacock, he shoved aside the massive oak door and slumped in the last unoccupied chair by the bar. As well as being the town pub, it also served a reasonable meal, and many tradesmen took their midday meal here. Today, the crowd even included ladies, though to call them such was a bit of a stretch.

Old and weathered, they were dressed in vibrant homespun garments and were clucking like a pair of hens, their loud laughter testament to how freely they had imbibed of the pub's specialty ale. If he weren't mistaken, one held a fat cigar between her bony fingers. It was this woman who caused the hair on the back of his neck to stand on end. Her raspy cackle, shrewd stare, and wiry gray hair reminded him of the old crones from *Macbeth*, and he couldn't suppress the shudder which licked the length of his spine. He'd never before wished women weren't allowed in men's establishments, but he'd never encountered such contrary females who were content to drink and smoke like any man. Shrugging off his discomfort, he signaled for the barkeep and resolved to pay the women no mind.

Soon a glass filled with amber liquid appeared before him.

"Leave it," he said to the barkeep, indicating the near empty bottle of whisky the other man held in his hand. He nursed his drink and reclined in his chair, his long legs crossed out in front of him. His shoulders slumped in resignation as he swirled the golden liquid in his cup, contemplating his new orders.

Though the explosion which had killed Beatrice presumably also had killed Henry Michelson, the notorious smuggler, his superiors at the War Office weren't convinced he was dead. Since the night of Bea's disappearance, field officers had reported seeing Michelson in northern France and Paris. As an agent, and one familiar with Michelson, his organization, and his movements, Thomas was ordered to travel to France and to verify the authenticity of these claims.

Nothing would give him greater satisfaction than for the rumors to be true, so he could rid the world of the man responsible for so much death and heartache. Michelson had plagued his life for too many years. It was time for him to die, and as Michelson's bastard, he'd decided he'd deliver the final blow.

Tension gathered in his shoulders, and he pushed aside the unease which accompanied needless violence, forcing himself to relax, a difficult feat when the women two tables over had resumed their obnoxious cackling. The urge to throttle them into silence was strong, and almost negated his vow to never harm a woman. Disgust curled his lips, and he pushed his glass and bottle away. Too much drink and not enough food had soured both his stomach and his mood. Drunkenness was tolerable if the drunkard was affable. Thomas was not, and the last time he had over-imbibed, he'd come close to shaking some sense into Beatrice.

"The daft woman. As if she can dismiss me from her life with placid ease. The next time I see her, she and I are going to have a long talk about the state of our relationship. No more pushing me aside. She's going to be mine. If she's alive." His fingers itched and grabbed the half-empty tumbler of whisky. He swallowed and finished the bottle, his burst of bravado fading as he recalled she was most likely dead.

His stomach growled, reminding him he hadn't eaten since early morning. Dejected, drunk, and now famished, Thomas stood on shaky legs and weaved his way among the tables, eager to go home and eat. His cook undoubtedly had something prepared for him, something, he hoped, to rival the enticing aromas of his companions' meals in the small pub. He settled his account with the barkeep, and as he bid the owner a good afternoon, the wiry-haired woman's jarring, raspy voice penetrated his inebriated fog and jolted him to soberness.

"Pulled her out of the water almost ten weeks ago. She was nigh on dead when my grandson fished her out. Stabbed in the chest, leg a mangled mass of scorched flesh, but I managed to pull her through," the cigar-smoking woman said to her companion.

"Where is she now? Did she return to Guernsey when your grandson brought you?" the woman's companion asked.

"No, I left her on Herm with my grandson."

Thomas didn't hear what else the woman said, his mind consumed by the possibility Beatrice and this poor, wounded woman on Herm were one and the same. In his single-minded pursuit to find Beatrice, he had never even considered Herm. *Of course. Herm!* The current could have easily carried her east instead of to Guernsey, despite the bigger island's proximity to the explosion.

The urge to kick himself for failing to consider the possibility almost outweighed his desire to leave and sail to Herm this instant. With renewed hope, he calculated how long it would take him to row to Herm if he left now. He was so lost in his planning, he missed the speculative gleam in the old woman's eyes as he hurried out of the bar.

Chapter 16

Reading, England, May 1801

Bea's head pounded and light blinded her. Fatigue bound her limbs to her side, and she was unable to wiggle her fingers, let alone raise her arms to shield her eyes from the light.

"Drink this."

A welcome coolness rested on her lips as tepid liquid dribbled between them, though most of it ran over her chin and pooled onto her neck. She whimpered, now noticing the parched condition of her mouth and throat. "More."

An arm came around her head and lifted. The cup returned, and this time, she concentrated on the uncooperative muscles in her mouth and jaw, commanding them to tighten and drink. She was rewarded when most of the liquid slid down her throat, the rest slipping out the corners of her mouth. Exhausted, her head lolled, and the strong support lowered her the remaining distance to the awaiting pillow. "Thank you."

"Can you look at me?" a soft voice asked.

"Too bright." Padded feet walked away from her, and she heard the heavy snap of fabric falling in place. Darkness descended and banished the bright glare which had frozen her eyelids into immobility. They fluttered open.

Nausea roiled in her stomach, and she snapped her lids closed. "The room is spinning." Bile rose in her throat, and she swallowed, forcing herself to remain calm.

A sharp pain lanced her side, and she winced. "Why does it hurt to breathe?"

She heard a rasp and a snap. A whiff of sulfur teased her nostrils. Panic lodged in her throat as hazy images of pain resurfaced. This smell she knew. Once it had been a source of comfort. Now it was a potent warning of future pain.

"Hush, child," the voice soothed, patting her on the arm. "I lit a candle. Its flame is tiny and will not hurt you. Open your eyes and see."

Her head hurt too much to shake her refusal, and something about this voice brooked no argument. Though the words were calm and meant to comfort her, she caught the underlying order in the quiet command. Unwilling to provoke the steel underneath the silk, she obeyed. She caught a fleeting image of a tiny fire-flame and a concerned face before the room spun again.

"Keep those eyes open. Focus on the flame. All else will fade from view if you but focus on the flame."

As hypnotic as the flame, so, too, did the woman's voice captivate. Weak and enfeebled as Bea was, she was helpless but to obey. There was something entrancing about the dancing orb as it shimmied and twisted in the air. Even behind her lids, the flame flickered, and within its pulsing, life-giving rhythm, she relaxed.

"Gack!"

Plump fingers pried at each eyelid in turn,

disrupting her constrained calm, and she was forced to watch, helpless, as the writhing orb came ever nearer. Her chest tightened again, and her legs twitched in a restless, age-old dance, transmitting the urgency to flee, to escape the pain she knew the flame possessed.

"Hold still. I'm almost done." With a final look, the old woman retreated and took the flame away. Bea relaxed, her shoulders slumping in relief.

"Where am I?"

"You're at Sir Wickes's country home, my lady. In Reading."

"Sir Wickes?"

"Aye, lass. He's the one which found you after the horrible accident."

Bea remembered. "In the kitchen." Pooling blood...her maid's frantic screams...the knowledge her own death was imminent... The memories resurfaced so vividly panic rose and swelled again.

"How long since I've been here?" she asked.

"You've been asleep about two days, my lady. Sir Wickes brought you from London on Monday, and I've been tending to you since then."

"Who are you?"

The other woman moved about the room, lighting several more candles. When she returned to the bed, Bea saw a kind, middle-aged face framed by graying auburn hair. The candles cast a soft glow in the room and wreathed the efficient woman in a saintly glow. She was an angel, though of death or life remained to be seen. Bea hadn't decided if living was preferable to the blessed oblivion of death.

"I'm Mrs. Smith, Sir Wickes's housekeeper. My father was the local doctor, and he took me on his rounds. Taught me everything he knew," she said, unmistakable pride coloring her words.

Though indebtedness of any kind chafed, she was alive because of this woman's skilled hands. "Thank you." She was alive, yet much remained unclear. Someone had taken her away from the horrible house and nursed her back to health, but for what reason? To be hanged? Her throat ached, and she swallowed to keep those vile tears at bay. Her resolve was no match for fatigue and fear. *What have I done?*

Restless fingers curled in the bedclothes as she remembered how they had curled around the knife's wooden handle she had plunged into her husband's stomach. Her own stomach churned, and bile rose to coat her throat. She had killed her husband was what she'd done.

"I know it isn't easy, child." The healer's gentle touch as she wiped away the lone tear startled Bea from the spiraling descent to madness. Gentle kindness, not pity, greeted her panicked gaze. She had expected pity, had been on the receiving end of such looks for the endless eighteen months of her marriage.

Marriage. More like a prison sentence. Fear licked up her spine, and she shuddered, pulling the blankets closer to chase away the memories of those horrid months.

Servants who had heard her screams late at night could scarcely meet her gaze the next morning, and those who did managed guilt-ridden sympathy at best. She had long since developed an immunity to such comfort, yet pity, no matter how undesirable, would not have caused her to sob in earnest.

"There, there, my lady." Mrs. Smith sat on the bed.

"It wasn't right what he did to you. He's gone now, and you're safe. Sir Wickes won't let anything happen to you."

"But Mrs. Smith, I don't know a Sir Wickes. How do I know he's not a former companion of my husband? How can I be sure I'm safe?"

The woman clucked her tongue and took Bea's hand in her own. "Oh, you poor dear, I didn't know you had no acquaintance with the master. No wonder you're shaking so."

"Who is he? Please, Mrs. Smith, is he kind?"

"I suppose it has been many years since last we met," a deep voice said.

Mrs. Smith dropped Bea's hand and stood. "There's the master now, my lady. I'm sure you'd like to make his acquaintance again. Can you brave a little light if I reopen the curtain? The sky has darkened a bit."

Bea turned her head into the pillow and listened as muted footsteps, now two sets, moved about the room. Once again there was a heavy snap of fabric as Mrs. Smith pulled back the curtains, and Bea flinched when the light streamed into the room. The housekeeper had been right. Clouds had rolled in to darken the sky, allowing muted light to illuminate her sickbed room. Her vision adjusted to the brighter interior, and she concentrated on her clutched hands until the room came into focus. Once the room stopped spinning and her vision cleared, she looked away from the knotted piles of bone and flesh clutched on her stomach to examine her room.

A soft blanket of white wool draped over her torso and legs, tucking into the base of her bed where a sleek, polished footboard jutted past her feet. Next to her lay a small cot piled with blankets. Her nurse must have been sleeping there. Pale, eggshell-blue papered walls had colorful landscapes hung at varying intervals on three sides, and a bank of windows comprised the wall opposite her bed, flanked by heavy, dark-blue curtains. The sky had darkened even further in the time it took to explore the room, and she was able to see much better in the softened light. It was a well-appointed room, and judging by the solid furniture, tasteful decorations, and carpeted floors, Sir Wickes, whoever he was, didn't lack for coin.

He, along with the door, was on the one side she had yet to inspect. Though he had said not a word, she knew he was waiting for her to complete her survey of the room before speaking. *It's now or never.* She had suspected before looking he'd be large. His presence by her side radiated power, yet even this knowledge had not prepared her for the man himself.

Sir Wickes was huge. Tall-statured and broad-shouldered, the man towered above Mrs. Smith. Intelligent gray eyes held her own, though she wasn't fooled by the complacent smile on his face. This man was dangerous, and panic replaced the fragile toehold she had gained to remain calm.

Mrs. Smith stood by the man smiling at her, oblivious to the power radiating from him. Bea tried to warn the older woman, to plead with her to run, but her words were trapped and no sound emerged from between her open lips. She was helpless but to stare at the two, and pray no lasting harm would come to either of them.

"There, Mr. Wickes. I told you she would awaken

today, and with color in her cheeks, too. Why, my lady, you seem even better now than when you first awakened. I'll run to the kitchen and bring a tray now you are awake. I won't be but a moment." With a swish of her skirts, Mrs. Smith turned and left.

Bea had a vague notion the housekeeper had left the room but was too busy tensing her leg muscles, to see if she had enough energy to run, to pay heed to the gentle woman's comings and goings.

"You do remember me," Mr. Wickes said.

"You knew my husband," she whispered, fear hoarsening her words. "You were friends." Bea inched away from the towering man and teetered on the edge of the bed. One foot snaked out from underneath the blanket and rested on the carpeted floor. She balanced her weight on her bent leg and calculated the distance to the door.

"Acquaintances, yes. Never friends. We had limited business dealings together, nothing more." Mr. Wickes walked to the other side of the bed and readjusted Bea so she was once again lying in the middle of the bed. He sat beside her and cradled her head in one hand.

"How did you…what are you…" He'd been silent and stealthy, surprising for one so large, yet his presence by her side confirmed she was far weaker than she'd imagined. She had not even noticed him walking around the bed until he was next to her. He sat on the bed, and his weight on the mattress pulled the blanket tight over her legs, confining them into immobility. Weak as she was, he'd trapped her, and there was no place for her to hide.

Quite simply, Sir Wickes overwhelmed her.

"Here, drink this." He held up a glass Mrs. Smith had placed on the nightstand on her lips, but she set her lips into a mulish pout. "Drink," he ordered. Terrified of his booming voice and his large stature, she obeyed.

After he was satisfied she had drunk enough, she pulled the covers to her chin and resisted the urge to sleep. "What are you going to do with me?" Exhaustion weighted her limbs and eyelids, numbing her to all else save slumber's beckoning pull. She stopped struggling, yawned, and closed her eyes. Before oblivion claimed her, she heard his soft reply.

"You've lost your way, my lady. I'm going to help you find it again."

Chapter 17

Herm, Channel Islands, September 1810

Thomas had found her once when she needed him. He'd do it again. An optimistic deception but necessary to bolster his faltering strength. For hours he'd rowed, impatience causing him to act with uncharacteristic rashness. The possibility Beatrice was on Herm had spurred him to action, and he had taken a small schooner out, refusing even to wait until the evening's tide, when the promise of a helpful breeze and rocking waves would have sped along his journey.

The island was a speck in the distance, though each time he rested his arms and looked behind him it grew in size the longer he rowed, the jagged shoreline becoming clearer and more distinct with each sure stroke through the water. He gritted his teeth as raw skin chafed with the constant friction of his palm against the wooden oars, but he pulled on.

Sun-gilded waves beckoned, and the temptation to take a quick dip to cool off and ease his aching muscles threatened to overwhelm his sense of duty to complete his mission and find Beatrice.

"Liar," he snorted. "Beatrice has never been a mission, not since the day I found her among the carnage of Darimple's madness."

She'd filled a part of his life he'd ignored for so

long he'd forgotten it existed. Even now, many years after her dependence on him had faded, he craved her—her wit and humor, her smiles and companionship—they were as necessary to his survival as nourishment or sleep.

To stop searching was to admit she was gone. For as long as he rowed and continued to look, Beatrice lived.

A splash, followed by a feminine squeal, alerted him to the presence of another in the warm, September water. He was closer to the island than he had calculated. Nostalgia, transporting him many years into the past, had occupied his mind and distracted him from his approach to the island. With renewed vigor, he pulled harder through the water, squinting through the fading rays of daylight to see where the sound came from. A blurry silhouette, bobbing in the water, stared back.

His vision adjusted to the light and to the mysterious female splashing out of sight. He was able to make out the sandy beach and massive, rugged rock outcroppings jutting in the water. It was by one of these immense boulders where he saw her, frolicking in the waves.

She was nude, or at least he supposed she was, for she kept to the rock's lengthening shadows and remained underwater save for her head. There were moments she popped above the water and he spied expanses of naked skin marred by sodden, snake-like tresses, almost black in the fading light.

"What a bold creature to stay in the water playing when a stranger approaches. Most likely not Bea."

Beatrice was ever cautious and would have swum

away, sought shelter, and been prepared to attack before any intruder would even have noticed the ripples her hasty departure would have caused. Defeat weighed like a stone around his neck, and the oars cut a sluggish swath through the darkening waves.

The shore was close now, yet a quick glance to the rocks where the shadowed swimmer had been hiding revealed nothing but lapping waves. Scanning the beach, he looked for any sign she had gone to shore. Finding none, worry took root.

"I hope no harm has befallen her."

"Careful, or you'll row over me." The fine hairs on his arm raised at the voice's familiarity.

The woman, who had pulled herself to the lengthening fingers of sunlight splaying across the water's surface, waved at him and swam behind the craggy ledge. He caught a glimpse of her curvy backside as she pulled herself onto shore and wrung out the water in her hair. She turned her profile to him, and his heart stopped.

"Bea!" he shouted, too afraid to hope but helpless to stop.

She peered over a large boulder, her familiar heart-shaped face and lush lips so welcome a sight her face blurred and wavered, emotion clogging his throat. *It is her!* Frantic to be near her, he jumped out of the boat and dragged the vessel the remaining distance to shore. Once on dry land, he ran, stumbling through the wet sand in his haste to see her.

Now clothed in a light shift, she ran away from him, peering over her shoulder, fright etched on her pale face. Though exhaustion lay heavy upon him, he lengthened his stride before she had put too much distance between them.

"Oh, my God! It is you." He searched her face, afraid to take his eyes from her, and when unable to resist, he cupped her cheeks to caress her soft skin. His fingers trembled, and he worried he had been clumsy and hurt her when he saw her flinch.

"I'm sorry. Please, forgive me." *For hurting you now, for sending you to danger, for not being there when you needed me most.* His faults were numerous, and from the continued look of fear on her face, he had much for which to atone. He'd have to seek her absolution later, after he had assured himself she was real. Because he feared she'd run away, and because he could no longer help himself, he enfolded her in his arms and buried his face against her neck.

"Who are you...mphf?" But her question was to remain a mystery, for he captured her lips with his and kissed her. Not wishing to add to her distress, he kept his kiss chaste, praying she recognized how his mouth paid her reverence and respect. The rounded curves he held in his arms and the gentle touch of her mouth against his brought him a measure of peace he had not experienced since the night she had gone missing. He was home.

Breaking off the kiss, he tucked her head onto his chest, and the hole he had carried with him since her ship had exploded shrank.

"Beatrice, the world declared you dead, but I refused to lose hope. I've been looking for you for months, determined to find you." He cradled her face in his large hands again, letting a shaking thumb glide across her cheek and over her swollen lips. For endless moments she stared at him, confusion replacing fear.

While she studied him, he waited.

What does she see? Will she turn me away?

She nipped at his thumb resting on her lower lip, and he groaned. Perhaps he was to be forgiven after all.

"T-Thomas?" She loosened her arms from his tight hold and ran her hands over his face. "Is it you?"

Thomas's stomach clenched. Something was wrong with Beatrice. Not knowing what, all he could do was offer her comfort, but when he wrapped his arms around her shoulders, she flinched and pushed away. His arrival was not the happy reunion he'd expected. Instead of bringing joy, he'd brought pain and confusion.

In her haste to leave him, Bea stumbled and fell to the sand. He offered his hand to help her rise, but she raised her hands over her head as if protecting herself from a striking blow.

"Don't be afraid. I'd never hurt you. Tell me how to help you." He crouched on the sand, careful to maintain a comfortable distance between them.

She whimpered and clutched her temples. "My head. What's happening to me?"

Chapter 18

Reading, England, July 1802

"What's wrong with her, Doctor?" Mr. Wickes asked, his hushed whisper carrying to where Bea lay on the bed. She rolled on her side and faced away from the two men carrying on a whispered conversation within the confines of her room at Mr. Wickes's country estate.

"She's experienced a trauma, Thomas. You can't expect her to recover instantaneously."

"But her body has healed."

"Yet her mind remains trapped in the horrors of her past."

Bea tried to ward off the images the doctor's statement resurrected, and failed. It was true. Her body was no longer wracked in unbearable pain. Broken ribs had healed, bruises had faded, but the images of her dead maid and her husband's ugly sneer before she plunged the knife into his belly had not disappeared.

"What can I do to bring her back?"

She covered her ears with her hands and moaned. *Leave me to die in peace, Sir Wickes.*

"Give her a purpose, Thomas, and a reason to live."

The men's voices faded away, and Bea was once more alone.

Quiet and alone. How I like it.

Why, then, was her melancholy worse now in their absence than in their presence? Curling in a tight ball, Bea rocked herself and stared at the wall while her life, pitiful as it had been, played before her.

****

"Who are you?" Bea asked. She had jolted awake in one of Sir Wickes's many guest bedchambers to the unsettling sensation someone was watching her sleep. Her instincts were right. A man sat on a chair near the windows, his features obscured by the encroaching darkness.

"What are you doing here? Where's Mr. Wickes?" When he failed to respond, she rolled over and pulled the covers to her chin, dismissing the rude man and his officious silence. *It's the doctor keeping vigil to ensure I don't expire while in his care.* As quiet as the room was, she listened for a rustle of clothing, a shifting of limbs, or some indication the man in the corner was leaving. If possible, the room quieted even more, until the whoosh of pulsing blood deafened all other sounds. "Doctor Maxwell, I'm fine. You needn't remain here with me. I simply need rest." Having dismissed the man in the shadows, Bea resolved to put this strange interlude from her mind. When the man neither answered nor made any move to leave, worry clouded her mind.

He is not Mr. Wickes or the doctor. They are both too polite to remain silent and ignore my questions, so if it's not either of them, who can it be? An unpleasant notion wiggled its way to her conscious mind. Perhaps it was someone to avenge her dead husband. Though Mr. Wickes had assured her the double murder of her husband and maid was blamed on a botched robbery by an escaped felon, Beatrice did not believe such a matter was so easily explained away. Someone had to question why she alone survived. This man, it seemed, was he. *My time has come.*

Beatrice tried to convince herself she cared not if the man was intent on killing her. By the time she had composed herself enough to talk to him, she was pleased to hear her voice did not betray her extreme panic. "If you're here to kill me, please get on with it. I've been dying in stages for almost two years. Death and a quiet afterlife will be a pleasant reprieve from this business of living."

There was a rustle and a shift, and Bea listened in mounting horror as the man shuffled to the bed. He was here to kill her. Her eyes slammed shut and she knew a moment's panic before her hand closed around the knife she had stored underneath her pillow. Grasping the hilt in her hand, she flung herself off the bed, sprang to her feet, and charged the intruder. She had only a vague idea where he was standing, for the room remained concealed in shadows, but she hoped he'd not expected her to fight back. It didn't matter. He was faster and more skilled and had her pinned against the wall in a matter of seconds, her own knife pressed against her throat.

The man remained cloaked in darkness, though his pungent pipe tobacco was not as reticent. The smoke curled around her head and into her nose, the bitter taste coating the back of her tongue. It was the same tobacco her husband had used. Panic threatened to close her throat, yet she managed to speak around the lump. "Please. Don't kill me."

"Why not?" the man said, his soft question punctuated by an odd lilt. "You were ready for it moments ago."

Those blasphemous words had been true, but with her own death imminent, she saw the lie behind her casual request. Her fight to survive, however hopeless, proved it.

"I'm not ready to die."

He pressed the knife closer. "What did you say?"

"I'm not ready to die! I want to live!"

The knife's pressure eased, and she was released, her knees buckling from the stress of her encounter. She sat hunched on the floor, gasping, and crying out when several small flickers cut through the gloom. As she watched, more light appeared to chase the shadows away, and her familiar room took shape. Two familiar booted feet strode into her vision.

"Mr. Wickes? Someone tried to kill me."

He crouched to her level and took her cold hands in his. "Not kill you. Shake you out of your stupor, maybe."

"You planned this? After everything I've been through, you ordered someone to attack a defenseless, wounded woman?"

"I asked a colleague to help you. He said you were hiding, protecting yourself from further harm. The barrier you erected worked too well, and it has prevented you from living. When I told him about you, he feared you were preparing to die."

"He's right. I was, but I am no longer, Mr. Wickes, so please refrain from sending attackers to my bedroom in the future. My constitution cannot cope with further trauma."

"You're wrong," the lilting voice said. "You fear the evil you have experienced has corrupted you, made you weak, but it has strengthened you beyond measure and given you the tools you need to survive."

A small man, no taller than her sister Evie, stepped out from behind Mr. Wickes's shadow and stood before her. His wrinkled face and dark brown eyes held a lifetime of happiness and sorrow, and she flinched from the pain she saw lurking there. He wore his long black hair loose about his shoulders. Clad in a flowing white shirt, the fabric draped over his torso and his legs to conceal the loose-legged black trousers which almost dwarfed his feet.

"Who are you?"

Mr. Wickes stood and helped Beatrice to rise before introducing the strange man to her. "This is Jones. He does side jobs for me when needed, is an accomplished thief, a skilled fighter, and has become a friend in the years I've known him. He has agreed to train you."

"Train me? For what purpose?"

Jones approached her, and fearing a reprisal of his previous activities, she plastered herself to the wall he had pinned her to moments ago. "You hold on to your anger and fear like a shield. I can show you how to harness those emotions and wield them to your advantage." The musical cadence of his speech soothed some of her frightened nerves, but his plan to help her left her panicked.

"You want me to learn to fight, Mr. Wickes? Ladies of quality do not make a production of our anger or resort to fisticuffs when events do not turn in our favor."

"The moment you defended yourself against your husband, you forfeited your right to be called a lady of quality. It is time for you to become something more."

She hung her head, for it was true. Her actions separated her from her peers, and she'd never again be counted in their ranks. To survive, she had sacrificed her chance to live a normal life as suited a woman of her station. Life as she'd understood it was gone.

What does he mean by "to become something more"? The path he'd have her trod was dark, uncertain, and full of pitfalls and lurking enemies. Mr. Wickes's idea to train her intrigued her, though fighting accomplished nothing save to rid herself of unwanted guilt and anger. She didn't see how this choice offered anything but danger, and she'd lived a lifetime of danger in the eighteen months of her marriage. Another path presented itself, one which led to a quiet country home on a small, overgrown road. It offered anonymity and peace if she but asked for it. *But what to choose?*

Strong fingers cupped and raised her chin. "There is only forward," Jones said. His gaze cut through her silence to the turmoil within.

What if forward is as frightening as what lies behind? But the longer she stared at Jones, the more certain she was of what to choose. Her quiet country cottage faded, for rustication, even peaceful rustication, was its own form of cowardice. Hiding herself away from the world served to prove her dead husband had been right—she was a cowering weakling. More of his taunts returned to replay in her head, and anger, never far from the surface, rose and screamed in protest.

You were a stupid ass, George Darimple, and if you weren't already dead, I'd kill you again. There is

126

nothing weak about me.

"Jones is going to show you how to channel your anger and use it for some good. He's going to help you clear the muddle in your head and give you a purpose for leaving your bed each morning. He's here to teach you to cope," Mr. Wickes said. "Please, give him a chance."

"What is it you want?" Jones asked, his lyrical tenor a steadying melody to her mind's discordant harmony.

For the first time since the night she killed her husband, she was asked to choose. The idea she was at liberty to do so was freeing, and she made a tentative peace with this new path she had chosen. "I want to live."

Maybe because Jones was also something more, he heard her unspoken plea to belong and be useful in those four words, for he said, "You have my word, Beatrice Westby. When we are done, you will thrive."

Chapter 19

Herm, Channel Islands, September 1810

Beatrice had suffered since the accident, if the sobbing, moaning bundle of femininity in his arms was to be believed. "Ah, don't cry, sweet Beatrice. I can't stand it when you hurt." Thomas wrapped his arms around her again and held her until sobs no longer wracked her body. "Better?"

"All day my memories have been pounding on the door to my consciousness. You, though, were the key." She nuzzled the soft skin bared by his unlaced shirt. He forced himself to relax under her inquisitive touch. She wasn't ready for a renewal of affections. She needed time to reacquaint herself with him after the events of the last four months.

"Has everything returned?"

"Most. The events before the accident and my arrival on Herm remain fuzzy."

"They'll return when you're ready. Try not to worry about it."

"You smell nice," she said, her sweet voice thick with her tears.

He laughed. "I'm filthy and covered in sweat."

"Hmm. I disagree. Cloves, bergamot." She rubbed her nose along the corded ridge of his neck muscles and sighed. "And sweaty man. My favorite." Her sigh of delight coupled with the small wiggle of her hips had him taut and at attention. Thomas was near to expiring. When she molded her legs around one hard thigh and smashed her breasts against his chest, he promised himself never to bathe after exercise if this was the response he could expect.

Hell, he'd roll around in the mud to experience the same tantalizing inspection of his person. Her arms snaked around his neck, and she rested her head on his collarbone. Her plump lips, scant inches from his own, begged to be kissed. Lowering his head, he touched his lips to hers. A breeze fluttered the leaves and sent his long locks, now loose from his queue, flying around his head and lashing their faces. Bea stiffened in his arms.

"I remember," she whispered and fell from his embrace.

Thomas lifted her from the sand and cradled her in his arms, spreading warm kisses over her face. He walked away from the shore and sat on the ground, his back resting against a large tree. She held onto him and let go when he tugged his shirt over his shoulders to wrap around her chilled body.

"Your hair. You're wearing it longer now."

"My hair?" He freed a hand and pulled the mass of it over his shoulder away from Beatrice. "Of what import is my hair?"

"Sandalwood. You must have taken to using it after I left. When the wind whipped strands of your hair across my nostrils, I smelled it. It clings to the ends."

"I don't follow. You love the scent and begged me to try it. You're not pleased?"

"Michelson wore it." She snorted. "More like bathed in it. It clung to anything he touched. After months of travel with the man, I became conditioned to hate it. Now I can't smell it without it conjuring the specter of the man's twisted smile and his beady, calculating eyes." Bea scooted off his lap and crawled several feet away from him. Finding a spot on the sand, she hugged her knees to her chest. "Until you bathe, I prefer to keep my distance. I know it's you holding me, Thomas, but a part of me imagines it's him. I'm sorry."

"I shall bathe as soon as possible," he said, hoping his words did not betray the anger brewing within him. Even now, with the man rumored to be dead, he came between him and the ones he loved. Yet another reason to despise the man. He'd almost killed Beatrice, and his greedy, grasping specter stood between their reunion.

He longed to touch her, but he let his hand fall when he saw her flinch. Guilt competed with anger, for if he weren't mistaken, she had suffered endless torments on her most recent voyage with Michelson.

And I'm the one who sent her to the snake's den.

"The accident left you confused?"

"For a while, yes. Events from early June are returning to me." A shudder wracked her small frame. "I was so scared, Thomas. The blast came earlier than planned, and I couldn't get out in time. Michelson had me trapped. He stabbed me under my heart and almost killed me. When the staircase fell and trapped my leg, I knew I was going to die. Michelson jumped overboard before the explosion. Jones stayed till the end, and we were able to heave the burning wood off my leg. Everything after that is a bit of a blur. I jumped and swam away from the ship, knowing if I were caught in the explosion I'd die. Sometime later, I found a plank and crawled onto it. No rescue came, so I prepared for death."

"We were out there looking for you, but the remaining gunpowder caught, the ship exploded, and we had to return to shore."

"By the time you had people searching, I was on the other side of the explosion, floating away on the current to Herm."

"And here you are."

"Luka found me. He pulled me out of the water and brought me here."

"Luka as in your childhood sweetheart?"

"As in not my husband."

"You married him while stranded here?"

"No, but I did in a dream."

He'd ignore her ramblings about dreams for now. There were other more important details to discover, like what had this man done to his woman all these months. "After abandoning you a decade previous, he saved you?"

"He and his grandmother. When I awoke, I didn't remember anything from the last ten years. I was eighteen again and married to Luka. My memories stopped the night before he left me, and for whatever reason, he never corrected me."

"Did the blackguard take advantage of you? I'll run him through, if he did."

"He didn't. I—" She shook her head and turned her face away from him.

"Tell me."

"Once I had regained some strength, I repeatedly threw myself at him, convinced we were married. He refused each advance, showing more restraint than I did, and prevented me from doing something to cause us both regret."

"Seeing him hasn't resurrected any tender sentiments, has it? You won't mourn him again?"

"Beatrice!"

"Speak of the devil," she said.

"The man himself?" Thomas asked, squinting to see this man who once held his beloved's heart. "I can't make out much in the darkness."

"He's coming from that way," she said, and jerked her head toward Luka's approximate location. "I'm over here, Husband," she called.

Thomas smirked. "Even I recognize the bite in your tone. He'd have to be an idiot not to hear your displeasure."

"Oh, he'll know, all right. He is going to get a piece of my mind."

"Tris," Luka cried, and Thomas burned with jealousy upon seeing Beatrice's unguarded reaction to this man's arrival. Peace. He brought her a measure of peace Thomas had never been able to provide. It was soon gone, though, and anger twisted her classic features to a rage-filled mask of pain and betrayal. She stood, crossed her arms, and waited. Thomas leaped to his feet and joined Beatrice, offering her what comfort and protection she'd allow him.

Luka appeared from the gathering darkness and sprinted the remaining distance between her in seconds, gathering her in his arms. "I've been looking for you all day. Where did you go?"

She wiggled out of his arms and took a step back. With hands planted on her hips, she lowered her eyebrows and pursed her lips to scowl at him. "Of what concern is it to you? We're not married. In fact, you left me at the altar some ten years ago. Any obligation or sense of duty dissolved the night you abandoned me." Thomas placed a comforting arm about her shoulder.

Luka leveled a hostile glare at him. "Who's this?"

Bea hissed a warning. "None of your business. You have long since ceased to have an opinion on my life and my relations."

"I'm Lady Beatrice's friend and companion, Thomas Wickes. Since *The Stallion* sank, I've been searching for her all these months."

Luka crossed his arms over his chest. "I fished her out of the water and brought her here to be tended. Had I known she had someone waiting for her, I would have left word last I was in Guernsey."

"No matter," Thomas said. "I'm here now."

"Good. You'll be able to help her fill in some of the blanks surrounding her accident and any prior events."

Thomas increased his grip on Beatrice's shoulder, a silent warning for her to guard her secrets around this man. Though they may have once been betrothed, this man, *this Luka,* didn't need to know what had happened to her on the ship. Beatrice patted Thomas's hand and squeezed his fingers, telling him she needed no such reminder. He removed his hand and said, "Yes, we'll have to talk, but first, my lady, shouldn't you go inside? It must have been a trying day for you, becoming lost, rediscovering your memories. A good night's rest is what the doctor ordered."

"I agree with him," Luka said, and grabbed her arm. "You've had a rough day. Best you go inside. I'll fetch you supper once you're settled."

A scowl marred Bea's face, and she crossed her

arms over her chest. "I will go to bed when I decide to. There is much yet to say."

"And it can wait until tomorrow, Tris."

"I agree," Thomas said as he grabbed her other arm. "You are looking a bit peaked, my dear. You should go to bed."

"How dare you dictate to me, Thomas," she said. "You waltz in here almost three months after my accident and presume to command me?"

"Waltz?" he asked, hard and defiant. "I spent those months combing the islands for you, most often by myself as I mucked through untamed wilderness on Guernsey and her surrounding islands. As for waltzing in here, it took me five hours to row from the mainland to Herm. I hardly call hours of rowing a pleasant evening in a ballroom."

"Yet it took you three months to come here. Did Herm even cross your mind, or were you too focused on your other interests to come find me?"

"Finding you has consumed me since the night you disappeared."

"Why didn't you come here? This is the most likely location for the currents to take me. Perhaps you weren't searching as diligently as you claim."

Now it was Thomas's turn to splutter. Luka's muffled snort of laughter angered Thomas and drew Bea's attention.

"As for you, you spineless, weak-willed seducer of young girls' innocence!" Luka's laughter ceased, and he scowled at her. "I cleaned your damned fireplace, cooked your meals, and mended your socks and drawers. My memory was gone, and you took advantage of me. You could have treated me with kindness, but instead you tormented me. I passed many a sleepless night worrying I had disappointed you, when all along you were laughing at me, reveling in my ineptitude."

"Come on, Tris. You put me in a difficult position. Try to look at it from my perspective."

Bea raised her hand to stop his defense.

"I am through with both of you, and now I will go back to the house because I am a bit tired. I will get my own food tonight, and I will put myself to bed when I am good and ready." She turned on her heel and stomped across the sand to the cottage, the slam of the door's wooden plank a thunderclap of foreboding and retribution yet to come.

Chapter 20

London, England, May 1810

Beatrice was furious. Through clenched teeth, she smiled and feigned interest in Lord Smith's lengthy narrative on the merits of raising lambs versus pigs as he twirled her around the ballroom floor of her sister's betrothal party. *Country lords should not come out of rustication.* This one, especially, and his incessant chatter about his sheep proved his heart remained in Northumberland. *And with his livestock.* Rumor had it, though, Lord Smith was on the prowl for a new wife, his previous one having expired after the expulsion of their third child. A braver woman than she was needed to take on the man's brood and his ovine companions. Hence her ire. Her talents were better employed at subterfuge and misdirection, not engaged in idle conversation with a sheep farmer, of all people.

Thomas Wickes would explain his purpose in requesting she entertain Lord Smith. *If I ever find him.* She scanned the ballroom again, searching for a familiar set of broad shoulders and gray eyes, but there was no sign of the man. Bea conceded defeat. Despite his height, Thomas blended into a crowd like a master pickpocket. He'd announce himself when he was ready.

Whereas I am all too ready for this dance to finish. I swear, if he tells me about spring lambing— She suppressed a shudder.

"My lady, are you well?" Smith asked. "You trembled."

The sheep farmer was observant as well as enamored of farming. Lovely. "I grow fatigued, my lord. The heat is stifling tonight, and the ballroom grows stuffy."

"By all means let us retire from the dance floor." He propelled her away from the crowds to a bank of chairs near the open balcony. Once seated, he said, "Allow me to fetch you some refreshment, my lady."

With her faithful companion occupied, Beatrice debated escaping but stopped herself when she recalled her objective. She was to stay with Lord Smith until the supper waltz, and she mustn't fail. To do so was to admit she wasn't ready to progress to more difficult and demanding tasks. She owed everything to Thomas. Disappointing him was not an option. No, she'd stay with Lord Wooly, to prove to Thomas Wickes she was more than prepared to engage in this new assignment. Years of training and preparation would be wasted if she fell asleep before Lord Smith shared his secrets with her, though. *Why does the man have to be so dull?* Thirty long minutes stretched before her.

"Here you are, my lady," Smith said as he returned with two glasses of punch. Seating himself next to her, he offered her a glass, which she sipped, studying the man over the crystal rim.

Of above-average height, he was solid and fit, though he was no young dandy. Medium-length brown hair silvered at the temples, and kind brown eyes crinkled when he smiled or laughed. With a strong nose and patrician features, his looks were a testament to some distant Roman relations. His mouth was lush, full, and out of place on his classic features. He was not bad to look at, but handsome was too generous a word and ugly too severe. She found him interesting. There were worse men with whom to pass a half an hour.

"I must admit, Lady Beatrice, I was surprised to receive your introduction. We don't exactly move in the same circles."

Gaining an introduction with Lord Smith had worried her until she recalled that, as the sister of the bride, she'd be in the receiving line with the family. A discreet word to her mother, and Beatrice secured a lengthier introduction than was normal. His surprise at her interest was evident, for Beatrice moved in the highest of circles within the ton. Even her turbulent marriage and the resulting scandal when she shed her husband's name had done little to dampen her reception with the *haute monde*. Lord Smith, however, came to Town but rarely, and when he did, stayed to the shadows or the game room. Tonight, she had ensured he'd spend at least some of his time with her by requesting a dance with him. Though he might take no pleasure in balls and wish for the company of his furry, ovine companions, he was polite enough to acquiesce to her request. "I'm sure I don't know what you mean," she said and removed her fan from her wrist to wave in front of her flushed cheeks.

His teeth flashed white in the soft glow from the wall sconce. "I'm sure you do, though let's not argue."

"Is it so difficult to conceive I might find you attractive and wished to be introduced?"

He laughed, a great barrel-chested laugh which had her smiling in spite of herself.

"Look at you, and then look at me. I beg no false praise; I am simply pointing out the obvious."

She closed her fan with a snap and tapped him on the forearm. "Beauty can be as much a curse as ugliness, though you are far from homely, Lord Smith, and you know it, too."

A ruddy flush tinged his cheeks, but otherwise, he ignored her compliment. "How do you mean?"

He's modest. Why this information surprised her, she couldn't say, so she stored it away for further examination at another time. "People look at me and make certain assumptions. Men in particular have one idea in mind when they call or pay suit, while women take an almost immediate dislike, fearing any association with me will show them in an unflattering light. It's lonely."

"I never saw it in those terms before. You have experienced much loneliness, my lady."

It was a statement, so much worse than had he asked her. A question was laughed away or avoided. Fact was not easy to dismiss. His shrewd deduction hung between them, and once again she was taken by surprise. He proved to be more intuitive and empathetic than she had credited him for. Because he'd cut through much of her posturing, she decided to be truthful.

"I'm a person the same as you or anyone else, longing to make a connection. Few take the time to get to know me, and so I am labeled and placed with those who are like me. It's discouraging." A servant walked by, and Beatrice placed her empty glass on his tray, her melancholy stronger now she had told this stranger such a revealing part of her personality. She was lonely, yet so was he.

"We are not at all dissimilar. Perhaps I asked for an introduction because I saw in you a reflection of what is inside me, someone who is a little lonely and out of place. Perhaps I wished to see beyond your public mask and discover your true self. Can you imagine a situation such as I've described?"

He took her gloved hand in his to brush a soft caress over her knuckles. "You honor me, my lady."

Bea squeezed his hand and stood. "It is warm. Could I interest you in a stroll through the garden?"

She took Lord Smith's arm, and they descended the stairs leading into the gardens. The terrace was a-twinkle with flickering torches lining the groomed walks. The scent of gardenia and orange blossom bushes, wheeled out from the green house earlier in the day, wafted on the breeze. Flowers bloomed from every plant and bush until the garden seemed like a carpeted wonderland. "How do you find our small piece of paradise? Does it compare to the gardens bordering your estate?"

"It far outshines mine. My mind has been preoccupied as of late, with concerns about the farm and my own offspring taking most of my concentration and time. I fear the gardens have fallen in disrepair since my wife's passing."

"My condolences on your loss, my lord. Raising three children and managing such a huge enterprise as your farm must be overwhelming at times, and all without the support of a mate."

"I admit it is, though the children haven't complained. My parents have come to stay for the duration, until I find a wife. Their presence has been soothing."

"Family can be so comforting during difficult times. Do you have siblings?"

He hesitated, and her intuition flared. *I've hit a sore spot. He avoids my gaze and has refused to answer my question.* Wickes's odd request for her to engage the man held its first glimmer of interest, and she cautioned herself against rash behavior.

"I have two sisters, Lord Smith. Amelia is younger by almost three years, and Evelyn, whose betrothal ball this is, is the youngest by five years. But I ramble. This must be public knowledge," she said, hoping if she talked about her family he'd be more inclined to share about his.

"I understood you to be the oldest, my lady, though your sisters' ages in relation to yours was unknown. How could I not have heard of the three Westby sisters? Even in the wilds of northern England your beauty is as lauded as is the unfortunate curse which has plagued you three since your childhood."

"Our beauty is lauded? How delightful!"

He led her to the lit gazebo. "Ah, so we are going to ignore the entire subject of the curse?"

"There's not much to tell. My father wished to punish us for a lie we told, so he hired a gypsy woman to curse us. His intent was to make us suffer for a couple of days before telling us it was all a hoax. Little did he know we would believe such a fool notion." Beatrice walked the perimeter of the gazebo and paused to twine her finger around some creeping ivy climbing the gazebo's latticed sides. "My sisters abide by the curse's constraints."

"Not you, though."

"Not I. Of the three of us, I find logic and reason

eclipse superstitious belief."

"You say your father did this to you and your sisters? Even as angry as I've been at my children, hurting them in such a heinous manner has never crossed my mind."

Beatrice rejoined Lord Smith where he had taken a seat on a bench. "You are a better father than mine. Relations are much like eggs. There's a rotten one in every bunch."

"They can be disappointing."

"We have an uncle on my mother's side whom no one speaks of. Bad business during the war. He backed the wrong side. We're not to talk of him."

"Why did you?"

"To show you many people have disappointing relations, yet here we are in a fragrant garden on a warm spring evening enjoying ourselves. Disappointing relations aside, their decisions cannot stop our amusement unless we let them."

"Mine could prove disastrous for succession should anyone find—" He shook his head. "Never mind, my lady. As you say, it is a beautiful evening, and I'm a fortunate devil to have the loveliest of ladies gracing my side."

"You flatter me, sir, in the same breath you insult me. Am I such an empty-headed bundle of fluff you would not trust me to protect your secrets as I trusted you to protect mine? For I assure you, were my uncle's exploits to be made public, we would be ostracized from polite society."

"I meant no offense—"

"But you did offend. By valuing my physical appearance and denying the use of my considerable intellect, you relegate me to a position of window ornamentation—pleasant to behold but useless, nonetheless."

"Apologies, my lady. My wish was not to offend but to spare your sensibilities. My brother and the problems he has caused are not worth your notice."

"They are if it continues to trouble your mind. Come, my lord. You have become too accustomed to guarding your thoughts. Allow me to ease some of your burden. Even if there is nothing I can do, sometimes sharing one's problems can lift their heaviness."

His brows furrowed in concentration, and he deliberated over her words.

She counted the number of couples strolling through the garden as he struggled to reach whatever conclusion was awaiting him after her declaration.

"Andrew," he said.

"What?"

"If we are sharing each other's confidences, you might as well call me Andrew."

Bea's spine relaxed an imperceptible inch. He had decided to confide in her after all. It was better this way, for him to trust her. She'd not have to use her considerable charms to coerce his secrets from him. Seduction was not unpleasant; however, she had come to like Andrew Smith in their short acquaintance, and she didn't want to see him hurt.

"Andrew, how pleasant to make your acquaintance. You may call me Beatrice."

"The pleasure is all mine."

She smoothed her skirts before clutching them together in her lap, a sign of how nervous he had made her. *Drat. This country lord is more suave than I had anticipated.* To avoid the peril of further missteps, she had to redirect the conversation to safer waters. Thomas would bemoan her lack of restraint were he to discover how a simple country lord had discomposed her.

"You are a charmer, Andrew. Best be careful, else we shall find ourselves in front of the minister before week's end."

"Beatrice, you do flatter me, but you are too expensive for everyday wear."

She swallowed a sigh of regret and the bitter sting of rejection. True, she'd tolerated this man's attentions with restrained irritation less than an hour past, but he'd shown himself to be a gentleman and a more intuitive conversationalist than she had credited him to be. She liked him, and though she had no desire to wed ever again, rejection was unpleasant, so she laughed instead. "You're right. I'm much too costly for a gentleman farmer such as you. Since you have delivered a kind set-down, my amazing intellect will be here in London and not in the wilds of northern England to face certain boredom and stagnation. Avail me now of your worries, and between the two of us, we'll decide what, if anything, is to be done."

"Somewhere in there was an insult, Beatrice, but no matter. Like your uncle, my brother backed the wrong side."

"He has not reconciled with you?"

"No, and I doubt he ever will. It is too late for us anyway."

"I'm sorry for your loss. To lose a brother, even one who was adrift, cannot be easy."

"What? No, I meant he's thrown his lot in with a wicked bunch of smugglers. He's their captain, if you can believe it, and for all I care, he can go hang. He made his choice, and now he can live with the consequences."

"He sounds like my uncle. He joined with some smugglers, too, but these men were smuggling guns and money to French soldiers. I'm ashamed to call him family."

"Anthony, too."

"Anthony's your brother?"

"Anthony Longe. He took my mother's maiden name when he chose this dark path, the one bright spot in this whole sordid affair. That and he has decamped far from here, in the village where my mother grew up. No relations remain in Maryport, and none who live there remember my mother's family, for they moved away when my mother was a mere infant."

She scooted closer, bridging the gap between them, and rested her hand on his thigh, a calculated but necessary move. His trust was essential. Yet when the muscles underneath her hand shimmied and bunched, she admitted there might have been an ulterior motive behind her shrewd deliberation. She'd wanted to see if he was as solidly built as she'd imagined. "Maryport is near the Lake District, isn't it?"

He removed her hand to trace lazy circles on her palm. "Hmm, my estate is not far from there."

"I've longed to travel there, but an opportunity has never arisen."

"Perhaps one day you'll have reason to do so."

"Your secret is safe with me."

"As yours is with me."

She leaned closer until her face was but a whisper from his. "I was right, you know."

"About what?"

"You are a man worth knowing. Even a pretty window ornament can recognize a man of quality."

"Thank you, though I must admonish you against calling yourself names. You are no empty-headed bundle of fluff, my lady, but kind and wise and—"

She pressed her lips to his and kissed him to stop his words, for in her heart, she knew otherwise. Conniving, lying, and manipulative were more apt terms. With every caress, coy glance from beneath her lashes, and shared confidence, she'd manipulated his responses to her, playing him like a fiddle. Her conscience pricked at her deceit, because even though she had promised to never reveal his secret, she was going to do what she must and damn the consequences.

A charming flustered smile tugged on his lips as he pulled away. "Well, it's past time I return you to the ballroom."

"You're right. Father is going to make my sister's betrothal announcement before the supper waltz. I'd best hurry if I'm not to miss it."

They strolled through the garden and up the stairs in silence, Bea's mind too preoccupied with what had occurred in the garden to engage in small pleasantries and her body too aware of the man's strength beside her. The two slipped into the ballroom unnoticed, and Bea curtsied, prepared to leave.

Andrew stopped her and pulled her farther to the ballroom's shadowed sides. "May I request the privilege of calling on you tomorrow?"

Guilt lodged in her throat. He was a sweet man who deserved more than lies and intrigue. He deserved a loving woman, a partner to share life's burdens and a wife who'd not disgrace him. Grief replaced her guilt, for at one time, she'd have been willing to play the part. Gone was the wild, impulsive girl who had loved with abandon and believed anything was possible. Gone, too, was the calculating debutante who did what was necessary to ensure her love-child had a name. No more was she sheltered and naive. Fear, anger, regret—she'd experienced them all. Nothing, save a handful of charred cinders, remained of the girl called Beatrice Westby. Andrew Smith deserved better than what she had to offer.

"I'd be honored," she heard herself say. He beamed, and she dropped a brief curtsy, eager to be away. Slipping through the crowded ballroom, she rushed outside, her strides lengthening until she ran. She ran until her sides ached and her chest heaved, until exhaustion numbed her from the harsh realities of her chosen life, and when she could run no more, she returned to the house once again collected and in control.

What did it matter if an honorable man wished to court her? He was a job, nothing more, and she was a superb actress.

****

"Where have you been?" Thomas Wickes said, sneaking up the back servants' entrance. He ducked into Beatrice's old room in Westby Manor and closed the door. The festivities below stairs were waning, and tonight's events had left her exhausted. She experienced no remorse for leaving her baby sister's betrothal party early.

"Getting the information you requested." Beatrice slipped behind her dressing screen and removed her dress. With a shimmy, the golden silk pooled at her feet. Her stockings soon joined the pile of feminine cloth on the floor. Grabbing her dressing gown, she secured the sash and stepped from behind the screen.

She turned her back to Thomas and handed him her hair brush. One by one, Thomas removed the pins holding her honeyed curls in place and dropped them in Beatrice's open palm. "I saw you dancing with Smith hours ago. What have you been doing since then?"

"You're not my husband or my father, Thomas," she said, gifting him with an annoyed over-the-shoulder glare. "Something happened."

"Something? Or someone?" He pulled the brush through her hair, and she winced at the sharp tug of pain.

"Jealousy ill suits you, Thomas, and it is a tedious emotion. Since Lord Smith proved most cooperative in divulging his brother's name and whereabouts, I am in a generous mood and will not torment your green beast any longer. My sister was the reason for my tardiness."

"Amelia, I assume, since she went missing after your father's announcement." Thomas handed her the brush and shucked his boots before removing his cravat. Bea sauntered to the bed and slid under the covers, her bare legs and feet reveling in the luxurious slide of silk. Thomas's home, though modern and in possession of many luxuries, did not boast silk sheets, a serious lack of linens, in her opinion. She sighed and snuggled under the counterpane. "It seems my sister has eloped with your inside man, Tavis McGuire."

"What? Did he find what he was looking for first?" Thomas joined Beatrice under the covers and pulled her back into his embrace.

"I doubt it, since he was busy romancing my sister. My guess is they are galloping out of London, heading north to Gretna Green."

"Hell and damn." He blew out the bedside candle, plunging the room into darkness.

Beatrice yawned and relaxed in Thomas's embrace. "She seemed happy when I helped her climb out her bedroom window."

"Climb out a window? Amelia?"

"She surprised me, too."

"Tavis will have to wait. What of the information you learned?"

"Smith's brother is a smuggler and a ship's captain, most likely on *The Stallion of the Sea*. He has residence in Maryport. The man has been on the run for years. My guess is it shouldn't take much to convince him to retire and for me to step in as his successor."

"Explain to me why you're doing this?"

"Because you're too well known and too important, and I make a damnably good male. You can't fault my training, for it far outweighs anyone else's in the War Office."

"Someone else would have suited."

"Grumble all you want, Thomas, but it has to be me. After eight years of training, I'm ready. Master Jones has declared there is nothing left for him to teach me."

"Fine. We leave for Maryport tomorrow at first light." Thomas kissed her forehead, rolled over, and slept, his gentle snores a familiar comfort despite this night's revelations. He was a dear man and, much like Andrew Smith, too good for her. When they had embarked upon their affair more than a year ago,

Beatrice had warned him to tangle with her was to court disaster, but he had silenced her concerns with his tenderness and care. Her training might be complete and her emotions better controlled, but she was no worthier now than when she agreed to Thomas's mad proposal to mix business with pleasure. As Jones often said, one has to know when to walk away, and it was past time she ended her relationship with Thomas Wickes. He'd be better off without her.

She crept out of bed, careful not to disturb Thomas, and dressed in her traveling clothes, then snuck out of the house. By the time first light peeked over the horizon, she had fled London, leaving behind Thomas, Andrew, and any dreams of a happier future.

Chapter 21

Herm, Channel Islands, September 1810

Beatrice had run away from him again. "What the hell!" His bellow followed the emphatic door slam Beatrice delivered after scurrying away from him. Since arriving on this Godforsaken rock the islanders called Herm, nothing had gone to Thomas's plan. Instead of falling into his arms and renouncing any involvement between her and the Rom leader, Beatrice had been agitated and refused to accept the comfort he offered.

Jiggling the handle on the small cottage door proved ineffectual. It was locked. "Contrary female can't stay in one place," he muttered. "Not like I've spent months searching for her and want to be near her." Not as if he were anxious to hear how she had spent her time recovering after the accident. He shot an angry glance at Stefano, his imagination running rampant at all the liberties the man might have taken with his Bea. *Damn it! She's my woman!*

He needed answers, and he needed them before he strangled Beatrice's not-husband. Thomas pounded on the closed wooden plank keeping him from Bea, but Stefano pulled him back and shook his head. *God, even the man's name has me curling my lip like a wild dog.*

Thomas bristled and clenched his fist, knowing a good fight would clear the air and put some distance between him and this anger. Stefano, however, was oblivious to the gathering tension, or he didn't care. Either way, it made Thomas all the more eager to hit the man. Thomas balled and unballed his fist and reined in his galloping temper while the other gathered driftwood and other sizable logs from the woodpile next to the cottage.

"Why did you stop me?"

"It won't work. When she's in a mood like this, best to let it run its course and stay out of her way." Stefano dropped the gathered firewood in a pile and squatted over it, using his tinder box to strike a flame and coax a spark from the seasoned wood.

"What would you know about her moods? You haven't been around to see her moods since she left the schoolroom. A lot can change."

The wooden logs held the flame and soon a small blaze flickered from the pile of dead branches to chase away the cool night. "Of course not, no. Our acquaintance occurred when she was a young lady— serene, pleasant, and never rash."

"Sarcasm is not necessary." Thomas resisted the urge to stick out his tongue and squatted by the fire. *This man takes me back to my schoolyard days, when throwing rocks and sticking out one's tongue was the best rejoinder for an insult.* Much more time in the man's company and he'd regress to their cavemen ancestors of long ago, pounding his chest as he wrestled the other male to secure Beatrice's affections. Luka Stefano was not his favorite person.

"It is if you are too stupid to believe because I knew her when she was young I didn't experience the full sting of her spite. Once she told her father I had stolen one of his prized horses, and all because she caught a village girl kissing me. I tried to explain how the little village hussy had come on to me, but she was incensed and in retribution created a crazy story about me stealing a horse. We were run out of town because of her lie."

"You were the cause of the curse?"

"If you're implying I participated in such a ridiculous farce, you would be wrong." Luka poked at the fire, his expression unwelcoming.

"No, but her lie is what caused the curse."

"Yes."

"And all because you couldn't keep your hands off some rosy-cheeked village wench?"

"She initiated it, which everyone conveniently avoids mentioning, but yes. One indiscretion cursed Tris and exiled my family from England."

"So you're the injured party, hmm? To hear her tell it, you were the one who left her."

"I am aware of who left whom, but my reasons were not as unscrupulous as you have imagined."

"Why?"

"Because she was young and had never been farther than her father's townhouse in London. A nomadic lifestyle wouldn't have suited her."

"Or maybe a wife wouldn't have suited you."

"I made the best choice at the time. Everyone paints me as the villain, but I was barely a man, myself."

"Man enough to seduce her, get her with child, and leave."

Stefano lifted his head, and he stared at Thomas. "What do you know about our history?"

"More than you, apparently." Thomas reclined against the pile of firewood and crossed his arms over his chest, for all intents, a gentleman at his leisure.

"Are you going to make me beg?"

"Are you going to be difficult when I take her away from here tomorrow?"

"No. I'll let her go, provided she tells me where the child is."

"You don't know."

"We have established there is much I don't know, so spit it out! My patience for this game wears thin."

"The child is dead. He died soon after his expulsion."

Stefano blanched, his pallid complexion visible even in the firelight. His discomposure almost stirred Thomas's sympathy.

"You lie."

"I'm sorry. You don't know?"

"When I left her, I took the family to Russia. We rarely go there, reserving it for times of great turmoil amongst nations. I needed to get away, somewhere far away where she'd not come looking for me. If she tried to send a letter, I'd not have gotten it until too late."

"Would you have come back if you'd known?"

"No. Yes. I don't know. I was a young man. My father's passing came as a surprise, and I was thrust into the role of clan leader. I was finding my way with my people. A wife and child would have made the transition more difficult in some ways and easier in others." There was a beat of silence. "Yes. I would have come back for her, had I known."

He snarled, his sympathy fading in light of Stefano's multiple transgressions. "You did more than abandon her. You ruined her life. When she discovered she was with child, she had to marry in haste. Within a month of your having left her, she married a marquis. He was a brute."

Stefano clenched his fists. "Her mistreatment during her marriage is to be laid at my door, too? Abandonment, death, and abuse—she has done nothing but suffer since I've left. Fool!" He grabbed a hefty log he had yet to chop and heaved it across the deserted beach.

"Temper, temper, Stefano. Flinging logs will not change what is past. Beatrice will still resent you, and your child will still be dead. I do regret telling you so baldly. Had I know you were unaware of the child's death, I'd have softened the blow."

Stefano plopped into the sand. "I didn't know. I've kept her here all this time, and I didn't know."

"Kept her here? She was too ill to travel. How did you keep her here?"

"I coddled her. Cooked her meals, laundered her clothes, and helped her heal. When she awoke, she believed us to be married. My grandmother asked me to continue the charade until her memories returned. She feared any unpleasant news would harm her worse than playacting as her husband. Believe what you will of me, but after my initial anger cooled, I wished her no ill will."

"To hear Beatrice tell the story, you tortured her needlessly and worked her like a serving girl."

"Not at first, but she was so persistent in her belief we were man and wife... The sneaky wench kept climbing into my bed or else she'd flit about the house half dressed. I was going mad!"

"So you devised a way for her to stay busy to guard her virtue?"

"Or mine. I didn't know what else to do. She was angry with me, all right, and botched every task I gave her, but it kept her out of my bed. I'd not compromise her, not when she was ill and adrift."

"But if she had been hale and her memories whole?"

"I'm noble, not neutered." Luka snorted and threw another log in the fire. "When I confronted her today, I told her we weren't married. Something inside her snapped. She cowered and winced whenever I came near. She called me George."

"Her husband. He was a mean son of a bitch. I'm not sorry he's dead."

"I'm glad, or else I'd hang when I returned to England to exact the pound of flesh he owes Tris."

Against his will, Thomas's attitude toward the other man softened. He questioned his own reactions in a similar situation, a young man thrust into a position of consequence, responsible for the lives of many. He might have left, too, and spared the woman he loved the hardships he'd have faced. As for the ridiculous farce and their pretend marriage, Thomas believed the man had not taken advantage of Beatrice and had done his best to see her cared for and safe. *Damn it. When I'm ready to punch the man and tear him limb from limb for harming Beatrice, he shows himself to be an honorable man who takes his responsibilities seriously.* Grudging admiration grew.

"There is a grave marker on my property in England. I had it erected when Beatrice came to live with me. You may visit, if you desire. She named the child Gabriel Lucas. The grave is empty, for the child's remains are not there. Beatrice does not know what happened to him after he died. The child's death and disappearance remain an open wound to this day."

"Thank you, Thomas. Maybe one day I will return to England and visit the boy's grave, but for now, I am needed elsewhere. Tomorrow I'll fetch my grandmother and wend my way to Russia, where my clan waits. Beatrice will be in good hands on her return to England."

"My journey, alas, is taking me to France. The man Beatrice fought the night of the explosion is rumored to be alive. Reports he has been spotted in Paris have arisen, and my superiors have ordered me to verify their truth."

"And if he's alive?"

"Kill him once and for all."

"And if you can't? Will Tris continue to be in danger from this man?"

"I'll stop him."

"How can you be so sure you'll succeed?"

"Because he raped my mother and forced her into a life of servitude, so it is my duty to see the evil bastard is wiped from existence."

Luka whistled. "Does Bea know about your vendetta?"

"To some extent."

"You mean to the extent you were willing to tell her."

"She was told he is a threat to her country. And he is."

"You used her."

"No more than you."

"I didn't knowingly send her to danger."

"No, you pretended an affection when none existed."

Luka jumped to his feet and towered over Thomas. "Don't twist what I shared with Tris into something manipulative and evil. I loved her so much I was willing to walk away, to set her free to love someone who could give her what she needed."

"She needed you, and you weren't there! I was left to gather the pieces of her failed marriage and her heartbreak over losing you. It took me years to win her trust, and years more to earn her love. Where were you? Don't tell me you loved her. Not when leaving her nearly ended her life."

"I may not have been there when she needed me, but I would have if I had known. I love her to this day."

"Not enough to stay, because once again, you're running away."

"Do not insult me by suggesting I'm a coward. I have responsibilities outside my own desires, so take your sanctimony and shove it up your arse, Thomas. What about you? You claim to love her, too, but not enough to tell her the truth."

Stefano snapped his jaws together, his silent fuming glare fuel for Thomas's own raging anger. His nostrils flared, and he calculated the distance over the fire, the urge to wrap his hands around Stefano's throat a physical ache.

He lurched when a stiff breeze carried through the clearing and sparks shot off from the main campfire. Both men jumped back to avoid the live embers. By the time the breeze settled and the flames no longer leapt out of its secure circle, Thomas's anger had receded.

Across the circle, Stefano had dropped his arms to his side, the black fire of anger receding and gusting away with the wind. He slumped to the sand, propping his chin in his hand. Thomas joined him.

"Neither of us has been honorable to her," Thomas said, breaking the awkward silence.

"I can't offer her more than when I left her ten years ago."

"And I can't tell her the truth yet."

"Neither of us deserves her."

"You're right. What are we going to do about it?"

"I'll return to my family and leave her in peace. My reemergence in her life has been tainted by lies and manipulation. In time, maybe she'll remember the good moments we shared with passing fondness."

"I was going to take her with me to find Michelson, but I can no longer countenance sending her to danger. I'll secure her passage to England, and find my father on my own."

"At least she'll be safe." Stefano grew quiet and sprawled in the sand, his soft snores an irritant grating on his already troubled mind.

Thomas stared at the flames long into the night. Restless sleep found him in the early hours of morning, and bird song heralded him awake. He rose and walked to the cottage, alarmed to find the door flung wide open. Someone had thrust a knife in the wooden plank. The sharp tip held a single piece of white paper. Ripping the paper from the knife's hold, he scanned the letter.

"Stefano, wake up! Damn it all. She's gone to France!"

Chapter 22

Maryport, England, May 1810

Maryport in Cumberland was a quaint village near the Irish Sea. Built on the remains of an ancient Roman fort, it integrated modern and timeless design to create a charming and unique town. Regimented cobblestone roads, enduring evidence of the Romans' far-reaching influence, took Beatrice to the town's center, where she found a local pub. With a few discreet inquiries, and several greased palms, she had the information she desired regarding Anthony Longe's whereabouts. Remounting her steed, she followed the paved road to the edge of town, where the newly erected lighthouse stood, a beacon of light for the distressed at sea. It also served as a notable landmark, for despite Anthony Longe's best efforts to remain hidden on the outskirts of town, his cottage's proximity to the lighthouse had ensured his presence remained fresh in the townspeople's minds.

Beatrice slowed her mount as the lighthouse came into view, and she spied the dirt road forking off from the main thoroughfare. With a flick of her reins, she maneuvered her mount onto the narrow path, careful to walk at a sedate pace lest her horse's hooves announce her arrival. Though the sea's crash and roar deafened most other sounds, she knew a man like Longe, a hired mercenary with a sizable bounty on his head, would be more alert to the minutest disturbances than most. Upon spying the house, a small, thatched, whitewashed cottage surrounded by towering trees and dense foliage, she dismounted and stole a quick peek through the dirt-smudged windows. Someone was at home, for a husky figure sat slouched in a chair before the hearth, a glass clutched in his hands. She tethered her mount at the back of the house and rubbed him with grass, promising him a more thorough currying when she finished her business with Anthony Longe.

After much debate, she had decided to present herself to Longe as a man. Though the idea to play the damsel in distress and use her considerable charms to coerce the man to do as she desired had its merits, she did not wish to appear weak, a distinct disadvantage when dealing with unsavory sorts. "At least I look the part," she said, glancing at her state of dishabille and grimacing. Her shirt was dirty, wrinkled, and coming out from her breeches, and a ripe aroma wafted from her underarms. Mud caked her boots and speckled her tan riding pants, and grime encrusted her fingernails and coated her face. Her golden curls lay like greasy ropes around her face, and she sighed, knowing the day she'd need to shear her locks was fast approaching. After a halfhearted attempt to straighten her person, she tucked her golden curls under her cap and knocked on the cottage door.

The door slanted open, and two hard eyes peered through the crack. "What do you want?" a gruff voice growled.

"You Longe?" she asked, careful to lower her voice to a harsh rasp. She tugged the cap farther over her forehead and took Longe's measure. Not as tall as his brother Andrew, the man before her possessed the same chestnut locks and brown eyes, but where Lord Smith's had been warm and open, his younger brother's possessed a hard, calculating glint.

"What's it to you?" he sneered, spitting on the ground

She was undeterred by his bristling anger and rested her arm on the jamb. "I've business to discuss with the one they call the Pirate Longe."

"We've no business together, stranger, and it's to your fortune we don't. Heed my warning and be gone before I decide you are worth my notice." He tried to close the door, but she had inserted her foot between the door and the jamb and braced her shoulder against the solid wooden plank. He scowled.

"You're captain of *The Stallion of the Sea*. I'm your new first mate."

"Ho-ho! Someone esteems himself in high regard. You're nothing more than a puny stoat, no more fit to be my first mate than you are to shine my shoes." In his amusement, Longe had released his hold on the door, and she took the opportunity to shove her way into the cottage.

His scowl deepened at her intrusiveness, and she recalled one of Master Jones's earliest lessons: *An angry man is a malleable one, for anger overpowers judgment.* As long as her behavior continued to upset him, she had the advantage. Best to press forward before he grew wise to her game. "But first mate I will be, for I assure you, as fierce as your reputation as pirate smuggler, I am better." She walked to the sideboard, selected a glass, and poured herself a sizable amount of whisky from the opened bottle. Sidling to the small table, she turned the chair around and straddled the seat.

He remained wary, but he grunted and sat opposite her. "Such boastfulness for one so young and frail. The first storm we'd encounter at sea, and you'd be knocked overboard, or you'd be green at the gills and puking all over the deck. No, you're no sailor, boy. Who filled your head with such optimistic drivel?"

She drained her glass and set it on the table with a clank. "Do not confuse size with strength," she said, pleased to note his increased color and agitation. "I have been trained by the best."

"Who would take on such a weakling?"

"Have you heard of Ching Shih?" He blanched, and she laughed. "I see you have."

"You lie. How did you, a mere nothing of a boy, come to be trained by the pirate queen herself?"

Beatrice had lied. Oh, she knew who Ching Shih was. Master Jones had instructed her on the woman's influence when she had sailed to China seven years ago. Chinese sailors under Master Jones's command had taught her everything she knew about sailing and commanding a ship and had ensured her safety while she was learning. Never having met the woman was a mere technicality. It had, however, been a possibility, for the woman dominated the China Sea. From all accounts, she was fierce, and her rules were law. Everyone who sailed knew it, too, but Beatrice had never had the bad fortune to experience her laws firsthand. Longe, though, didn't need to know that particular detail.

"As I told you before, I was trained by the best, and

I will be your first mate, if not captain," she said. She selected an apple from the small bowl in the middle of the table and took a bite, almost choking on the first bite from restrained laughter. His eyes bulged, and a vein in his forehead throbbed. *Finally. I've pushed him to the edge. Now to tip him over.* She grimaced and spit the apple piece onto the floor. "What a mealy piece of shite. Is this the caliber of food the dread pirate eats? Whoever told me you were a man of discriminating tastes was wrong. You're no better than the locals, drinking the tavern piss the pub keeper passes for ale. I'd sooner sail a dinghy with a leper than serve under you."

Longe's nostrils flared, and the acrid tang of sweat mixed with violent excitement hung between them. Her own pulses sped in anticipation. "You insolent little pup. I ought to wring your neck for such disrespect."

"Do it."

His hands on the scarred wooden table twitched, and she tensed her leg muscles, springing from her seat as he lunged for her across the table. He roared and threw the table against the sideboard, and turned, a rage-filled mask contorting his placid features. She watched him from the open doorway and sprinted as he chased after her. When he was halfway out the door, she slammed the door on his arm, trapping it between jamb and rough wooden plank. He grabbed her and wrapped an arm about her waist, pulling her in to a one-sided embrace. Instead of struggling, she released the pressure on the door, twined her arms around his neck, and pulled herself over his head to perch on his shoulders. With her thighs wrapped around his neck, she squeezed until he staggered and fell to his knees.

When he pounded the ground with his hand, she pushed him to the dirt and released him from between her thighs. The man collapsed and rolled over, cradling his injured arm.

"Who are you?" he gasped, gazing at her in disgruntled admiration.

"I am Captain Allen Braithwaite, and I am your salvation, Anthony Smith," she said, using his given last name instead of the pseudonym under which he sailed. "And I am here to steal your command."

****

After some cursory snarling, an unfortunate reprisal of Longe's attempt to strangle her, and a heated discussion in which her elbow remained lodged in the man's trachea and her knife blade a whisper from his cods, Anthony Longe agreed to cede his command of *The Stallion* to her.

Two weeks later they approached the eve of his departure. They had arrived in Oban several days past and were waiting for their employer to finish some business before sailing for Southampton and on to France. Beatrice had grown to admire Anthony Longe, and while his choice of career was at odds with her sense of duty, she could not fault the man's work ethic or leadership. He ran a tight ship with absolute discipline, and while the sailors were thieves, they maintained a strict ethical code which ensured the safety and prosperity of everyone who sailed. His ship was well run.

"My ship, now," she said, and took in the sparse wooden furnishings in the captain's quarters and her few belongings she had just transferred to the room. She settled on the comfortable wooden chair near the window, ran her hands over the smooth arms, and sighed. She'd done it. Lady Beatrice Westby, former society beauty, had commandeered a ship.

"I'm in the room, Braithwaite," Longe said. "You can wait to do your gloating until I'm on shore."

She snorted. "You're halfway out the door as it is. Let me have this moment."

"Females. You're all the same. You can't help crowing over a victory, whether you're in the drawing room or in the captain's room."

"What did you say?" Tightness coiled in her stomach, and she stood, her muscles tensed and ready to attack if provoked.

"I know you're female, Braithwaite," he said.

She clenched her fists as her heart beat a rapid staccato in her ears. *Lord, I'll have to kill him.* Killing had been part of her training, and though she had not done so since her husband, she was prepared. *Or at least I hope I am.* Longe was a grumpy, scowling bastard, but she'd come to like him in their short acquaintance. Despite her best efforts, she blanched.

"Don't get all fidgety on me now," he said, waving his hands to have her resume her seat. "I've known for a while. I'll not share your secret as a result of my departure."

"How?" she asked, and slumped in her chair.

"Your scent. The day you tracked me to my cottage, you wrapped your legs around my neck. Over the sweat, dirt and horse, I smelled your feminine heat. It's unmistakable."

"Since then? Does anyone else—?"

He shook his head. Most of the crew find you a bit puny, but all agree you're fierce and not to be crossed.

You'll not have any problems commanding them once I'm gone."

"Why?" she asked, and hoped he understood what she was asking.

"I'm not saying I haven't liked my life, but smuggling to the French has never set well with me. I had convinced myself it didn't matter because I couldn't see who was being hurt by my actions. Talking about my brother with you, hearing about his deceased wife and his children reminded me who I was. It became more and more difficult to reveal your identify the longer we remained in company."

"Thank you. Will you return home?"

"I might, to say goodbye before I leave for the Americas."

"Your brother wants to see you," she said. "I know it would mean a lot to him."

"And your family? Do they know what risks you take?"

"No, and it's best if they don't. My younger sister has recently eloped. She and her husband live not far from here. Though I miss her, it's best to remain in the shadows."

"What a lonely life."

"It's a path of my choosing. I have no regrets."

"After a lifetime of shadow, I have many and wish to fix some of them, if you're ready to take me to shore."

"Yes. If we leave now, I can be back before my employer returns." The two left the room and walked mid-ship toward the shore dinghy hanging from the side. They lowered the dinghy into the water and clambered down a rope ladder to board.

Once they each had oars in hand, she asked, "What is Michelson doing here anyway?"

"Something to do with his son. He's been obsessed with some red-haired society miss who eloped and jilted him. He's going to try and convince the girl to leave her husband."

She pulled her oars from the water. "The red-haired woman sounds like my sister. If they have her, she is in serious danger, for there is no gentle convincing with this family."

He put his oar over his legs and slapped his thigh, as though pieces to a puzzle he couldn't see fell into place. "It all makes sense, why you targeted *The Stallion* and how you came to possess such skills as a captain and a fighter. You know Michelson. You've been planning this for years," Longe said. "Given who your sister is, I even know who you are."

"Please—"

Holding up his hand, he stopped her frantic plea. "Don't fret. Your secret is safe with me, but now I'm curious as to what prompted you to choose this life."

"Michelson has ruled my family with power and wealth for too long. My father is a weak man and has never defended himself to Michelson. He sold my sister Amelia to Michelson's son Jeremy in exchange for cessation of aggressions between the two. When my sister eloped with her husband, I imagined her to be safe. Fool! I should never have left her."

"Recriminations do nothing but intensify guilt. Trust me. Action is better suited to the remorse churning inside. Let's row. He has a private home near the beach. If they've taken her, she'll be there."

The two rowed in silence and soon landed on

shore. They pulled the boat onto the sand and concealed it with some large branches. "I leave you here," Longe said. "I can't risk Michelson seeing me and taking action against my brother and his children. In another life, I could see us…" He shook his head and smiled, the first genuine smile she'd seen on his rugged face since their introduction. "Good luck, Captain Braithwaite." He kissed her on her bearded cheek and fled, his escape cloaked by the inky darkness and the roaring waves pounding on the shore.

Chapter 23

Dielette, France, October 1810

Thomas and Stefano steered the sailboat to shore on the western coast of France and docked her in Dielette's port. A return of rainy weather and choppy seas delayed their arrival, and Beatrice had almost two weeks' head start. Thomas was frantic, though he'd not admit to such an emotion. Not in front of Stefano. The man had been insufferable and smug their entire two-week sea voyage, having read Beatrice's note and learning he, Thomas Wickes, was responsible for her late night departure to France. In her scrawled note she had pinned to the door, Beatrice confessed she'd heard the entirety of his conversation with Stefano. She'd discovered his parentage and had decided their entire relationship, which was built on a small omission on his part, was a fictitious fairytale he'd woven to gain her cooperation in his vendetta.

Barmy female. Thomas had never questioned Beatrice's mental state before, but this twisted logic convinced him her mental faculties remained addled. A pretty female traveling alone across war-torn France was concerning enough, but when the woman was a befuddled and lethal Lady Beatrice Westby, Thomas's level of concern elevated to near historic heights of agitation. He must find her—and soon—or risk losing her forever.

A patrol of French soldiers passed by their hiding spot, and they retreated farther into the shadows. "We need some sort of transportation," Thomas said. Obtaining any sort seemed an impossible task, as large numbers of French soldiers swarmed the port. They'd been lucky to avoid detection thus far, using the cloak of darkness to conceal their entrance. He'd not risk their luck and tarry on the docks much longer.

"What do you recommend? A coach? The public roads are unsafe, and any horseflesh capable of pulling a rig has been conscripted to Napoleon's army."

"Walking will take too long. Beatrice has been gone for almost two weeks. She could be anywhere."

"Or she is where she said she would be in her note, investigating reports of Michelson's whereabouts in Paris."

Thomas didn't like Stefano's answer any more than he relished the idea of walking across the battlefields of northern France to Paris. He ran his hands through his hair and scrubbed his face with his palms. "I need to find her, Stefano, but first we need to hole up someplace safe."

Stefano beckoned. "Come on. There's a small pub not far from here. During the day it's swarming with officers, but this late at night it might be less crowded."

Entering the pub, Wickes pulled his sailor's cap low over his forehead and found a table in a darkened corner while Stefano bought each of them a pint. When he brought them to the table, Stefano slid into the empty chair next to Thomas's own and took a long swallow of his ale. Thomas stared into the foamy liquid, worry churning his stomach.

"Why the urgency to find her, if not for your sense of guilt? You did mislead her, and as she said in her note, she is more than capable of caring for herself."

"We didn't leave each other on the best of terms. When she left me in London early in May, she went north to find the captain of *The Stallion of the Sea*. I followed and reunited with her in Oban, where we had an ugly disagreement. She boarded the ship and sailed south, while I remained behind to fix a mess her father had made. In her absence, I was shot and could not travel to Southampton as soon as I would have liked, and I feared she'd have sailed before we could talk and finalize plans. With the deluge of rain this June, I was able to intercept her one night at a local pub before she sailed, when she terminated our romantic relationship and told me she was retiring from a life of espionage once the final job was completed. There was no time to convince her otherwise, and I didn't take it well."

"Why did she end things with you?"

"She said she had used me enough, and I was too good a person."

"Implying she wasn't. How ironic, though, for her to leave to avoid using you when you have been doing the same your entire relationship."

"The irony is not lost on me, Stefano," he said, his voice a thunderclap of anger. "Regardless, guilt festers within her and she blames herself for what her husband did to her. She has also never forgiven herself for ending the bastard's life."

"You didn't tell me she killed her husband."

"I didn't want to overburden your conscience, not after I told you so poorly about your child. It haunts her to this day. His death and the loss of her child."

"My poor Tris. Such a hard life she has led. It explains why she screams at night."

"You've heard?"

"It's…unearthly. I asked my grandmother about it. Aba said she had experienced great anguish, and her mind suffered. I can't even imagine the pain she has had to endure. A lesser woman would have broken."

"Hell, anyone would have broken after the horrors she's lived. I want to help her, but she said she doesn't need me anymore."

Stefano smirked and rocked back in his chair. "So to prove her wrong, we're going to chase her across a battle-strewn country to find her."

"She needs me, even if she's too stubborn to admit it."

"Maybe she's not the stubborn one."

"When we find her and she tells me to go, I'll go."

"But not without a fight."

"No, which is why I must find her. I love her."

Stefano's arms bunched and tensed before he sighed. "*Merde.* Why did you have to go and say that?"

Thomas stiffened, crossing his arms over his chest. He didn't know what Stefano was about, but he was positive he wasn't going to like it. "It's true, and what's it to you? I said it before."

"Not like this. Not like she was your entire world."

"It's none of your business whether she is or not."

"It is now." Stefano stared at his glass, his jaw clenched, as if he were coming to some decision. He heaved a sigh and nodded once. "I can get you to Paris within a week, if not sooner."

"What? How?"

Stefano pushed up his sleeves. "Do you trust me?"

173

"Not particularly."

"You haven't a choice. Do you speak French?"

"Yes, but—"

"Sorry, Thomas. Don't take this the wrong way." Stefano made a fist, reared his arm back, and punched him in the face.

Blood gushed from his nostrils and dripped to his mouth, the iron tang coating his lips and tongue. "What the hell?" He was wiping his nose with the back of his sleeve when the bastard hit him again. Thomas ducked, rallied, and managed to clip Stefano's jaw before the nomadic traitor kneed him in the stones. Thomas dropped to the ground and gasped.

"*Salaud*! Quiet, you filthy *anglais!*" Stefano yelled. "*Gardes!*"

Several French soldiers who had been drinking in the next room came running, including a young *capitaine*.

Thomas's instincts screamed at him to stand and defend himself, but the pain was too intense. Luka solved the problem for him, yanking him from the floor and plopping him in a chair. With a length of rope from round his waist, Stefano tied Thomas's hands behind his back. He was stuck.

The young captain sneered at Stefano before taking Thomas's chin in his hand. The French officer studied his face and spit on the floor. "Who have we here, peasant?"

Stefano crossed his arms over his chest, towering tall and massive as a stone slab. Thomas had never seen anyone as formidable as Luka Stefano. He was no lightweight himself and had, therefore, underestimated the man. Staring at him now in the dim light from the tavern lanterns, civility's thin veneer vanished and revealed him as the warrior he was. "A gift for General Reynard." Thomas registered the moment Stefano's expression changed from grim to dangerous. The young captain did not do so and sneered at his own peril.

"What do you know of Reynard?"

"Enough. You will take me to him."

"Reynard has moved on to Paris. Besides, I'd sooner take a pox-ridden whore to Reynard than a half-breed mongrel like you."

Stefano stalked closer to the captain, towering over the smaller man. He smiled, a wicked flash of gleaming white teeth against bronzed skin. The captain gulped, his Adam's apple bobbing from nervousness. "What message do you want me to deliver?"

"Tell him the French Wolf has brought him an English dog."

****

Much of what occurred next was clouded in a haze of pain and betrayal. Once the guards were convinced of Stefano's identity, Thomas was trussed like a Christmas goose and thrown into a rickety cart. He slept and awoke to a gentle swaying. Various barrels and boxes surrounded him, the smell of salt air coated his tongue, and the loud groaning and creaking from shifting deck slats oriented him soon enough. He was at sea. From the dim light, stale air, and cargo piled around him, he was in the hold. "Where are we going?"

A hard poke in his ribs roused him, and he tilted his head back, squinting to see who had found him. Stefano loomed above him, his grim expression and palpable worry poor compensation for wounded pride. Thomas scowled.

175

"Good. You're awake. I brought you some whisky to dull the pain and see to the cuts on your face." Stefano untied him and handed him the bottle.

Thomas hefted the bottle in his hand like the stones in the schoolyard of old, calculated the effort to raise the bottle over his aching head, and winced when a raw wound stretched and opened on his jaw. Better to use the liquid inside to cleanse the wounds before bashing Stefano's brains with the empty bottle. Several questions lurked, waiting to jump out, but he recalled the most surprising revelation Stefano's betrayal had revealed. "You're the French Wolf? We've been hunting you for years. You've stolen hundreds of thousands of pounds in supplies meant for British troops. You're a wanted man."

"By the French, as well. I've angered many people."

"For what? To secure Napoleon's reign?"

"I told you not to take it the wrong way. It's nothing personal. England was once my home, as is France, but I needed coin. My people were starving, and scavenging provided for them when nothing else did."

Stefano offered his arm and hoisted him up. He snatched his arm away and rubbed his jaw, glaring at the man. "I should kill you, for no other reason than because you throw a mean right punch. My jaw is throbbing."

Stefano crossed his arms over his chest and widened his stance, unconcerned Thomas had threatened to kill him. "We were in a difficult situation and needed a quick way to get to Paris. Across land was near impossible. We'd be stopped and questioned, or worse, conscripted. This way, we're avoiding the majority of the fighting and will be escorted directly to Reynard. You'll be with Tris before week's end."

"Not if I'm a prisoner." Thomas rubbed his wrists, the rope burns raw and painful, and prodded his ribs. He cringed but a more thorough prod didn't reveal any were broken.

"You won't be. I will."

"What?"

"I don't need to escort you to Reynard's camp. Others have delivered goods I've salvaged, so it won't be unusual for me to refuse to continue into Paris. When we near the city, we'll switch places, and I will be taken to Reynard instead of you."

"We look nothing alike, and despite the young captain's obvious fear of your reputation, it has not rendered him witless."

"Our builds are similar enough I will pass for you."

"You'll be killed."

"Probably."

"But why?"

"My time has come. The choices I've made to ensure my clan's survival have muddied my morals until I've had to search to find the man I once was. This is the right choice for me. No one needs me. My clan is taken care of, as is Tris. You'll see she's happy."

"What are you saying, Stefano?"

"One of us can have her, and it's not meant to be me. My destiny lies in a Paris prison. There are consequences to my actions, consequences I have avoided for years. No more. I won't die a coward."

"If you were planning on turning yourself in all this time, why did you have to hit me and turn me over to the French? I could have presented you and spared us both this ruse."

"There was a chance you'd be taken too. Your French is not as good as you believe, and your acting skills are questionable. I saw how you tried to hide your anguish over Tris's defection, and you failed miserably. Better you were unconscious and unable to open your mouth. Otherwise, you'd have given us away for sure." Thomas's inner child heaved a huge rock at the man's head.

Stefano, oblivious to his turmoil, smirked and slugged him on the shoulder. "Plus, you're getting my girl. You owed me some pleasure for my sacrifices."

Gratitude for Stefano's gift moved him beyond his petty jealousies, and he held out his hand. "Thank you. She will want for nothing the rest of her days."

"Assuming you can convince her to return with you."

"I'll do my best. She's worth it."

"I have one favor to ask before we part."

"Anything."

"Tell her I love her."

Chapter 24

The Stallion of the Sea, The Atlantic, June 1810

Beatrice closed the door behind her and rested her forehead on the wooden plank separating her from her sister, Evie, and the man who had stowed aboard *The Stallion of the Sea* to claim her. Alfred Coombes was a brave man, full of shrewd logic and integrity. He was also the perfect man for her headstrong little sister. Beatrice couldn't be happier the two had found each other, and she prayed she had the strength to say goodbye forever.

Slipping between the shadows, Beatrice hurried across the deck, down the ladder to the hold, and through the connecting passage to the galley. There she prepared for her night's work. Poison, Master Jones had said, was as intricate and demanding a mistress as physical combat, and Beatrice had bedded this particular lady for years. She'd studied which plants rendered a man immobile but aware, ideal for a particular brand of torture, and which killed within moments. The sleeping draught she had gifted her sister Evie on her eighteenth birthday was a potion of her own design, ensuring the victim would pass an oblivious afternoon none the wiser. It was this potion she now prepared.

The galley cook was abed, so Beatrice moved

about the room unhindered by her attentive crew or her own attempts to be a man. After so many weeks, playing the part of Captain Allan Braithwaite came more easily with each passing day, though the continued ruse was tiring. The sooner this job was finished, the sooner she could leave this life behind. Thomas hadn't believed her when she'd broken off their professional and romantic relationship, a week past in Southampton, but she'd never been more serious. The game's cost was too dear, both physically and emotionally. It had been years since Beatrice had experienced any emotion other than the ones demanded by the part she played; it was impossible to distinguish between the two. Hence the decision to retire after this job. After the ship exploded and Michelson was dead, her debt to Thomas was paid. If Thomas had an inkling she viewed their relationship as such, he'd have terminated the professional aspect years ago. But a debt was owed. Thomas had saved her, given her a purpose, and taught her the skills she'd need to never be at a man's mercy again.

She removed from her inner coat pocket a sachet containing her own blend of dried plants and stirred them into the pot of boiling water. Soon, a steady vapor arose from the water, dangerous if ingested. Taking out her pocket watch, she marked the time. Thirty more minutes of boiling, and the mixture would be ready to process. She sat at the small table Cook kept in the galley and removed an object from her breast pocket, unable to resist pulling out the worn parchment despite her efforts to ignore its presence.

Unfolding the letter, she traced the neat hand, her heart pounding in her chest at the man's bold scrawl.

He'd written her. The letter had awaited her at the local pub in Southampton, and had she not met Thomas there before sailing, she'd never have received it.

Dear Captain Braithwaite,

Imagine my surprise when last week my brother came to visit. As you know, we've been estranged for years. At first I was unwilling to meet with him, but when he told me of your sister, a young woman named Beatrice, who had convinced him to attempt reconciliation, I was intrigued and flattered. When I discovered how she had worked so diligently to ferret out my secrets and arrange this meeting, flattery devolved to cynicism. I had enjoyed the company of your sister and had imagined a mutual attraction, though now her interest in a middle-aged country farmer makes more sense. I did visit your home to ask permission for a courtship, but your sister had gone. I can assume she was not ready for what I had to offer, and I regret the missed opportunity to know her better. She was a lovely young woman, a little lonely and sad despite her pretty smiles and engaging conversation.

My brother has informed me of your career, Captain Braithwaite, and from comments my brother has made, the path you are on is equally lonely, as well as dangerous. You have my gratitude for finding and returning my brother to me for even such a brief period. One day I'll repay the favor. Perhaps, Captain, much like my brother, you are in need of a friend. If such a day arrives, I would be honored to be one for you.

Sincerely, Lord Andrew Smith

P.S. Before he left, my brother gave me your most likely direction, so do not fear either he or I will compromise your chosen course. He bade me tell you it's never too late to leave and find a new path.

She put the letter on the table with a sigh and stared at Lord Smith's signature until the ink blurred. When she'd left Anthony Longe on the beach in Oban, she'd told him she had no regrets. The inked parchment in front of her was proof enough she lied. For one night, she was Beatrice Westby, society beauty and companion to a charming gentleman. It wasn't real, though. None of it had been. Beatrice was a part she played to acquire what she wanted. Captain Braithwaite was as authentic as her society self, and she was left with a hollow sensation akin to dread. For years, she'd played a part to achieve one goal or another, and with the end near, she had no new persona to take on. The idea of finding and adopting her real self was daunting. *What if I don't know who I am?*

"Lord, I hate being maudlin." She tested it out and found it was true whether she was playing a part or being herself. "At least I know one true thing about myself."

"Is everything ready for tonight?" Jones asked, interrupting her self-pitying. He sank onto the stool opposite her.

She tucked the letter under her hands. "The sleeping potion is almost done, and I'll set the fuses once the evening meal is complete."

"What's in your hand?" Jones, drat the man, missed nothing. He eyed the parchment until she tucked it away in her jacket pocket.

"Nothing. A letter for someone who no longer exists."

He pinned her with an assessing stare, and she resisted the urge to fidget. Dissembling with Master

Jones was ineffectual and a waste of time. He was a ferret, able to seek out the truth amidst a mountain of lies.

"Do you know why I agreed with Thomas's plan to train you?"

"I assumed it was because you are friends."

"Thomas Wickes is an honorable man who inspires great loyalty but rarely friendship."

"If it wasn't friendship, why?"

"Because I knew what it was to be lost and alone, powerless against those who would seek to exploit. The day in your bedroom when I attacked, I saw something in you."

She snorted. "Most likely fear. You had me pinned to the wall and shaking in my night rail in under a minute."

His lips curved in an approximation of a smile. "Yes, there was fear, but there was also light. For despite the darkness which had all but consumed you, I saw a spark, a part of you which refused to give in. That's why I agreed to train you."

She studied her hands, clutched white in anxiety and unspoken fear. "What if I'm not the same person anymore?"

His exasperation colored each word. "Of course you've changed. Everything changes."

"But what if the change isn't good?"

"What is it you are afraid of?"

"I'm afraid I've lost myself, that without this life, I don't know who I am anymore."

"Look at me." He took her chin in his weathered brown hands and studied her for countless moments.

"Well?"

"I have seen your soul, Beatrice Westby. Kind, witty, generous, and terrified, you hide yourself so others won't guess at your pain."

She flinched and jerked her head away. His hands dropped to the table. "He has been dead for years. My actions have nothing to do with him."

"The lies you tell yourself! You knew who I was talking about without hearing his name. Of course he has everything to do with the choices you've made these last eight years, and he will continue to influence them until you give yourself permission to be human. You made a mistake a long time ago and have punished yourself since."

"You and Thomas are the ones who taught me what I know. You gave me this purpose."

"We gave you a way to channel your pain. What you did with it afterwards was your decision."

"But Thomas…I owe him a debt."

"At no time did your imagined debt outweigh your desires and goals. Had you wished to stop, he'd have directed your energies to something else. You alone chose this life. Not Thomas, not me, and especially not George."

"It's all my fault. All of this, the baby, my marriage, it's my fault. I'm to blame."

"Beatrice, what happened to you was not your fault. George Darimple was an evil man, and you were unfortunate enough to be his property. But his actions do not define you. They do not decide your worth or your value. They do not dictate who you are. You alone control how you see yourself."

She clutched the older man's hands in her own, her throat thick with unshed tears. "I don't know anymore who she is, Master Jones," she whispered. "Tell me, please!"

He stood and pressed a soft kiss to the crown of her head. Squeezing her hand, he said, "You will rediscover your spark and find your way home when you're ready, Beatrice Westby. I promise." Master Jones bowed and left the galley, plunging her into a dark despair.

A loud hissing signaled its need for attention as water from the boiling pot roiled over the sides onto the fire. She checked her pocket watch. Her thirty minutes were over. She removed the pot from the fire and prepared the potion for the evening's meal. After cleansing the galley of all traces she'd been there, she wrote a letter to her sister Evie, blew out the candle, and sat at the little table. As darkness faded to dawn and sounds of the crew's awakening rustled around her, she contemplated Master Jones's words, but she was no closer to deciding whether this night she'd live or die. Sighing, she heaved away from the table, walked through the hold, and went onto the deck to watch the sunrise.

There was nothing left but to wait.

****

Everything had gone wrong. Correction. Almost everything had gone wrong. Her sister Evie was off the boat, which was now a raging inferno primed to blow. Michelson, who was not drugged into indefinite sleep with the rest of the crew, had awakened to find her checking the fuses.

The potion hadn't worked. Michelson stood tall and angry in the hold, the grogginess from the herbal tea she'd mixed hindering his movements, for he weaved on unsteady feet across the hold and tripped on barrels blocking his path. With a thud, he fell to the floor, and she did not stop to question her actions. She lit the fuses.

Her original plan called for her to be miles away, rowing to Guernsey, when *The Stallion,* her cargo, and the traitors who called her home exploded and floundered at sea. Michelson, damn him, had ruined everything, and if she didn't want to perish with the ship, she needed to flee.

Sprinting to the exit, she climbed the ladder, yelling, "Michelson's awake! Jones! The fuses are set! Cut the rope now!"

She heard a piercing scream, followed by a large splash, relief swift to replace her initial concern. Her sister and Mr. Coombes were off the ship. Now to ensure she herself didn't die with the rats. Running across the deck, she climbed onto the quarterdeck to better prepare for Michelson's attack. She did not wait for long. Fire licked the wood, escaping from below deck, and the man emerged from the hold illuminated by the orange flames wending their way across the wooden floor. He was wreathed in smoke, his gruesome features contorted to a feral mask of savage intent. Beatrice had long suspected the devil was real, and an involuntary shudder wracked her small body. She was going to die.

"Cap'n!" Jones yelled, and she turned her head. A flash of steel flew through the air, and she caught her sword. Jones ran to her side, and the two crouched in position. She watched and waited as Michelson removed a sword from the scabbard at his hip and charged, leaping to the quarterdeck with agility and speed.

He circled her and snarled. "You're Westby's git, aren't you, girl? And if I'm not mistaken, Thomas Wickes's pet project. I recognized your Chinaman. You call him Jones. Thomas loves collecting the outcasts and giving them a second chance. I can't believe he convinced an intelligent woman like you to do his dirty work, but my boy was too much of a coward to face me."

She pushed this new information about Thomas aside, not ready to contemplate what Michelson had revealed. If the traitor was to be believed, Thomas had been using her for years. She hated being someone's pawn in a game to which she understood only part of the rules. Anger prompted her to speak with uncharacteristic boldness. "Nobody sent me," she said. "Wanting to kill you has nothing to do with Thomas Wickes and everything to do with me. You've ruled my family for too long, Michelson. Killing you will be a pleasure."

The stairs were close, and there was a chance she'd survive if she could dive overboard before the fuses arrived at their target. Already the ship listed and groaned as fire ate through the ship's wooden hull. Soon, the hot licking flames would ignite the gunpowder and they'd all be dead. Fighting was never her first choice. She'd flee if given the chance, but he had her boxed in between her cabin and the rails. There was no room to run; she'd have to fight.

Jones kept by her side as she circled Michelson. Seeing an opening, Beatrice lunged, but Michelson had been expecting her first move. He parried, and the two clambered across the deck, the ring of steel against steel competing with the sizzling crackle of burning wood.

Jones fought behind, forcing Michelson to divide his attention between the two. When smoke wafted from below deck and surrounded the three, cloaking them in a thick, pungent haze of charred wood and imminent demise, she lost track of Jones and Michelson. She kept the cabin wall to her back and skirted the perimeter of the quarterdeck, using the railing as a guide.

Jones lay on the deck; a large welt in his head bled onto the deck floor. The reassuring thread of Jones's pulse against her trembling fingers soothed her initial panic, yet the momentary distraction cost her. A keen slice of pain ripped through her torso, and she cried out. Metal pierced the tender skin below her breast, and she staggered and fell to the ground. The smoke cleared, and Michelson stood over her, his dark, leering face resurrecting forgotten panic and fear.

"A pity. You were smarter than I expected and even had me fooled, until your sister was brought aboard. The similarities were too prominent not to question your true identity. Some discreet eavesdropping outside your cabin, and I had enough to put together who you were, Beatrice Westby. Your reputation is well known to private entrepreneurs such as me and my associates." He shook his head and clucked his tongue. "How unfortunate reports exaggerated your skill with the blade. It makes killing you less exciting."

She gathered the remnants of her strength and plunged her sword in the man's foot. He crumpled and fell to his knees. They stared at each other for endless minutes, both panting in pain, before Beatrice reared back her arm and punched the man in the nose. Pulling herself to her feet, she stood over him and pressed the tip of her sword against the older man's neck. She stomped on his sword hand until he released his weapon. When she kicked the sword away, it clattered against the wooden deck.

"A notable difference between the two of us, Michelson. Killing you brings me nothing but satisfaction." She had tensed her arm, prepared to drive the sword through, when he held out his hands.

"If you kill me, you'll never know."

"Know what, you foul old man?"

"Where your son is," he said. Her sword arm faltered, the pressure on the man's neck eased, and he smiled, a gruesome mockery of mirth. "Correct, Captain," he said. "Your son."

"You're wrong, Michelson! He's dead! My husband told me—"

"And your husband was honest, was he? A kind man, one who would never beat his wife or servants?"

"He's dead," she repeated, though with less conviction.

Michelson threw back his head and laughed, a wild, frantic chortle which rose above the fire's sizzle and hiss as flames crept along the deck below them. "No, he lives, and I know where he is."

Not dead? Impossible! *Yet haven't I hoped he was alive?* Her arm trembled, and the sword shook in her hand. Triumph blazed from Michelson's black soul. *No, Michelson must die.* The debt she owed to Thomas was so close to being paid. She raised her sword, swung, and let it fall to the deck. Some things were more important than honor. "Go," she said. "Get out of here."

Michelson needed no further encouragement, for he stood. Before launching himself from the railing, he said, "Bring me Thomas, and I'll tell you what you want to know." In a moment, he was gone, the splash below confirmation he had landed in the water. Michelson would live. He was too stubborn and too evil to do anything but. She'd find him, and when she did, nothing short of a miracle would prevent her from discovering what she desired.

A loud groaning crack filled the silence following Michelson's departure, and Beatrice had mere seconds to dive out of the way as the main mast crashed to the deck. Though she avoided being crushed by the burning timber, she was now pressed against the stairway. It creaked and groaned before shuddering beneath her. She fell to the main deck as flaming chunks of stair crashed around her, trapping a portion of her left leg.

"Jones!" she yelled, hoping her friend and mentor would awaken and hear her cry. "Help!" She screamed until her voice was hoarse, all the while pushing at the smoldering wood with her hands. Skin, raw and charred, peeled off her hands, and she fought back an overwhelming urge to give in. "Jones!" she tried again.

"You let him go," Jones said as he stumbled over from where Michelson had felled him. Finding the two discarded swords, he used them to heave the remaining pieces of stair off Beatrice's leg.

She wriggled her leg from underneath the heavy weight, each movement a fresh wave of torment as pain licked through her body. "My son's alive, Jones. He knows where my son is."

"If you can believe the word of a murderous traitor," Jones said as he lifted her off the ground and helped her to the railing. Each agonizing step sent a jolt of pain through her body until she shook from the effort to remain upright. She clutched Jones's waist and turned her face to his, the familiar lines and wrinkles visible in the harsh, orange glare. A popping noise sounded from below, and *The Stallion* listed to the side. They were out of time. The fuses had found their target. "I have no other choice."

"Go, and find your son. Make your own path, and leave this world of secrets and danger behind."

"Come with me, Master Jones. We'll find him together."

"What was my first lesson?"

Tears having nothing to do with the pain in her body plopped on her cheeks, and she shook her head even as she said, "Know when it's time to leave."

He hugged her and said, "God be with you, Beatrice Westby." With a final bow, Master Jones stood as she pulled her burned leg behind her, grasped the rails of the tilting deck, and threw herself in the ocean's inky embrace.

Her son was alive, which was reason enough to live.

Sara Ackerman

Part III

"I've not considered my future. Someone else has done it for me. In twenty-eight years, nobody ever asked me what I wanted. Now that the future is mine, I'll tell you exactly what I want. As soon as I figure it out for myself."

~Beatrice Westby

Chapter 25

Paris, France, October 1810

Beatrice awakened to the muted sounds of grunting and a woman's high pitched squeal. Her heart pounding, she scanned the cramped, dim room, looking for a familiar sight to ease the panic her abrupt arrival to consciousness brought. A gentle snore focused her gaze on the lumpy cot adjacent to her bed. From her candle's muted light, she saw tousled brown locks and a snub nose poking out from above the threadbare quilt.

"Amy," she whispered, latching on to the name like a rope in a storm. Her memory continued to play tricks on her mind, but she would remember the child's snore for the rest of her life. The young girl, who was no more than twelve, had a musical nose. Every night for the past six weeks, Amy's whistling nose had serenaded her to sleep. It was maddening and endearing, and raised her protective instincts toward the child. Another grating laugh followed by a lusty moan penetrated the thin walls. These sounds she knew as well. One of the girls was entertaining a caller. Sleep's tenacious hold cleared, and she remembered.

She was in Paris at Madame Cosette's brothel, one of the few safe refuges for a single woman traveling in Paris. Most madams did not allow a single, attractive woman to stay at her home without the rough slide of sheets at her back, but Madame and Beatrice had a long history.

Cosette, a petite Frenchwoman with chestnut locks, wide, chocolate-colored eyes, and an oval face, had been a downstairs maid in her husband's London home when the pretty girl had caught her husband's roving hands. As with all his possessions, he had soon injured Cosette, and the girl feared for her life. Beatrice hadn't hesitated to help her, knowing all too well the cruel sting of George's spite. The girl had to leave. One day when George was out of town on business, she gathered her meager pin money, sold what jewelry was hers, and helped Cosette disappear. It took Bea six weeks to heal from the broken ribs George gifted her after discovering what she'd done. Years later, Cosette had written her and promised safe haven if she were ever in Paris. After fleeing Herm, she called in her favor and presented herself on Madame Cosette's doorstep late one chilly September night. She'd stayed with Madame since then.

The squealing and grunting from next door stopped, and Beatrice flopped her head back on the pillow. Now what? She was awake with no one but herself to talk to.

Time was a luxury she could ill afford. A life such as hers required dedication and meticulous attention to detail. Lives depended on her clarity of mind, so she focused on what she could control. Only in rare moments did she indulge in retrospection and regrets, a tedious and self-serving pastime in her opinion. Since arriving in Paris, she'd had nothing but time. Time to obsess about her son and whether Michelson had been lying. Time to dissect the meaning behind Thomas's and Luka's beachside conversation. Time to drive herself mad with waiting.

Six weeks had passed, and she'd yet to discover Michelson's location. She twitched under her bed sheets and ground her teeth together when Amy's nose hit a piercing note.

"For heaven's sake, Amy. Be quiet!" she hissed.

Amy's incessant whistling ceased, and her roommate snorted awake. "Did you say something, Beatrice?" she asked, her sleepy blue eyes struggling to open.

Contrition ate at her. Amy woke early and worked late. The child needed her sleep. Bea forced a gentle smile. "Go back to sleep. I'm sorry I woke you."

"Another bad dream?" She was awake and full of sympathy, having experienced Bea's nightmares before. Amy swung her legs over the bed, wrapping the quilt around her shoulders. She padded the short distance between their two beds and nudged her leg on the bed. "Move over, Bea. The floor's cold."

Scooting to the far side of the bed, Bea held open her blankets while Amy crawled in. The child curled like a kitten in sunshine and was soon asleep, her whistling fainter than before.

Bea flung a protective arm around the girl and snuggled in. The night was cold, and Amy's company helped chase away the chill. *Poor child.* Orphaned at the age of eight, she had been sent to Paris by her maternal aunt when it became too difficult to feed and clothe her along with her own children. Cosette had found her wandering the streets, a ragged urchin with more fleas on her than on the dogs she bedded with, and took her home. Amy had worked for her ever since, helping Cook in the kitchen and running small errands for the girls. At twelve years old, she'd seen more heartache and pain than most adults see in a lifetime, yet here she was in Bea's bed, offering comfort. She was two years older than her own child.

What is he like? Is he quiet and sincere, like dear Amy, or does he possess a wild streak like me and Luka? Is he even alive? Her arms ached to hold him, and a fierce longing, never far away, consumed her. She hated this constant worry and questioning. Action suited her, not this uncertain limbo. Cosette had cautioned her to be patient, a trait she'd barely mastered. She was doing all she could; all the girls were. Every day she went to the market with Amy to inquire after any men matching Michelson's description. Amidst fondling and kissing, the girls questioned their callers, and Cosette placed a discreet word in a high-ranking French official's ear, requesting information should he come across any. They'd found nothing, and Bea feared Michelson, and the location of her son, was gone.

Michelson could be anywhere by now. Paris was the most likely location, given the news Thomas had shared with Luka regarding what his superiors at the War Office had learned. Men like Michelson went where the fighting was the heaviest, to profit from the misfortune and despair which followed a war like the plague. Since Napoleon's recent marriage to Marie-Louise of Austria in April, the fighting had eased in the capital, and the majority of French and British troops fought on the peninsula. News from the front was infrequent, but yesterday word had arrived that Wellington had stopped an attempted invasion of the

Iberian Peninsula. The French retreated after suffering serious losses, and tensions in France's capital had been high since then. To ensure her safety, she'd have to refrain from asking questions about Michelson and caution Amy and the girls to cease for now, as well. When the news of this defeat faded and other battles caught the public's interest, she could resume her search. Until such time, she'd harness the often praised but seldom practiced patience. Maybe she and Amy could refashion some of the girls' discarded gowns. Amy was growing like a weed, and her work dress skimmed her knees. It was time for some new clothes, and though she was less than a proficient seamstress, she understood the basics and had nothing but time to practice. A new dress for Amy would bring a welcome distraction while she waited. Settling on a plan, she snuggled against Amy and slept.

****

The next morning, Bea talked to Cosette about making Amy a new day dress, and two of the girls volunteered their old gowns to be remade for the young girl. Amy heard her planning and almost burst from excitement. After a morning of constant pestering, Bea relented and took the girl to the front sitting room to measure and pin the fabric.

"Hold still!"

Amy wiggled and grabbed a swath of blue satin. "Look at the colors! I've never seen such a beautiful blue."

"If you move one more time, Amy, I swear you'll get pinned in your soft derriere, and I'll not be sorry."

The child froze, doing a grand imitation of a statue save for the impish smile on her face. "I'm sorry, Bea.

199

It's exciting to have a new dress. I promise not to squeal if you stick me again."

"Again? I was being careful," she said around a mouthful of pins.

Red stained Amy's cheeks. "Ah, I meant to say if you stick me. Again."

Bea sighed. "Has it been bad?"

"A few dozen pricks. Didn't hurt at all."

"Liar," Bea said, pulling on one of the girl's fat, brown braids before peeling back the pinned cloth. "I'm done with you anyway. Off to the kitchens with you. Cook was baking bread earlier today. Go and pester her for a change."

With a smile and a wave, Amy skipped out of the room. Bea gathered her supplies, pulled a chair near the window, and stitched. An hour later, Bea had sewn the skirt to the sleeve, her head ached, and her fingers bled from her sheer ineptness. "Damn," she said. "I'm never going to finish."

"You have other talents, my lady," Cosette said. The woman had entered the room without her awareness, an unheard of feat mere months ago.

She scowled. "You shouldn't arrive unannounced. It's not polite."

Cosette laughed. "I knocked and called out twice. You were engrossed in your sewing."

Bea showed her the skirt. "I'm awful. At this rate, I'll never finish her dress."

"Give. I have some free time the next several nights. I'll see what I can do."

"But I promised Amy I'd sew it."

"We've seen how well your attempt has gone, *mon amie*. It'll be our secret. You can give it to her and be the heroine. My gift to you."

Bea resisted the urge to protest, for the woman had more than repaid whatever debt she imagined she owed her. However, Cosette was as stubborn and proud as she, so Bea passed over the fabric with a smile and said, "Thank you."

"Now, I've brought you your tea. Cook was in a generous mood today, so we have an apple tart, fresh bread, and some aged cheese."

"Won't you stay?" Cosette never did, though, and Bea was unsurprised when she declined yet again. She viewed herself as the help and Bea as the lady of the house. Despite years of separation and dramatic changes for both of them, Cosette treated her as an honored guest.

"I'll be in my room attempting to, ah, undo all your hard work. Enjoy." Bea poured herself a cup of tea, but Cosette paused at the door. "Oh, you have a visitor. I forgot to mention it."

"For me? Is it Michelson?"

"Come, *chèrie.* You know a man such as he does not pay social calls. No, I was referring to a tall, handsome man who claims to be your fiancé."

"I don't have a fiancé."

She shrugged, a delicate lift of her shoulders, and said, "The man is here. Shall I send him in?"

Curiosity, as it was wont to do, prompted her to say yes, and when she looked through the door and met a pair of steely gray eyes, her heart warmed. In spite of their recent separation, he was a dear friend.

"Thomas! What are you doing here?"

"You didn't expect me to sit back and rusticate on Herm when you decided to take on Michelson by yourself."

"My decisions can have no bearing on your actions, Thomas. We are no longer involved."

His gray eyes darkened to forged steel. "Damn it, Beatrice! Of course they do!"

"Why? Because you take responsibility for me?"

"We've been together eight years, my lady, so yes, you are my responsibility."

"You saw to my education, Thomas. I assure you I am prepared for any eventuality. Tea?" She arranged a cup and poured, her movements precise and graceful in spite of the turmoil his presence had brought. Even though she had terminated their relationship, he had found her and was behaving with more than a little possessiveness.

He ran a frustrated hand through his hair and sat.

"How did you find me?" she asked when she had passed him his tea.

"I was there when you received the letter from Cosette. I assumed you'd come here, as the war has limited the establishments taking in boarders."

She raised the porcelain cup to her lips and sipped. "I'm disappointed, Thomas. Six weeks have passed. I expected you much sooner."

"We encountered some difficulties." He gulped the hot liquid and replaced his cup on the table, rubbing his hands together as he looked over the refreshments.

"We?" She arched a brow and stared over the rim of her cup.

Thomas grunted and placed some bread and cheese on a plate. "Stefano and I traveled together."

She returned her cup to its saucer, filled her plate, and sat back determined to enjoy her tart, a rare treat given the shortage of supplies in Paris. Luka Stefano and his choices were none of her concern, and she refused to let him spoil her afternoon. "He is continuing his journey east?"

"When we left Herm, Russia was his destination. I did mention we had some difficulties. He was captured and is being held prisoner in Paris."

Her fingers slackened, and her plate slipped from her hands to the floor. It landed with a dull thud. For a moment, she was unsure what had happened, but Thomas pointed to her feet and spied her discarded plate. "Oh, how clumsy of me," she said, bending over to retrieve the fallen pastry. A knot formed in her stomach, and she pushed back the panic which arose the moment he'd told her Luka had been taken. She returned her plate to the table, her appetite having disappeared, and smoothed her skirts. "Captured. What an unfortunate turn of events. He was most anxious to travel to Russia. Will he be released?"

"Unlikely. He's being held on several charges, desertion and theft the two most serious of his crimes."

"Desertion? He was in the army?"

"More like he provided the army with certain services and did not inform his commanding officer, General Reynard, he was not returning."

"How can they charge him if he was not enlisted in the French army?"

"It seems Reynard took exception to his failure to bring in an English captain along with the supplies the captain was said to be smuggling. Stefano sent his men with a quarter of the estimated shipment, the rest having exploded and sunk to the bottom of the ocean, and he kept the captain."

"Me." She stood and paced to the window, inaction unbearable given this distressing news. Pressing her fingers to the cool windowpane, she tapped her fingers to help her focus on Thomas's narrative. Each word he spoke, her finger pulsed on the glass, creating a soothing rhythm to calm her heightened emotions.

"You are not responsible for his choices, Beatrice. He was hell-bent on revenge, and all his other obligations faded into the background when he found you. He wasn't going to let you go."

"How did this general even know Luka had captured me?"

Thomas set his plate on the table, stood, and walked to her perch by the window. He towered over her, and for this moment, she permitted his strength to bolster her own. As she sagged back into his embrace, he wrapped his arms about her waist and hugged her close. "When Stefano's men returned to the mainland with the supplies, the general asked if there were any survivors from the explosion. One of the men slipped and mentioned you lived. Reynard let the two men go, having no further need of them, and waited for Stefano to return to France."

Her voice wobbled when she asked, "Will he hang?"

"It's almost certain. He's a good man and did what was necessary to guard the welfare of his clan. Do not judge him harshly."

She turned in his embrace and rested her head on his shoulder. "I don't. Luka is a good man. My regret is for the suffering I've caused him."

"I admit my own intentions toward him were not always honorable, yet he sacrificed himself in the end.

When it became clear travel from the coast to Paris was near impossible, he arranged to turn himself in, ensuring our safe passage to Paris but condemning him to death."

She shivered despite herself. "Did he have a message for me?"

"He told me to tell you he's always loved you."

"Oh." She moved outside the comforting familiarity of Thomas's arms and returned to her seat by the fire. "Thank you for telling me. It couldn't have been easy for you to hear."

Thomas ambled over to the fire and leaned his arm against the mantel. "No, but I have hope, where he does not."

"Hope?"

"I mean us."

"Thomas, there is no us. I've explained this all to you."

"Yes, you've explained," he said, an angry frown twisting his handsome features. "How prettily, too, did you tell me we no longer suited and you had decided to end our relationship. But you left before I could tell you no...no, I don't agree. I won't let you go." He grabbed her by the arms and pulled her from her chair, taking her mouth in a bruising kiss. With her arms pinned to her sides and her legs trapped against the solid brick surrounding the chimney, she had nowhere to go. She screamed, the sound muffled against Thomas's lips, and pushed against his shoulders. When he wouldn't release her, she bit his lip, yelling to let him release her. Rearing back, he grabbed his mouth and glared at her. She stumbled backward until half a room separated them.

Her body trembled, whether from the unexpected savagery of Thomas's kiss or from the helplessness which had overwhelmed her when he had trapped her, but she was angry. "You force me and take what you want, is that right, Thomas? Because from where I'm standing, the one difference between you and George is he's dead and you're not."

"God, Beatrice. I'm so sorry," he said, and advanced, cutting the space between them in half.

She had moved nearer the door by the time it swung open and Cosette entered, followed by Amy. "We heard a scream. Is everything all right in here?" Cosette asked, placing a comforting arm around Bea's waist.

Her smile when it came was tight. "Everything is fine, thank you. Mr. Wickes is leaving."

"Beatrice, please listen." He attempted to pull her to him, but Amy and Cosette stepped in front of her.

"She has asked you to leave, sir. I will show you the way out." Amy opened the door and pointed to the gaping space. Thomas took his leave, pausing to gift Bea with a contrite grimace, before Amy herded him out of the house. The door's slam reverberated through the house, causing windows to rattle and more than one soiled dove to yell at Amy to be quiet.

"Well, *amie*, this calls for something stronger than tea, *n'est pas?*"

Bea rested her head on Cosette's shoulder and held Amy's hand as the two women talked and laughed, doing their best to cover Bea's unnatural silence. Once in the kitchen, Cosette opened a bottle of wine, and the two women drank while Amy coaxed Bea into talking about her adventures at sea, until Cook shooed them out so she could prepare dinner. It wasn't until later in the night when all business had concluded and the house was fast asleep that Beatrice identified the emotion Thomas's brutal kiss had resurrected. For the first time in eight years, she had been afraid.

Chapter 26

Paris, France, October 1810

The next morning dawned early, and the cold air nipped at her poor nose, which had the misfortune to poke over the covers. Bea groaned, her head throbbing, and tried to open her eyes. Her lids fluttered but refused to open. Pulling the blankets over her head, she attempted to go back to sleep, but the incessant ache pounding in her temples demanded attention. Her legs fell off the side of her bed, and she slumped to her knees, her torso nestled in the bed's warm cocoon.

"Get up, lazy bones." Small hands grasped her waist, tearing her from her cozy bed. Bea, surprised by the sudden removal from her warm nest, slumped and sprawled on her stomach on the cold floorboards. Amy's high-pitched giggle broke through the haze of pain and caused the ache to worsen.

Amy knelt on the floor and rubbed Bea's back. "Cook said to give you this." A small cold glass pressed against her cheek, and she squealed. A tumbler full of greenish liquid rested by her nose. "She said it would help with your headache."

Bea struggled to her knees and clutched the bedpost, taking the glass and swallowing the liquid in one gulp. She gagged but managed to keep in the vile concoction.

"Madame Cosette wasn't as lucky as you. She lost her stomach after the first swallow."

"I am unaccustomed to imbibing strong spirits," she explained. "However, I have never had a queasy stomach." The traitorous organ roiled, and she pressed the back of her hand to her mouth.

"You and Madame were funny last night," Amy said, taking the glass from Bea's lax fingers. "But Madame warned me not everyone is as good-humored after so much wine."

The nauseating sickness passed, and Bea flopped on the bed, a leg dangling off the edge. "Madame is right, as usual."

Amy pushed her leg aside and sat on the bed. "Madame also said you might be cranky this morning, and I am to help you with your toilette."

"For someone who couldn't stomach Cook's drink, Madame is a font of wisdom this morning. How long has she been awake?"

"Oh, hours. After she was ill, she was her usual cheerful self. Shall I help you dress? Madame is holding breakfast for you."

Bea snorted and rolled onto her back. It figured the petite Frenchwoman, shrewd entrepreneur, competent seamstress, and humanitarian, could also hold her liquor better than she could.

Easing onto an elbow, she shook her finger at Amy. "You can tell Madame she can go—"

"Madame said you might be saying something inappropriate. Get up. I'm starving."

Bea allowed herself to be pulled to a standing position while Amy clucked and fussed and tugged her into a day dress. When she slipped on her shoes, she wobbled, and her stomach bucked. Bea clamped her lips together and grimaced at Amy, who yanked her by the hand and led her down the stairs to breakfast.

Fresh bread and eggs greeted her in the kitchen, and she pushed past Amy to run out the back kitchen door, losing the contents of her stomach in the bushes.

Cook was waiting with a glass of water and a chuckle.

Amy's face split in a wide grin. "Didn't you tell me you were never sick to your stomach?"

Bea growled, and Madame's lips curved in a sly smile.

"What's so funny?" Bea asked.

"You. Come. Dry toast is the perfect remedy for one who is never sick."

She slumped in a chair, rested her elbow on the table, and propped her tired head on her hand. "Are you laughing at me?"

"But of course," Cosette said, sipping her morning coffee.

"No one laughs at me," she grumbled, reaching for her toast. "And no one orders me about," she said over a mouthful of toast, glaring at Amy.

Cosette's mirth bubbled and tinkled, surrounding her in its cheerful sound. "I know. It's about time someone did."

She ripped off another piece of bread and chewed, her thoughts as dark as the cloudy morning sky.

Traitor. But whether she was referring to her mutinous stomach or her amused friend, she was too tired to decide.

****

Bea dragged in a deep lungful of crisp October air.

Cosette had suggested a walk after luncheon to help clear her mind, and loath as she was to admit it, the woman had been right. Fresh air and time away from the brothel had helped bring some perspective to Thomas's arrival and the unexpected turn of events yesterday afternoon had brought.

The little park two blocks from the brothel was deserted, as most sane individuals were inside on such a gloomy day as this, and though the flowers had long since died and it had been years since there had been money to groom the walkways, someone had taken the time to ensure the main path remained open. She ambled on the garden path until she came to the park's center. A small patch of earth formed a square in the middle, and a stone bench adorned each side. She sat on one and watched the breeze whip the dead leaves around in the air. Dry and brittle, they fell to the ground, skirting in aimless circles on the path. "What a perfect metaphor for my life," she said and resisted the strong urge to pity herself. Since the blasted accident, nothing had been the same. Before, she'd been purpose-driven and in command. True, her life had difficulties, but they had kept her grounded and focused. Leaving it behind, though, was necessary despite the melancholy and listlessness. Thomas's arrival yesterday had anchored her aimless wanderings, for his company heralded safety and comfort. For a moment, she'd forgotten her malaise, even going so far as to allow Thomas's strength to bolster her own. Had he not lashed out and surprised her, she might have continued to equate security with happiness. His uncharacteristic aggression jolted her out of the complacent fog in which she was mired, and called to attention some harsh truths.

"Hello."

"Thomas," she said, resisting the urge to jump and flee. She had missed the signals someone approached. Though he had startled her today and frightened her yesterday, she reminded herself Thomas was the man who had rescued her from darkness and sheltered her for almost a decade. One action did not alter who he was as a person, and she owed it to him to hear his explanation. Even so, she clutched her reticule and the switchblade she kept inside.

"Cosette told me where you were. Don't be angry with her. I told her I had information about Michelson."

"You lied."

He took a precarious seat on the corner of her bench. "I was wrong yesterday, Beatrice. Anger and hurt at your rejection prompted me to lash out, and I behaved badly."

"I was afraid of you," she said, and watched as he lowered his head.

"I am so sorry."

"Never have you treated me with such roughness. It alarmed me, and for several moments, I was afraid."

"I know and I'm—"

"I *was* afraid, Thomas, and it took me a while, but I know why. Ever since we've met, you've cared for and cherished me. I've never wanted for anything while with you."

"You deserve to be cared for, loved, and protected."

"For a time, yes, I needed to be coddled and protected. You helped me heal, Thomas, and gave me a second chance."

He grasped her hands, his forehead drawn tight in his distress. "I'd give you more, if you'd let me."

"Perhaps you believe you can give me more, but you see me as the scared young woman you rescued, and no matter what I've accomplished, you will want to protect me. It's who you are."

"What are you saying?"

"I don't need to be sheltered anymore. I was scared for so long. It's almost as if my fear kept George alive. As long as I allowed you to protect me, my fear controlled me. He controlled me. Master Jones was right. He told me I decided how I saw myself, and for too many years I've told myself I'm a coward."

"Absurd. You're the bravest woman I know. There is no other who is as smart or as daring as you."

"Every time you sent me on a job, I was terrified."

"Why didn't you say?"

"Acting is a talent of mine, did you know? I played the part you wanted me to play because deep inside I knew myself to be unworthy of such a man as you, yet I wanted your approval with an ache that was almost physical."

"There's nothing for you to prove. If your fear is what stands between us and our happiness, cast it aside. I love you for you, not what you can do for me."

She cupped his dear, sweet face in her hands, her own heart breaking at his whispered admission of love. "Oh, Thomas. I do love you so, but don't you see? Our relationship was built on a lie. Every action, every word was constructed to win your approval, to ensure your support and protection. I can't continue to use you, nor can I stay in an unequal relationship."

"How can you say you love me in the same

sentence you end our relationship? My one desire has been to provide for you and see to your best interests."

"As long as I had your arms to embrace me when life became hard, I didn't have to confront what was bothering me. You took care of my worries and made my life so comfortable, I'd never have left."

"What I offered was better than your life with Darimple."

"Comfort can be as strong a prison as abuse. With few demands and the security of your home, there was no need for me to do anything aside from serve you. Everything you and Master Jones taught me detracted from my pain. Years of training conditioned me to hide the worst parts of myself, until I was more detached machine than flesh-and-blood woman. I had lost myself on the quest to discover my potential."

"Had you indicated you wished to stop working with me, I'd have arranged for something else, anything to ensure your happiness."

"You're not in charge of my happiness, I am, and it has been years since I've examined what brings me joy."

"My presence is not enough? The comforts of my home, the love we shared—they were not enough to ensure your felicity?"

"When you took me from my husband's house and invited me to your home, I was grateful. From this gratitude, an overwhelming rift split and a chasm opened between us. Helping you closed the gap and gave me a sense of accomplishment, yet I was not happy. If we were to pursue our relationship and marry, each day the debt I owe you would weigh heavier and heavier on my shoulders, until I grew to hate you for the position in which you placed me. No matter how hard I worked, I could never restore any semblance of equality between us, and I refuse to be in another marriage where I am inferior."

He was horrified. "There was no debt. Your life was not something which required repayment."

"It does in my mind."

"Not in mine." They stared at each other, the sadness on his face echoed on her own.

"There's no way around this, is there? You cannot be happy with me, and I can't be happy without you."

She took his hand and held it, a sad smile on her lips as she said, "One day you'll know happiness again, Thomas, and you'll be glad you waited. I promise." They sat for endless moments, each an island of pain and sorrow connected by a pulsing bridge of flesh and sinew. Though it hurt to end her relationship with the man who had given her second life, the decision to do so eased a tremendous pressure from her shoulders. Spring may have been months away, yet inside, where her hopes had lain dormant for years, they stirred and extended tiny green shoots which wrapped her heart in renewal and warmth. A biting breeze whipped through the park, stinging her cheeks and cooling her nose. It was past time to leave.

"Winter is coming. I can smell snow," she said, looking to the low-hanging distant clouds.

Thomas roused, squeezed her hand, and stood, folding his hands behind his back. "You hate winter. I can't imagine you are looking forward to endless months of cold and biting winds." She hated the lines of pain etched on his handsome face, but she was not responsible for his felicity or despair in life. Her life was hers to control.

"The season is for introspection, a time to sit back and reevaluate one's life. Introspection is tedious, as is idleness, for each brings whispers from the past which are difficult to ignore." She stood and straightened her cloak. "But it's also difficult to travel in winter, so I'll have to stop running and confront some of my faceless demons. It's past time."

Awkwardness hung between them. He cleared his throat. "It's getting late. Shall I escort you home?"

"Thank you, Thomas. I'd appreciate your company."

Sometimes one must set out on her own two legs to see where life leads, and sometimes one must be wise enough to accept assistance. Bea's legs were strong and eager to find a new path. Taking Thomas's arm, she didn't mind at all when he leaned against her side and clutched her arm for support.

Chapter 27

Paris, France, December 1810

The next six weeks passed in a flurry of activity. Determined to save Luka, she shifted her attentions from finding Michelson to locating her childhood sweetheart. In the midst of endless queries, false leads, and fallen hopes, Bea also explored what it meant to be a woman and mother, in the hopes of finding a new path. Within the safety of Madame Cosette's walls and the help of the assembled female population who lived there, she tackled all the feminine arts, save for the skills which made Madame Cosette's house popular. Sewing, as she had discovered with Amy's new dress, was not her forte, yet neither was cooking, baking, needlepoint, nor pianoforte. She was useless at being a woman, and discouragement combined with the cold, gloomy weather to heighten her melancholy.

"Perhaps you are approaching this situation from the wrong way," Cosette suggested. "You were abysmal at such tasks before. Why is now any different?"

"I wasn't ready to take on a woman's duties before, but now I am. Yet even as I attempt to behave within society's constricts, there is no place for me. I am destined to never fit in."

"You have other talents, *mon amie*. Why belittle

those skills at which you excel? Sewing a button or baking a cake has not served you in finding your Luka. It is time for you to embrace your unique skills and use them to find this man before he dies."

Bea mulled over Cosette's advice for hours before she donned a cloak and ran to the market. There was a baker who seemed to know when certain regiments were moving or when they were staying put. He conducted most of his business when regiments of troops were on the move, establishing his cart along the main route out of town. She had commented to Amy it was as if he were a mole, able to discover secrets others wished to possess. Her quest to discover her femininity had distracted her from following through immediately on her hunch, and weeks had passed without further questioning of this baker.

But Cosette had been right. She did have other talents. Within five minutes of finding the baker, he had told her where they were housing Luka. A General Reynard held him in an abandoned garrison used to house lesser nobility during the Reign of Terror. Luka's execution was set for Christmas Eve, less than a week away. Bea had used her cunning and strategic planning during the last two weeks to plot how she was going to liberate him from his cell. The remaining task was to dress for her part.

"Oof, Cosette. Must you pull so hard?" Bea held on to the support beam in Cosette's upstairs bedroom and winced as the Frenchwoman pulled even tighter on the stays and her bosom pressed ever nearer her chin.

"You want your best assets to show, *non*? Cosette will pull until they are displayed like two ripe peaches ready to be plucked."

"More like two mangled peaches. I'll be lucky if these stays don't kill me."

"You English are so dramatic," Cosette teased. "We Frenchwomen know the importance of a good figure and its effects on a weak mind, while you English hide your assets under billowy fabric. Stays may be out of fashion in London, but to get anything done in Paris, a lady never leaves home without them." The Frenchwoman tied off the stays and walked around to face Beatrice. Plunking her hands on her hips, she let out a satisfied sigh. "*Voilà.* I told you they would do wonders for your figure. No longer do you look so bulky and bumpy like a man." She scrunched her nose and laughed.

Bea placed her own hands on her hips and let out a shaky breath. *Not so bad.* She sucked in a lungful of air and spots swam in her vision. Inhaling had just become much more difficult, and she paced the wooden floor until she had a comfortable rhythm established, with fainting a distant threat on the horizon. "Those bumps are called muscles, my friend, and they helped me to play a certain role."

"Now you are ready to play another role."

"Are the other girls ready?"

"Babette and Nicole are prepared," she said. "There will be no problems. Tonight will be *magnifique.*"

"And the basket?"

"Cook left it on the front table before she went to bed. Are you ready for the *pièce de résistance*?" Cosette pulled a red satin dress from atop her bed and held it to her shoulders. "Isn't she beautiful? It was my favorite. Alas, I have grown too skinny. Maybe once the war is over and there are no more food shortages, I will wear her again. Hands up."

Bea obeyed and shivered at the luxurious slide of satin over her smooth skin. The dress fell over her bosom and hugged her hips, gliding in a waterfall of red satin to midcalf. The skirts were full and the neckline low. Cosette propped her chin on her fist and examined Bea, a critical frown on her pretty face. "Something is not right. You are not fluffy enough." The woman gestured toward her own chest. "Hold still." Digging in Bea's bodice, she grabbed her breasts and arranged the flesh until it overflowed the bodice, her nipples peeking above the red satin.

"Cosette! Must you be so familiar?"

She waved her hands in dismissal. "What is a little flesh between friends? You English are so prudish. Sit. I will apply your rouge."

Bea sat on the bed while Cosette applied rouge to her cheeks and kohl to her eyes. When she was done, she handed over a mirror, and Bea was surprised at the transformation. Her golden curls were piled atop her head, and several longer curls trailed over her shoulders to caress the bare skin on her back. Her eyes, so pale and odd, were vibrant against the dark kohl on her lids, and her pale skin glowed from the gentle hint of rouge.

"You are an angel, a temptress sent to earth to see the fall of man," Cosette said. "They will be unable to resist you."

Bea turned her head and examined the graceful arch of her neck and the long sweep of her lashes against her cheek. "A fallen angel, perhaps. Heaven wouldn't take me."

"*Précisément.* You are entering the garrison, *mon*

amie, not heaven, and dressed as you are, they will gift you the keys before opening the gates."

Bea studied her reflection and traced the contours of her features, a frown replacing her earlier delight.

"What has you so somber? Cosette has performed a miracle. The men, they will dance in the streets, while all the women will weep for your beauty."

"Beauty is a shell, prized if unblemished. Yes, you have transformed me, my friend, yet not all blemishes are visible. Even now I see myself in the glass and cannot countenance what appears there, for I have already lived several lifetimes. But it shows no wrinkles or age spots. There's no softening of skin around my neck and cheeks, no gray at my temples. You call me angel and temptress, while others have christened me strategist, spy, captain, sister, weapon, wife, lover, and friend. Who is the real Beatrice Westby? The glass is warped, blurring the edges of her face, and her image grows fainter as the years pass."

Cosette's face joined her own in the mirror, her dark-haired beauty a sharp contrast to Bea's fair complexion. "I have seen your blemishes, *mon amie*, and I have witnessed your pain. We share a common history, forged in adversity and tempered by respect and friendship. You tell me your beauty is a shell, but I am alive because of the compassion in your soul. A beauty such as yours cannot be contained within. It shines for all to see. You do not see the remnants from the ravages of life because you have risen above the opposition and created your own way. You are all woman, Beatrice, whether you needlepoint and sing or you ride bareback and steer a ship. So I say yes, you are angel and temptress and strategist and spy." Cosette tapped her on the nose. "But whoever said you must choose one?" Standing, she bustled about the room, straightening the bedclothes and putting away the rouge and kohl.

Bea studied herself for several minutes before setting the glass aside. "Thank you, for all your help. I don't know what I'd have done without you."

"My Beatrice, you'd have found a way. You always do, but it wouldn't have been as much fun, *non*?"

Bea stood and hugged the smaller woman, laughing as she said, "No, you are right."

"Come. The girls await, as does your Luka. He sounds most fascinating, not at all serious like your Mr. Wickes." She frowned. "I cannot forgive him for how he treated you."

She agreed, though she did not dwell on Thomas and what had happened. Since the chilly October day when they'd talked in the park, she'd not seen him. He'd sent a formal apology and passed along any news he heard about Luka and Michelson, yet he did not return to Madame Cosette's. Thomas remained in Paris, though. He'd sent word a few days ago saying he had a solid lead on Michelson. The two of them would have to meet soon, for Michelson had been clear—he wanted Thomas in exchange for information about her son.

"He has apologized. I cannot stay angry at him forever."

Cosette paused on the landing and linked her arm through Bea's. "You are too kind. He does not deserve your forgiveness." They descended the remaining steps and walked to the foyer.

"I may have forgiven, but I haven't forgotten."

"Smart. A woman's memory is her only defense against such injustices."

A strangled giggle caught in her throat, and she coughed to hide her amusement. *If Cosette knew what injustices I forgot with Luka, she'd not be sending me off with a smile to rescue him.*

"Have you your knives?" Cosette asked as one might ask a lady if she has her reticule.

"Two, strapped to my thighs," she said before putting on her cloak and situating the hood. Babette and Nicole waited for her in the front foyer, the basket tucked under Nicole's arm.

"Ladies?" She ushered the two brunettes out the front door and into the chilly night. "Let's be off."

"Have fun taking over the garrison, my girls!" Cosette yelled from the door.

Beatrice grinned because, in spite of the potential for disaster, her heart was light. Terror did not consume her as it had been wont to do in the past. Planning this escape and working with Cosette and the other women of the house had given her a renewed sense of self. This purpose had lifted her lethargy and brightened her spirits. She was going to embrace who she was and save Luka. Maybe, as her friend had suggested, she'd even get the keys to the garrison. After all, an angel, even a reluctant one, had gates open before her.

Chapter 28

Paris, France, December 1810

The garrison was easy to find, despite the late hour and the falling snow, located near the center of old Paris. The three woman passed over the Seine, by the silent, towering Notre Dame, and along the Left Bank. After almost half an hour, they approached the crumbling stone edifice. Large gates surrounded the garrison, and two sentries patrolled the perimeter. The cold weather and the proximity to the holiday meant the garrison had a meager supply of guards. Taking these two out would be easy. Fifteen minutes later, she had timed each sentry's movements and was able to take them unaware. Some gentle pressure on each man's neck rendered them unconscious. Bea tied their wrists and ankles together before placing them in a nearby empty building so they were out of the cold.

"Come on," she whispered to the two ladies. "Time to enter the gates."

Bea stayed behind the women while the two brunettes approached the wrought iron fence. They lowered their hoods and unclasped the frogs holding their cloaks about their shoulders. After a cursory fluffing of their voluptuous assets, they called out to the guards by the front door. "It is so cold, *chéris*, and we have come with wine, a present from your General

Reynard."

A husky older man with graying hair stepped from the door's shadow and shone his lantern about the clearing. The light illuminated the two women and provided Bea with an approximate distance between the front gate and the exterior fence. The man with the lantern scowled. "Be gone with you. This is no place for ladies."

"Is that you, Claude?" Nicole said, cupping her hands over her eyes. "You know I am not a lady. Come, it is cold, and you know the best way to warm me."

A second man stepped away from the door, this one younger and leaner. "Nicole? Babette? What are you doing out on such a cold night?"

"Philippe," Babette all but purred. "We bring tidings of comfort and much joy. Let us in, and we will help you forget this wretched, cold night."

The older man hesitated. "*Chérie,* you know we would love to, but we are working. No one is allowed in or out without the general's orders."

Not one to be deterred, Nicole shoved aside her bodice and plumped her breast in her hand. "Are you saying you wish to pass on these? *C'est dommage.* More for Philippe."

With an odd grunt and a hasty jangle of keys, Philippe pushed aside Claude and opened the door. "Let's retire inside."

The three women followed Philippe through the gate and into the garrison, where a roaring fire blazed in a cozy room. A quick glance showed four cots, two of which were unmade. A table with the remnants of a meager supper ran in front of the fireplace, surrounded by several wooden chairs. "Who's your friend?" Claude demanded, pointing to Bea, who had not lowered her hood.

Babette removed her cloak, tossed it onto a chair, and warmed her hands by the fire. "A new girl. Madame sent her with her compliments."

Phillippe slapped Bea's rear. "Let's taste what Madame has offered."

Lowering her hood, Bea removed her cloak and gave Philippe a sly smile. "First some wine," she said, pouring five glasses. "You may sample all you like."

"À votre santé!" She sipped her drink while the other four drained theirs in a swallow.

Philippe whispered in Babette's ear, pulling her to an unmade cot. Soft laughter and muted moans arose from the bed, and Nicole straddled Claude. The man assessed Bea with banked suspicion.

"What's wrong with her?" Claude asked, turning away from his lover's avid kisses. "She's not participating."

Nicole yanked the man's face back to hers. "She's never done this before, so she's going to watch, and afterwards you can try her out."

Obvious excitement at the prospect of bedding an inexperienced courtesan refocused Claude's attention, for his excited grunts increased, and he shoved Nicole's gown about her waist. Bea sat back and watched, more than a little bored, judging time's passing by the amount of firewood in the hearth.

The sounds of coupling rose above the crackling fire and howling wind. *How are the two guards conscious?* The drugged wine should have taken effect, but both men were alert and engaged with two of Madame's finest. Unable to watch the couples in front of her any longer, she turned to the fire, whose warmth soothed her, and she slept. Sometime later, Nicole jolted her awake.

"They are asleep. Finally. I've got the keys from Claude's belt. You need to go down the stairs and to the left."

"How did you—"

"Trust me. It's better if you don't know what I had to offer to discover those details. Thank God he passed out before I had to deliver."

"Thank you, Nicole. You remember the rest of the plan?"

"You English worry too much. We shall be fine. A whole night of uninterrupted sleep? Consider it an early Christmas gift."

Keys and lantern in hand, she thanked Nicole, who waved a hand and shuffled to curl on a cot near Babette. She shut the door behind her and locked it, not keen to have an interruption as she searched for Luka's cell.

Following Nicole's directions, she descended the stairs, took a left and shivered. Her flesh dotted and she rubbed her arms, wishing she'd brought her cloak with her, but soon enough she'd be gone from here.

"Luka?" she hissed. "Are you here?"

"I'll be your Luka, pretty lady."

"Shut up," she yelled to the prisoner on her left. "Luka, where are you?"

"Tris?" A faint voice near the end of the cell block came to her.

She raced over the stone floor, her feet slipping on the icy rocks, and shone her lantern in the last cell in the row, fumbling with the keys in the lock as she spied Luka on the stone floor, cold and shivering in his thin shirt and breeches.

"What have they done to you?" she asked, kneeling by his side. Careful not to let him see how his appearance affected her, she remained impassive as she surveyed his swollen and bruised face and the dried blood staining his face, shirt, and the soles of his feet. Someone had taken a knife to the soles of his feet, the flesh cut to ragged ribbons. Her stomach rebelled, and she swallowed to avoid vomiting. How was she going to get him out of here?

"God, Tris. It is you." He clasped her arm with surprising strength. "You have to get out before they come back."

"Shh. I've taken care of the guards. I'm here to get you out." She helped him to a sitting position and looped her arms about his waist. With a giant heft, she helped him to rise, his body stiffening as his feet made contact with the floor. "Can you walk?" she asked as she wrapped her arm about his waist.

"Yes," he said on a ragged exhale. "Take me out of here." They hobbled through the passageway and up the stairs, the tension from Luka's body unmistakable. Once above stairs, she unlocked the officers' door, grabbed her cloak, and left, ensuring the door was once again locked. It was essential the two courtesans not be found guilty for colluding with her. If they were asleep and locked in the room, they'd no more be suspect than the officers locked with them.

Wrapping Luka in her warm woolen coat, she dragged him the rest of the way out of the garrison. They stood outside the gate, snow falling about them. "What are we waiting for?" Luka said, slurring his words. "We need to be away."

"Our ride is coming." She crossed her fingers and prayed the other gamble she had taken two weeks ago would be fruitful.

Another fifteen minutes passed, and she worried she had pushed too hard, until horse hooves announced their ride's arrival.

"You're late. Help me get him in the back of the wagon."

The baker jumped from his seat and supported Luka's other side. Between the two of them, they hoisted him into the hay-filled wooden wagon. Bea tucked an extra blanket around Luka, took her cloak and wrapped it around her own shivering shoulders, and climbed onto the seat next to the driver.

"I almost didn't come."

Bea unstrapped a knife from her thigh and proceeded to pick her nails. "I know." She plunged the knife into the wood between them. "I would have killed you."

Even in the muted light from the storm, she saw him gulp. "I know."

The rest of the journey passed in silence. By the time the wagon arrived at Madame's home, the sun was poking purple and orange fingers in streaks across the horizon. Madame stood in the doorway, wringing her hands. "You are late," she whispered to Bea as she and the baker maneuvered Luka in the front door.

They went to the front sitting room, where a cot was ready, and deposited Luka on it. The baker straightened and said, "Our business is concluded?" he asked.

"We are through. You keep my secret and I'll keep yours. If not—"

"Yes, I know. I'm dead."

"Glad to see we are in agreement."

"*Mon amie*, what did you do?" Cosette asked after showing the baker the door. She brought with her a basin of warm water, some washing cloths, and several lengths of linen.

Bea carried the basin to the bed and dipped in a cloth. With gentle strokes she wiped away the blood and dirt marring Luka's face. He remained silent, his eyes closed, though his shallow breaths told her he was yet awake. "I used my unique talents, as you suggested."

"You've accepted your strengths as well as your limitations?" Cosette dipped a rag in the wash basin and wiped his hand.

"I've accepted I'll never be a normal woman."

"Thank God," Luka whispered.

Both woman burst out laughing as a smile tugged the corner of Luka's mouth. Tension fled from Luka's body as Bea pressed a chaste kiss to his lips. His brown eyes flickered once and closed, his breathing deep and even.

Chapter 29

Paris, France, December 1810

"He's grouchy," Amy said as she exited Madame's front sitting room. "I wouldn't go in there if I were you."

Bea ruffled Amy's hair and propped the door open with her hip, balancing a tray holding Luka's noonday meal. "Thank you for the warning. I'll do my best to manage."

"He called me a gabby little magpie," Amy said in a huff.

"I'll talk to him and suggest he apologize," she said.

"Don't bother. I told him he was an odiferous swine with the sensibilities of a weevil."

She laughed. "What did he say to such flattery?"

"Hmpf. He grunted and said for a verbose baboon, I was both insolent and gutsy."

"Sounds like you handled him," she said, pushing the door farther open and sliding a foot through.

"What does insolent mean?"

"Ask Madame. His food is getting cold, and you know he'll grouse if it gets much colder."

"You're going in?" To Bea's nod, Amy said, "Don't say I didn't warn you."

She entered the room and set the tray on a table by

his bed before sitting in a chair near his head. He scowled.

"Did the magpie squeal on me?"

"Amy mentioned you were in less than an amiable mood."

"Noisy girl. She prattled on for hours about one thing or the other, and when I suggested she close her mouth and listen for a change, she compared me to a pig. Someone needs to teach the girl some manners."

"The girl has fine manners. You happen to provoke the worst in her, though I don't know why. You are two of my favorite people, and I'm delightful."

"You meant to say we're delightful."

She grinned and poured him a cup of tea. "I rarely say what I don't mean."

"Fine. I'll apologize to the girl tomorrow."

"I've brought you luncheon."

"Is it something more than the broth and toast Cook's given me for the last week?"

She removed the warming cover with a flourish. "Voilà! Porridge. I made it myself."

Luka's pale face blanched even more, and she had to bite her cheeks to prevent herself from smiling. "I'm not hungry," he said, turning his face to the wall opposite her. "I'm tired."

"Too bad. Cook will be so disappointed you didn't try any of her coddled eggs or the strawberry preserves she found in the root cellar."

"Coddled eggs?" he asked. Lifting himself on his elbows, he scooted until his back pressed against the bed's headboard. Bea helped him arrange his pillows before showing him the other delights Cook had prepared for him.

"Hmm, smell this apple tart. Cook's a bit sweet on you and told me she's going to put some fat on your bones." He licked his lips and snatched the tart.

"I wouldn't want to hurt Cook's feelings," he said, his mouth full of food.

"Of course not. If you do find yourself hungry after all this, Cook did prepare the porridge, too. I'm well aware of your opinions on my cooking."

"I'm too satisfied with all this food to feign anger at your slight deception. You are a horrible cook."

"It has come to my attention," she said. "However, I possess other skills and enough money from my dead husband's estate to ensure I never starve or go without clothing."

He paused, an egg-laden fork suspended between plate and mouth. "This is the first time you've mentioned your unfortunate marriage to me."

"In all fairness, our time together was a bit surreal, and when I regained my memories, I left for France, and you were captured. With your sickness, there hasn't been an opportunity."

"Do you want to talk about him?"

Surprise rendered her mute. "What? No one has ever asked me to talk about what happened. Thomas was one of the few people who knew about it, and he insisted it was healthier to push the events aside and focus on the present."

"Thomas isn't here, so what do you want?"

"I'd prefer to never mention him again, but I might have to."

"Events such as what you experienced can infect a person's soul. They fester and spread the longer they are ignored. Sometimes it's better to purge all the ugliness to kill the infection, allowing for growth and an opportunity to heal."

A decade had come and gone, a decade fraught with pain, danger, and self-doubt, yet less than ten minutes in Luka's company and he already pinpointed what had bothered her about her relationship with Thomas. She had needed to talk about the events of her marriage, but Thomas assured her there was no need; she was safe with him and never had to relive those awful moments again. Yet the same comfort had caused the rift between them to increase until his love had smothered her, and she was stifled by his over-protectiveness. Luka read her like a well-loved book. After all these years, he understood her story, her motivations, and her desires. She would tell him what she could.

"He was an awful man, possessive and insecure. There were times I convinced myself I deserved his punishment, for I was planning to perpetrate a hoax by passing off our child as his. After the child died and he knew what I had attempted, his punishment worsened. Every day was a fight for survival. One day, he pushed too far, and I fought back, though being his victim."

He grabbed her hand and squeezed. "I can see how you might blame yourself. No man likes to find his child is not his own; however, what he did to you was inexcusable. The urge to blame yourself will never fully abate, but over time you will be able to forgive yourself for being human."

Master Jones had said the same thing. She tested out the idea of forgiving herself, trying to remember the young woman she'd been. Scared, alone, and heartbroken, her younger self had made the best choice, given her circumstances. Empathy for her eighteen-year-old self, not the typical pity, welled inside her, replacing some of her shame with calm acceptance. She was human, and though mistakes were part of life, there was one event for which she might never absolve herself. "It has been difficult to forgive myself and let go of the past because my mistake cost us our child's life."

"What has changed? Our child is dead. Surely you do not blame yourself for actions out of your control."

"For almost ten years I have, and I imagine it will be several more years before I can fully let go. Something has changed, though. Our son is not dead."

His hand in hers trembled, and she grasped it in both of hers.

"Beatrice, no, he's dead. You want to believe he lives to remove some of the guilt, but he's gone. You have to accept it. Don't torture yourself or me with this madness."

Her laugh when it came was a harsh bark. "Ten years I mourned our child. You've known about his death for a few months, while I've lived every day of those ten years believing my actions caused our baby's death. Don't talk to me of torture, for I have lived with this guilt for a decade. But no more."

"Be sensible, Tris. You're talking nonsense."

"Listen. He lives, Luka. Gabriel is alive," she said, uttering her son's name for the first time since his birth.

"No, you want to believe—"

"I know it. Before the explosion, Michelson told me he knew where our boy was. He said to find him and he'd tell me where our son is."

"Even if the man was telling the truth, he might be

dead. It's been months. Thomas said he had some leads, but if he hasn't found him yet, it's unlikely he ever will."

She pushed his hands aside and jumped from her chair. "Why are you saying this? Michelson knows where our son is. I sense it here." She thumped her chest. "Why are you taking this from me?"

"To pin your hopes on the word of a madman is foolishness and will bring disappointment."

"I have no other hope. He must know where he is. If not, it will be unbearable. It will be like...like..." Her words hitched in her throat, and she pressed the back of her hand to her mouth, shaking her head as silent sobs shook her body.

Luka struggled to rise and winced as he hobbled to her on his injured feet. "You have your hope, Tris. Take it and hold it tight, for as long as you believe, he lives in your heart."

"I will find him. I will find our son."

He hugged her close and rested his chin atop her head. "I know you will."

****

The ladies moved Luka to an upstairs bedroom the next day, as his feet had healed enough to allow him to walk up the stairs, thus freeing the front sitting room for Madame's girls to entertain callers. He settled in Amy's bed, the young girl having offered her space to Luka after he apologized. In his apology, he'd mentioned she had a feisty spark like Beatrice and a kind heart like Madame Cosette, and Amy, loving no one more than she did those two women, melted under the man's charm, giving him her bed and moving into Cosette's room with joy.

Bea busied herself in other parts of the house, doing her best to avoid her room and the man occupying it. His reaction to her news was underwhelming. Their son was alive, and he acted as though she brought him news of his death. Niggling doubt took root. Maybe Luka was right. Maybe she was wrong to hope, and with no hope, what were the chances she and Luka could have anything more than friendship? His duties resided with his clan, and hers was to their son. A relationship between them was as ill-advised as it had been ten years ago. Yet those tiny tendrils of hope which had grown and encased her broken heart in warmth refused to die. They clung, stubborn and resolute, and thoughts of a future in which she had both her son and Luka elated and terrified her. Hope was a fickle creature and more often than not heralded despair. She'd had sorrow enough and did not look forward to its resurrection. There being no other choice, she avoided her room to prevent the heartache arriving on the heels of hope and asked Cosette to take his meal to him once more.

"You can't ignore him forever, *chérie*," Cosette said. "Best clear the air, else you won't sleep tonight."

"I'm not sleeping in my room with him. Luka has vacated a bed. I'll use it tonight."

"The girls are entertaining callers in the sitting room this evening. Unless you wish to join them, sleep in your room. There are no vacancies. So many lonely men at the holidays. So much money for Cosette."

"You, my friend, are a devil in satin slippers."

She lifted an elegant shoulder. "Some things are universal. Money and sex, and I like them both. Many houses close for the holidays. They are shortsighted and lose paying customers. My house and the girls are, how do you say, open for a good time. We are full this Christmas."

"Your grasp of English expressions amazes me."

A sly smile graced Cosette's ruby lips. "I am as good as my teacher, *non*? Don't presume because I am such a gracious hostess I didn't see the rolling of your eyes or hear the way you complimented me. Dry as toast, you English. A compliment must be given from the heart, sincerity throbbing in each word."

Cosette grabbed her hands, her brown eyes kind as they looked in Bea's. "For example, I have seen such improvement in your needlepoint. How proud I am of you for your hard work."

Her head hurt from the change in subject, but the earnestness of Cosette's words lessened much of the frustration any conversation with Madame fashioned. "Truly? Do you believe someday my stitches will be as even as yours?"

"*Non*! I made a little joke with you. See the difference? You believed my compliment because I was sincere, but in my mind I was saying it in your dry voice because, as you know, you are horrible at the needlepoint. What a clever trick!"

"Not clever but mean! You said one thing but meant another."

"*Oui*, because I told you my trick. Had I remained silent, I would have known the truth, and your face would not look like that, all pinched and disapproving." She twisted her own face into a grotesque version of Bea's minor chiding frown.

Bea smoothed out her features and stamped her foot. Her brows contracted and her mouth pursed again.

"What does any of this have to do with my taking a tray to Luka?"

"Much like my small lie, you are playing a mean trick on him. He is alone and wounded, but the woman he cares for is avoiding him. You are scared, I know, but he doesn't need to know, eh?"

"You're telling me to lie to him?"

She waved her hand as if swatting away a bothersome fly. " 'Lie' is such a harsh word. I'm suggesting you see him, and if you must run and hide in your mind, do so. Don't allow him to imagine, as I do when I see your rolling eyes or hear your biting words, what he's done to deserve your displeasure."

Equal portions of horror and guilt assaulted her, and a hot flush stole up her chest to stain her neck and cheeks. "Cosette, I'm sorry. You are a dear friend. I meant no disrespect."

Cupping her cheeks, Cosette said, "I know, and I even understand. Your foul moods come and go and have, for the most part, lessened since you came to stay here. Remember, not everyone is as good a mind reader or as forgiving as me." She pressed a kiss to Bea's forehead. "Your man, for one. He was morose when I took him his luncheon, and had you seen the way his eyes lit with excitement and then faded when he saw me, you'd not have kept him waiting this long."

Bea grabbed the tray from the table by the stairs, took a step, and paused. "I don't want to hurt him."

"Of course not. You obviously love him."

"I do," she whispered, testing out the idea in her mind.

"Love is not the evil you imagine it to be. You have accustomed yourself to running when emotions intensify. Slow yourself and remember the joy love brings."

"I'm terrified, Cosette. The last time I risked my heart, it didn't end well."

"This time neither of you have any place to run. It's Christmas Eve, snow has made travel all but impossible, and the man is as weak as a kitten. Let him love away some of your fears."

Bea vacillated between hysterical laughter and terrified tears. She settled on scowling disdain. "I said I love the man, not I'm eager to warm his sheets! Besides, he's injured, or have you forgotten."

"But you will be warming his sheets. Whether you are clothed or not is for you to decide. I needed your bed for the holiday entertainments and for an unusual request from a regular client. Now's your chance to see if his important parts work or if they froze and fell off in his cold, damp cell. Either way, I'll have cotton for my ears by the bed, in case," she said. With a wink and a saucy swish of her hips, she sashayed out of the foyer. Bea stared after her for several dumb seconds, the unsettling realization she had been duped penetrating the confused jumble of her mind. In the space of fifteen minutes, Cosette had exposed her selfish actions and explained how she was hurting others by pushing them away, had tricked her into admitting her love for Luka, and because of the Christmas rush, had boxed her in to sleeping with him for the foreseeable future. Shaking her head, Bea ascended the stairs. The cruel vagaries of fate had cheated her friend, for if Madame had been a man in charge of military strategy, the British would have already conceded defeat.

Chapter 30

Paris, France, December 1810

Bea watched Luka eat in silence, having already picked over her meal and set it aside. Her appetite had disappeared the moment she settled in next to Luka on their bed.

"Why aren't you eating? Did you cook?" His handsome face crinkled in amusement, and hers did the same, happy to see the transformations a week of healing had begotten. The bruising had faded to a light yellow instead of the angry purple marks he'd had when she first found him, and some proper nourishment had added a healthier glow to his wan skin. He'd even gained some weight, for gauntness no longer plagued his face, and the added flesh softened the sharp contours of his collarbones and shoulders.

"Someone is doing better, if you have enough energy to tease."

"Seeing you brightened my spirits."

Those five words returned the uncomfortable awkwardness which had hung between them since her arrival. "You're quiet again," he said, setting his fork on his plate. "What did I say?"

"I'm sorry for avoiding you today. It's not you... it's me."

"So you were avoiding me. I wasn't imagining it."

"Cosette helped me to see a few important truths. I've kept everyone at arm's length, too afraid to permit more than distant friendships or casual affairs."

"Thomas said you were with him for eight years. How is eight years a casual affair?"

She stiffened, anger at his presumptions causing her to lash out. "We didn't sleep together until about a year ago, though it's none of your concern."

"If we're to share a bed, I want your reassurance I'm not dipping my pole in waters where someone has already claimed the privilege."

"Do you hear yourself? As if I'd let you dip your pole anywhere near my waters after such a comment."

"Give me a break, Tris. My mind isn't as nimble as yours, and clever metaphors are beyond me right now, what with my injuries and the constant pain. Tell me the truth. Are you and Thomas involved?"

Overwhelming tiredness swamped her already frazzled nerves, and any energy she had to prevaricate and make him regret his word choice vanished after witnessing his quiet anguish. Her response mattered. "We parted ways, and have not been involved in any physical manner for almost seven months. I love him, and most likely always will, but I'm not in love with him, not the way I was with you."

"You were it for me. After I left you, I was unfit to mingle in polite company for almost a year. The pain from your absence was physical. I wasn't much use and had convinced myself being without you was worse than whatever fate awaited us together." He gave her a lopsided grin. "I left my family and had traveled halfway to your father's estate, ready to fall on my knees and beg for your forgiveness, when I received word you'd married and borne a child whose appearance did not mirror his supposed father. The anger I harbored for you burned with as much fierceness as the love I once carried. I left England determined to forget you. It was almost another year before speaking your name didn't cause me to erupt in uncontrollable rage. Revenge helped to remove the sharp edges. I have hated you almost as long as I've loved you."

"Why are you telling me all this? Do you seek to punish me? I assure you I have experienced all the retribution I can bear."

"When you washed against my boat at Herm and I recognized you, there were several dark moments when anger and vengeance overshadowed human decency, but time with you, even time spent with your unconscious body, erased any remaining fury. You wear my bracelet."

She clutched her wrist, the reassuring hardness from the copper face pressing against her wrist. "It's stayed on my wrist for years." *What does my bracelet have to do with anything he's telling me?*

"The explosion and the plunge in the Atlantic rendered you almost unrecognizable, and soot and ash covered you, coating your skin and uniform. Blood stained your jacket, and fire had left its vengeful trace along your leg. You were blue from cold and shock, I imagine, and your glued-on facial hair all but disintegrated. Smoke hung heavy on the water, but a patch cleared and the moonlight shone on our boat. It caught a flash of metal on your wrist, and recognition slammed me in the gut. I should have thrown you overboard and let the water rock you away to oblivion;

you were almost dead, but you wore my bracelet, a cheap trinket I had bought the girl I loved when we were both young and full of optimism. Your bracelet was all the proof I needed of your identity, and I wanted to exact my revenge, yet my heart, wherein lies fear to lurk, had me save you and beg Aba to help you live. I'd already passed a lifetime without you by my side; I wasn't going to make the same mistake again."

"Why tell me all this now?" Her throat ached with unshed tears, and she clenched her fist, those tendrils of hope growing and strengthening around her fragile heart. Time, whose passage had marked endless years of heartache and disappointment, seemed to suspend, and the room quieted in expectation, as if the universe itself awaited Luka's answer.

"Cosette removed your bed. She said we're to share this one. If you lay with me, I'm not letting you go this time."

Her heart thudded in her ears, and her mouth dried. Hearing those precious words, words she'd resigned herself to never hearing again, was enough to thrill and terrify her. His desires were clear, but whether she was brave enough to trust him again remained to be seen. She tried to stall. "I can sleep on the floor, if you wish."

For the first time in this impossible, revealing conversation, he was angry, for his brows furrowed and his lips thinned to a white slash against his golden face, yet his answer betrayed none of his inner turmoil. "No, I don't wish it. However, it is your choice."

Did he know the gift he had given her? The freedom to choose sang through her body, clearing the confusion in her mind and all but destroying the lingering fear she clutched like a battered shield to protect her equally battered heart. This one choice had set her free, free to love again. "Oh, I guess we'll be sharing the bed. Are you tired?"

He relaxed, his shoulders visibly slumping against the headboard, and sighed. "A little. I'm more cold than anything."

"Why don't I change and come under the covers? You'll be warm in no time."

She cleared off the dinner tray and placed it outside the room, locking the door before returning to the bed. She picked up the candle from the nightstand, ready to blow it out, but he stopped her. "Leave the light on. You could hurt yourself in the dark."

A shiver stole through her body, so she turned her back to him, unwilling to show him the panic his request caused her. Her body had withstood a decade of change, and doubts assailed her. *What if he does not find me attractive? How will I bear the humiliation?* She clutched her arms about her middle and whispered, "No more running." It was time to trust again.

Placing her foot on the chair by the bed, she unrolled her stockings and placed each one over the chair's back. She released the ties under her skirt holding her woolen underskirts. They, too, joined her stockings on the chair. Trembling hands fluttered to her hair, and she removed the pins holding her curls atop her head. The golden mass swung free, and she ran her hands through the silky tresses, the day's tension easing as her fingers massaged the tightness from her scalp.

"Um, I can't reach all the buttons on this dress." Looking over her shoulder, she saw him swallow and swing his legs over the bed.

"Stand between my legs," he said. "I'll do my best.

My damn hands are shaking."

"From the cold? Let me warm them." She twisted to hold them in hers, but he swatted her away.

"Right now the window could swing open and a foot of snow encase my feet, and I'd not be cold."

"All right. Are you overly warm? Feverish, maybe? Your voice is hoarse, and your cheeks are flushed."

He cleared his throat and said, "Stop worrying. I'm fine. Hold still so I can undo these buttons." As the fabric parted to reveal her back, his fingers caressed the exposed flesh, and gooseflesh dotted her skin. He finished undoing the last button, and she shrugged her shoulders out of her gown, letting the navy, woolen fabric hang about her waist.

"You're not wearing a shift," he said as he ran the back of his hand across the bare expanse of unclothed flesh.

"The underskirts are bulky enough. Though I don't enjoy the extra layer, it's practical in the cold. Something had to go, so my clothes were no longer smothering me." She pushed the dress over her hips and it pooled around her feet. The dress joined the pile on the chair.

"How I admire your practical streak." His eyes glittered in the flickering candlelight, and she frowned, placing her hand over his forehead.

"Are you sure you're not ill? Maybe I should get Cook." She walked the short distance to her wardrobe and pulled out a dressing gown. Returning to the bed, she straightened the covers over his torso, and frowned. "She'll have an herbal remedy for you, and—"

Luka grabbed the tail of her sash and yanked her gown open. With a tug, the fabric slid from her arms to land in a heap at her feet. "I don't want Cook. I am not ill. If I'm flushed, it's from helping you undress and imagining the curve of your breast filling my hand. Get under the covers, Tris."

Her mouth rounded to mirror the widened surprise of her eyes, but she slid under the covers. He blew out the candle and pulled her against his side, her backside nestling in the hollow made by his bent legs. A rigid hardness pressed against her bottom, and she moaned.

"Thank God *that* didn't fall off in the cold."

His muffled chuckle vibrated along her flesh where his mouth nuzzled against the tender skin between her neck and shoulder. "You worried for nothing."

"It seems I did. Perhaps had I been bolder I might have asked."

"Imagine how the conversation would have gone. 'Luka, have your manly bits shriveled off in the cold, by chance?' No, I much prefer you discovered it for yourself. Your throaty moan was reward enough for my patience." He cupped her breast in his hand, and she arched into his touch, pushing her bottom to nestle more firmly against his rigid hardness.

This time he groaned and increased the pressure on her erect nipple. "Your patience?" she panted. "You kept me in a heightened state of desire on Herm for months, refusing each of my advances. My patience should be commended, not yours."

"As if I would take advantage of an injured woman. You had no memories and would have grown to hate me." He flipped to his back, and she draped over his chest, tracing her fingers along the outline of his ribs, around his navel, and to the pulsing heat which was all him.

"You're injured," she said, giving him a gentle squeeze. She spread hot kisses over his chest and across his abdomen, the air expelling from his lungs in short bursts the lower her mouth trailed. "Maybe we shouldn't be doing this. I'd hate to bring you dishonor."

He tensed and muttered a curse as she kissed him on his throbbing tip. "Dishonor me. Please. I'm begging you."

She gave him another squeeze before releasing him. Draping a leg across his belly, she straddled his hips and tilted her pelvis until he was nestled firmly within her. "As you wish."

****

The church bells pealed the hour, and Bea roused from her cozy nest atop Luka's chest. She shifted off and cuddled close to his side. "It's midnight," she said, poking him in the side. "Happy Christmas, Luka."

"Hmm?" He wrapped an arm about her waist and buried his cold nose behind her ear. "You're warm, the perfect gift on a cold night."

"I've never been anyone's perfect gift before. What must I do?"

"It's not hard. You must be naked and in my bed."

"Are you there with me?"

"Of course."

"Consider me gift-wrapped and ready for you to find on Christmas morning."

He trailed his fingers over her belly and across her hips to nestle in the warm valley between her thighs. Nibbling her ear, he shifted his weight until he trapped her beneath him. "But I opened my gift last night. Now what will be waiting for me?"

She gripped his head, which had come to nestle on

her chest, his roaming mouth stopping to lave attention on each tender breast. "I can dress. You can unwrap me all over again."

He trailed his fingers over her sides with feathery strokes and growled, biting her ear. "You're not going anywhere."

"You'll be sad on Christmas day with no gifts to open."

He nudged her thighs apart and slid into her waiting body. "I'll survive," he said, his movements smooth and languid. "Happy Christmas, Tris."

"Happy Christmas, Luka."

Chapter 31

Paris, France, December 1810

Christmas morning, especially a Christmas morning after gifting herself to Luka three times, came too early. Snuggled in by his side under the warm covers, the insistent knocking on the bedroom door did not fully penetrate her sleepy fog. When the timid knocking increased to a steady pounding, Bea awakened, groaned, and shuffled to the door.

"Bea," Amy hissed. "Open the door. It's important."

"This better be life-or-death important, Amy. The cock hasn't even crowed." Unlocking the door, she glared at Amy. The child pulled her to the hallway, shoving a sealed letter in her hands. "This came for you. The messenger said it was urgent."

Turning the letter over, she saw Thomas's seal staring back at her, and she ripped through the wax. The letter was brief. Four words were written under a series of scrawled directions. "I've found him. ~Thomas"

"They've found him, Amy. I must go," she said. "Thank you. This means everything to me." She pressed a swift kiss to the girl's cheek. "Tell Madame where I am going. I'll leave a letter for Luka and be back as soon as I can."

After shooing Amy from the hall, Bea hurried

through her toilette and penned a brief letter to Luka. She kissed him goodbye, noted his cheek was like ice, and added more wood to the fire, watching to see the flames caught before grabbing her cloak and racing down the stairs.

The directions Thomas had sent her were easy to follow, but the snow doubled the time it took to reach the squalid bar where Thomas had spotted Michelson. By the time she trudged the twelve blocks through the ankle-high snow, the sun had risen and she feared she'd lost her chance to confront him. Rats like Michelson didn't stay in one place for any length of time. Thomas's tall figure, hunched against the cold, reassured her, and she sped the remaining distance, arriving winded, flushed, and wet.

"I didn't know if you'd come," he said in lieu of a greeting.

"We spent years to reach this moment, Thomas. Let's finish it."

"It's good to see you, Beatrice. You look wonderful."

"You're seeing things. The cold has reddened my cheeks, and my nose is dripping. My hair is an absolute fright." She held the limp curls and laughed.

"No, you're younger, as if a huge weight has been lifted. You look happy."

"I am," she said.

"Do you have your knives? The situation within might get dangerous."

"I do."

While he knocked on the door, she came to a decision. His gruff concern for her was endearing, and though they were no longer intimate, responsibility and affection for Thomas outweighed the voice in her head telling her to be quiet. "Thomas, there's something I have to tell you. Michelson, your father, he wants you."

"He's been weaving his web for too long; I'm aware of his desires."

"Before he jumped ship, he said he knew where my son is, and he'd tell me if I brought you to him. I believe he wants me to bring you to him bound and gagged. At least that's the impression he gave."

"What the—"

"It was never an option," she said, her words a tangled rush in her haste to reassure him she'd not betray his trust. "I wanted you to know his plans before we go in. I'll get the information without handing you over."

His voice was flat when he said, "He's lying to you."

"Even if he is, I have to find out."

"I know. Quiet, now. Someone is approaching." The door opened a sliver, and two beady, black eyes peered through the slit.

"What do you want?"

Thomas inserted his foot in the small opening and used his massive shoulders to wedge his way through the portal. "To come in. Your hospitality is appreciated," he said to the small, greasy man cowering in the foyer.

"You've no business here. Leave before I get it in my head to be inhospitable."

"Your bravery is admirable, barkeep, but we do have business here. Take us to the one called Michelson."

"Nobody here by such a name," the small man

said, his squinty eyes shifting about the room. Bea stepped forward to apply some persuasive pressure to the man's tender regions when Thomas strode forward, grabbed the man's hand, and twisted. A cracking crunch followed by an agonized scream set her teeth on edge. "You have three other appendages, sir. Unless you relish the idea of losing the ability to serve spirits and walk, I suggest you quit lying and take us to Michelson. Do I make myself clear?"

"Y-yes," the man whispered, his chin touching his chest. Gray hair obscured the man's face as he whispered, "This way." They followed the whimpering man past the bar, through an unlit hallway, and through a low hanging arch. They found themselves in a small stone room used to house barrels of wine.

"Don't toy with me, old man."

"P-please wait," he said, and removed a stack of wine barrels, empty judging by the ease with which he lowered them, and gestured to a narrow wooden door. "Through there. He locks the door from the inside."

"You have our thanks. Now leave," Thomas said, ignoring the man, the weight of his angry stare centered on the wooden door. Raising his leg, he kicked the plank. Two thuds later, the wooden portal lay in pieces on the stone floor.

"So you've found me, have you, son?" a weak voice called from across the room. Scanning the interior, Bea saw a small, windowless room with enough space for a narrow bed, a table, and a chair. There was no fire, and the sole source of light came from the candles burning on the table. She shivered, and rubbed her arms through her thick, woolen coat.

"It took a while, I admit, but we both know I'm

smarter than you."

"Who's with you? Is that Westby's git?"

"Her name is Beatrice," Thomas said through clenched teeth.

"So it is. You lived," he said, addressing her instead of Thomas.

"As did you," she said.

"A little worse off than you, I see. Lost my foot from the stab wound you gave me."

"We're even. The railing fell on my leg and burned it."

"Hardly even, but let's not quibble over details." He coughed, a harsh, barking rasp, and clutched his chest, wheezing until the attack passed. "I'm dying," he said by way of explanation. "The stab wound near killed me, and after my foot was sawed off, infection set in. Sapped my strength and weakened me something fierce. For months I lay at death's door, but knowing you hunted me is what kept me from dying."

"How touching, Michelson, but—"

His face twisted, an evil sneer turning his lips, tightening the scar on his face until it was a jagged red streak against his pallid complexion. "I wanted to see your face, you see, when I told you I had lied. You failed, Beatrice Westby, and should have killed me when you had the chance."

"No," she whispered, her knees weakening as her vision blurred. "You know. You have to know."

"Beatrice, steady," Thomas warned.

"The time for steady has passed, Thomas," she said. Unsheathing her knives, she closed the distance between her and Michelson, pressing the older man against the stone wall with her knife's blade. He laughed, a gruesome mockery of mirth. "Perhaps I misjudged you. Maybe you do have the grit to do as I ask."

"Make sense, old man, before I slice your throat," she growled.

"Kill me. Put me out of my misery."

"Happily." The knife pressed against the soft tissue of the man's neck. This time when he laughed, it was genuine.

"Don't you want to know why?"

"He's tricking you, Beatrice," Thomas warned. "End this now, and we can be gone."

"No. I want his explanation. Why now, when your death could have been a painless sleep aboard *The Stallion*? Why kill you now and not before?"

"I'm dying."

"Wrong answer."

"Hear me out. I've been ill, and no doctor, not in England or here on the Continent, can fix me. The end is near, or so I've been told multiple times, but it will not be a quick death. I will linger in pain for weeks, if not months, my mind deteriorating with each passing day until I am more animal than man. I had hope of survival when I made our bargain, a doctor in southern France who had treated someone with my disease and prolonged their life by years. After meeting with him, he's assured me of my fate. I want to die with some dignity."

"If what you say is true, why should I believe you?"

"Because I lied. Your son lives."

"This is another trick. Don't listen to him. Kill him."

"Quiet, Thomas. Let me think."

"What reason could I have to lie now? My fatal weakness has been exposed. I've asked you to kill me. There is nothing left with which I can bargain. You hold my fate in your hands. I can die a dignified death at your hand, and you will know where your son is."

She eased some of the pressure from the man's neck and stepped back. "What proof do I have you tell the truth?"

"You have none, Beatrice. Come on, let's go." Thomas tugged on her arm. "I was wrong to ask you to kill him. He's a mad old man who enjoys playing with people's emotions."

"His name is Gabriel. He was born in the year of our Lord eighteen hundred and one, on a cold winter's day. Skin the color of caramel and hair as dark as night, he resembled your Rom lover, didn't he?"

"This is all nonsense," Thomas said. "Your father could have shared information about the child with him."

"But your father didn't know the Cook delivered your son, did he? He also didn't know your dead husband took your sleeping child from your arms and ordered the Cook to kill him."

"What? Impossible, she never would have—"

"She didn't. Whatever happened to your cook? Curious, isn't it, how she disappeared soon after your son died?"

She rubbed her temples. The news Michelson shared was causing her head to ache. "I never noticed, for I was grief-stricken. Much slipped my attention."

"Enough, Father," Thomas said. "Stop playing with her."

"I'm not, son. I'm telling her what happened to her child. Surely every mother has a right to know where her child is."

"Where? Where is he?"

"The Cook fled your home with the child and begged for help from the one person who would not refuse her. He gave her a job on his country estate. He provided for the child and has seen to his education."

"Who? Who did this?"

"Your father. Gabriel Westby has been living on Westby Estate in York since shortly after his birth."

"Impossible. My father...he wouldn't have kept this from me."

"He would if your dead husband were alive and he was trying to protect the child."

"I never returned home after George died. Thomas, you told me not to look back. I wanted to return. I asked you to take me home, but you refused. You said it wasn't good for me. Why—" She shook her head and faced Michelson. "How do you know all this?"

The grin which graced his face was a true horror, and she flinched, backing farther away from the man and his madness. "Thomas, of course. Didn't you know? He and your husband were good friends."

"T-Thomas?" she asked. "Is this true?"

"Beatrice, I can explain," he said.

"Explain what? How you kept my child from me? How you watched me suffer needlessly for years while you knew all along?"

"Listen. You mourned Luka's defection almost as much as the child's death. If you saw the child, you'd be reminded of him and continue to grieve. My concern was for you."

"Stop lying to me! Had you considered my needs at all, you'd not have behaved so selfishly, Thomas. No more lies, no more manipulations. Whatever love I carried for you is gone. I can't even look at you."

She threw a knife at each of their feet and turned toward the door. "He's yours, Michelson, unless your son gets to you first."

Thomas audibly inhaled, a sharp whistle cutting through the palpable tension. "Beatrice, you don't mean this. We've chased him for years. Don't you wish to end this, help me wipe him from the face of the earth?"

She turned back. "Do your own dirty work, Wickes." She spat on the ground, the urge to plunge the knife into the man's breast as strong as the day she'd killed her husband.

Clenching her fists, she addressed the man who had caused so much strife for her and her family. "I've fulfilled our original agreement, Michelson, and brought you your son. I will not end your life, for a swift death is a mercy reserved for those who attained some dignity and honor in life. You had neither." She gestured to the knife lying on the ground. "Kill yourself and end your own misery, or die as a raving madman. As for him, I care not. Do whatever you wish to him." Turning on her heel, she walked the short distance to the door, pausing when Michelson's oily voice skittered across her spine.

"But my dear," he chuckled. "I already did."

He was a cruel man, but so was his son. The two deserved each other, and she half hoped they'd both meet their maker this day. Leaving the two men to their fate, she gave a terse nod, ran from the room, and burst from the sordid den of evil out into the cold, pristine morning. Gulping huge lungfuls of frigid air, she trudged back home, hot, angry tears dampening her cheeks.

"Stupid winter wind." She swiped the moisture away with numb fingers. She hated the cold, and she hated winter. Pulling her hood over her head, she stomped through the melting snow, courtesy of the sparkling sunshine and rising temperatures. In spite of the clear, calm weather, only Bea noticed the chilling cold. Only she hunched her shoulders against the biting wind.

****

"Madame wants to see you," Amy whispered, helping Bea remove her cloak and boots. "What happened to you? You look awful."

She wrapped her arms about her middle to warm herself, the morning's revelations having formed an icy ball behind her chest. "Is Luka awake? Perhaps Madame can wait until I've seen him."

"You will not put me off with your tricks any longer. We will speak now."

Something was dreadfully wrong. Bea had noticed the unnatural quiet and oppressive tension the moment Amy opened the door. The girl had been subdued and refused to meet her gaze. As soon as Cosette had stormed from the kitchen to the foyer, Amy had rushed away, her head bowed. Cosette was incensed. Energy sizzled from her friend like lightning before a violent storm. Bea tensed and located the nearest exits.

"You've managed to push away everyone who has ever loved you. You were making progress, confronting your fears and putting some of them to rest. I see you fooled even Cosette with your deception." The

Frenchwoman's serene complexion became ruddy as anger twisted her gentle features into a horrible mask of rage. "How could you hurt Luka? Hasn't he suffered enough?"

Bea stepped back, plastering her back to the foyer wall. "What do you mean? How have I hurt Luka? I did what you suggested. I stopped running, and I gave myself to him with no reservations. What did I do wrong?"

"Luka is gone," she spat.

"Gone? But why? I wrote him and said I was coming right back. I left the note for him to read."

Her friend's anger faded, though concern bracketed her mouth. "What else did this letter say?"

Bea scooted away from the wall and paced the tiny foyer. "I-I said Thomas had found Michelson, and I needed to go to him. I said I loved Luka with all my heart, but I would also never stop loving Thomas as a sister would a brother, and it wasn't right to abandon him after all he did for me."

"No, oh, no. How could this be?" Cosette scurried to the small escritoire which stood by the staircase and snatched a small piece of parchment. "Here is what he read." Cosette showed her a charred piece of paper with the words, "I will always love Thomas. I cannot abandon him, so I must go to him."

Bea's chest squeezed. "Where's the rest? This isn't the entire letter. Oh, God! This isn't what I wrote!"

"He came down the stairs and told me you must be off laughing with Thomas, your revenge against him complete. Luka left soon after. He's going to travel to Russia. Before leaving he asked me to relay a message. He said loving you cost him too much. He was done."

"No! I promised to be with him forever. Michelson...I had to go. I had to know if our child lived. I was coming back to tell him I loved him. I didn't push him away." She was babbling now, unable to stop.

Ruined! Everything was ruined. After a decade of running and years of guilt, she had found her happily ever after. Even if Michelson had played her false, she had Luka and the glimmer of hope. Her future had appeared before her, rosy and shining with love. Now it mocked her, this endless gaping void of nothingness.

Slumping to the floor, she wrapped her arms about her knees and rocked. "I was coming back. I love him," she said, repeating it over and over again.

"Ah, *chérie,* I'm so sorry I doubted you." Cosette sank to the floor beside her. Wrapping her small arms around Bea's shoulders, she pulled Bea to her breast.

Tears made speech difficult, and her words when they came were garbled, but her guilt was palpable. "He didn't trust me, not enough to love me. I was a fool to believe he'd love me again. I've ruined everything."

"Beatrice, you are a strong woman who has been placed in impossible situations. You have done your best to survive, but it has been recently you have allowed yourself to live. Push aside your shame and guilt. Live your life. Go, and find your man. He can't have gone far."

"He's gone, Cosette. Even if I tracked him and explained, I am not at liberty to pursue him. My son, he's alive. I was coming home to tell him. It was going to be a perfect Christmas."

Cosette hugged her and squealed. "But this is *fantastique!* Your boy is alive. How did this happen?"

Bea rubbed her temples, wiping the remnants of her tears from her cheeks. "My head aches, Cosette, and I'm tired. Can we talk tomorrow?"

"*Mais oui*. It has been a most difficult day for you. Tomorrow, we shall have a nice long chat and figure everything out. You'll see. Things will not look so gloomy in the morning."

Kissing her friend on the cheek, Bea stood and said, "Thank you, Cosette, for being my friend. I'll never forget you."

"Bah, who could forget *moi* when I am so fabulous? Go. Rest. We'll talk tomorrow."

Yawning, Bea trudged up the stairs and slipped into her room, sitting on the unmade bed. The sheets held the faint scent of their joining, and the icy ball in her chest clenched. Ripping the linens from the bed, she threw them into a corner, desperate to be rid of any memories she shared with Luka. Her shoulders shook, and her hands trembled despite the fire burning low in the hearth. Luka's absence chilled the room and stripped it of all color.

There was nothing left for her here. Luka was gone, and her son was alive thousands of miles away. The decision to leave took only a matter of seconds, while packing her bags used less than ten minutes. She sat on the bare bed, her bag at her feet, and waited. Hours later, when the house quieted for the night, she left Madame Cosette's and joined the shadows. She was going home.

Chapter 32

York, England, February 1811

York in summer was lush and green, with verdant hills, sparkling lakes, and ancient forests. Bea had spent a happy childhood roaming the fragrant valleys and woods, climbing rocky hills, and swimming in cool waters. She loved York, and had missed it with a keen ache in the years since her marriage.

Bea descended from the public coach and clutched her small carpetbag, the long road leading to her childhood home a winding, icy path. Her shoulders slumped. York in winter was depressing. Skeletal trees, boughs denuded of their leaves, stood as stark, aged sentinels across the countryside. Snow covered the lush landscape, blanketing the earth in endless white fields. Low clouds hung heavy on the horizon, and the scent of snow lingered in the air. She hated York in winter.

But York was where her son was, and so Bea squared her shoulders and trudged up the winding entrance, nervous flutters taking flight in her stomach. The journey from France had provided plenty of opportunity to plan her first meeting with her son. She would remain warm and affectionate but with a cool detachment. Embracing and other maternal gestures, she had decided, would wait until such time as they became better acquainted. There also would be no crying, lest she embarrass or frighten off the child with any effusive emotions. Should Gabriel rebuff her maternal advances, her partial disengagement would serve as an effective barrier against further hurt. Or so she hoped.

The path to the front door was shorter than she had remembered, and she arrived at the entranceway and the grand stairs leading to the massive double oak doors in less time than she'd expected. Grasping the solid brass knocker, she raised the heavy ring and let it fall, the loud thud an echo of her frantic heartbeat. The door opened, and the butler peered at her, shock and delight registering when he recognized who was at his door.

"My lady!" he said, his gentle blue eyes filled with a suspicious moisture. "You've come home." He took her bags and offered his arm. She entered the large, marbled reception hall, and squeezed the man's arm.

"Grant. You haven't aged a day," she said.

"My lady, you are a terrible fibber. I'm much grayer, and my old bones don't move as fast as they used to. My face also has a few more wrinkles than last I saw you, and my memory is slow at times, but even as old as I am, I'd never forget you. If I may be so bold as to say so, you have matured and are a handsome woman. You were a pretty girl, but now you possess a quiet strength. I see it about your eyes and the way you carry yourself. Maturity suits you."

"Your charm, sir, has not altered with age."

"We were all so sad to hear about your husband."

"His passing was unfortunate." When she'd made the decision to return home, she'd prepared herself to talk about George. There were few people who knew the real story behind her marriage. The rest were given the lie Thomas created when he'd taken her—her husband and maid had been killed in a home invasion. Grant's condolences would not be the first she'd have to sidestep, though time would ease the staff's curiosity and lessen their sympathies.

"I wasn't speaking of his passing, my lady. The man deserved what was coming to him. My condolences were for you and all the suffering you endured."

"You know about my marriage? Those eighteen months of our marriage are a guarded secret few souls possess. How do you possess this information?"

"When Agatha came to work here, your father told me and the steward about your situation. He wished to protect you, should you ever seek shelter from your husband. Had we not known what you were fleeing, we might have given away your location had your husband come looking for you."

"Who is Agatha?"

"She's the cook your father hired when she arrived with your child."

She licked her lips, her mouth having dried to dust at the mention of her son. "My child. He's here, isn't he?"

"Yes, my lady."

"I'd like to see Agatha, please, and talk to her before I meet my son." She wrung her hands, twisting her flesh in an effort to ease the enormous pressure which built and lodged in her throat. Grant placed his hands atop hers to calm the frantic motion, soothing the part of her which had been whirling out of control since arriving home.

He squeezed her hands. "Of course, my lady. May

I escort you to the kitchen?" He offered his arm, and Bea slipped her arm through his, grateful for the support.

"Please. I seem to be lightheaded after my journey. Rough seas, cold quarters, and cramped carriages have left me fatigued." They traversed the main hallway and entered a smaller hall at the back of the house, taking the servants' stairs down to the kitchen.

"Travel, especially a journey as lengthy as yours, can be tiring."

"A month is hardly a lengthy journey."

"But ten years is." The aroma of fresh baked bread and roasted duck wrapped her in familiar warmth, prompting her to forget Grant's cryptic comment about the actual length of her journey.

She entered the kitchen, the bright, sunny walls alight from late afternoon sunlight. "Mama used to love roast duck. We'd have it every Tuesday for dinner." The cozy kitchen looked as she remembered. High windows let in plenty of natural light, while a grand fireplace provided enough heat to warm the kitchen and the stairwell on the coldest of days. A large worktable sat in the middle, cluttered with various herbs and vegetables in preparation for the night's meal. Next to the stairs she had moments ago descended was a narrow, planked door leading to the root cellar. It was a picture perfect scene, save for the missing cook.

"Today is Thursday, but Agatha, well, some say she has the sight. This morning she prepared a duck for tonight's meal, certain someone was coming to call."

"Incredible," she said. "Did she know it would be me?"

"I didn't, my lady," Agatha said as she ascended

from the root cellar to the main kitchen. "Though it warms my heart to see you alive and well after all these years."

"Agatha," she whispered, rushing across the stone floor to embrace the older woman.

"There, there, my lady. Had I known it was you, I'd have prepared blancmange for dessert."

"My favorite. You remembered."

"There isn't much I don't remember about you, my lady." The mysterious comment, much like Grant's, left her puzzled, but Agatha offered her a chair and poured some tea.

"Grant? Will you join us?" she asked, turning to find the butler where she'd left him by the stairs, but he was gone.

"He's already had his tea. Besides, tears make him uncomfortable."

She opened her mouth to protest Agatha's assumption she'd cry when a plop of moisture landed on her hand. "Oh. I shall apologize later for causing him discomfort."

Agatha waved her hand and snorted. "He left because he was afraid he'd join in. You'd embarrass him if you mentioned it. Best to let it go."

She sipped her tea and fiddled with the porcelain handle. "Is my boy—is Gabriel here?"

"My lady, I'm a blunt creature by nature and nosey by habit, so I'm going to come out and say it. Where have you been for all these years?"

"Excuse me?"

"Your father left me with your boy years ago. When your husband was alive, visiting wasn't a possibility, but once he died, you never wrote or visited.

267

Why are you here now?"

Bea's face crumpled, so she ducked her head, the truth she had believed for so long pouring forth in a pained rush. "He was dead."

"You'd better explain." Agatha sat back in her chair, teacup in hand, and listened while Bea told her tale from the day after Gabriel's birth to a month ago when she'd discovered he lived. The tea had grown cold by the time she finished, and Agatha had mopped her eyes with a handkerchief so many times the cloth was a mangled, wet mess.

"Your father never told you? Any of it?" Agatha asked when she'd regained possession of her voice.

She shook her head. "Father was a weak man, and his actions were less altruistic and more self-serving. He was governed by cowardice. He's gone, at any rate. His reasons for keeping this from me will remain a mystery."

"For someone who was betrayed by her own father, you are more serene than I would have been."

"He saved Gabriel and provided for him when I could not. For those reasons alone, I can forgive him."

"Do you want me to tell you about your son?"

"Please," she whispered.

"He's such a sweet, sunny-natured lad. I could talk about him for hours."

"You love him," she said, saddened to have missed so much time from his young life.

"I do. We all do. He calls me Grandma, did you know? Grant is Pop, and Mr. Jackson, the steward, is Uncle Jack." Bea smiled. In the absence of his own flesh and blood, her son had found himself a family, a loving, nurturing one, from the sound of it.

"Mornings he has lessons with the local minister and his children. Uncle Jack walks him to the parish house and walks him home when lessons are done. He's real smart, knows his letters and numbers, and can already beat Grant at chess. Afternoons, he can be found out at the stables helping the groomsmen care and feed the horses. Most evenings I have to drag him from the stalls so he can eat his dinner. He'd sleep in a stall, if I let him."

"He's like me. I used to sneak to the stables whenever our governess turned her back."

"Aye, he does love his horses, though to be honest, his favorite time of day is when the supper dishes are cleared, he's been washed and tucked into bed, and we take turns telling him stories."

"What stories does he love?" She pictured herself taking over the role of storyteller at Gabriel's nightly stories, and longed to learn what interested him.

"We tell him about you. Grant and Mr. Jackson have years of stories about you and your sisters. Though our acquaintance was short, I told him of your bravery and your determination to protect him. I told him of your interests and your kind heart. We've kept him entertained with your exploits, your bravery, and tales of your cunning since he was old enough to hold a spoon."

"Does he hate me?" she asked, staring at her fingers, which were bloodless tangles of knotted flesh.

Agatha stretched her arms across the table and covered her hands with her weathered, work-roughened ones. "He loves you. Sometimes he's sad because you are apart, but we told him you were doing important work which required you to be away. Each year, he loses some of his hope for your return, but no, he will not hate you."

A door in the hallway slammed open, and a gust of cold air swept through the main kitchen. Agatha stood, waddled over to where Bea sat, and hugged her in a tight embrace. "That'll be him now. He'll be hungry. There's some gingerbread and milk on the counter. I'll be upstairs when you two have finished talking." With a final encouraging squeeze, Agatha left the room as a young boy ran in the room.

Rosy cheeks flushed from the cold sat under sparkling brown eyes that surveyed the kitchen as the boy stood with his hands on his hips. "Grandma, I'm starving. Is there any shortbread left?" He stuttered to a halt when he saw her, his brows crinkling as he puzzled out who she was.

Bea's chest tightened and her throat burned. Tears welled and splashed on her cheeks. Rising, she took an unsteady step toward him, all her careful plans forgotten after one glance at her child. "You look like your father," she said before reaching out a trembling hand to caress his black hair. "But you have my curls." Falling to her knees, she grasped his shoulders and pulled him to her embrace. "Gabriel, I've found you at last."

Thin and trembling, he stood in her embrace, motionless save for the frantic pounding of his heart. When his small arms wrapped around her shoulders and a little head buried itself against her neck, her heart squeezed, ready to burst from her chest.

"Hello, Mother."

Chapter 33

York, England, March 1811

The month following her reunion with Gabriel was the best and the most terrifying time of her life. Once the initial excitement of being reunited had faded, Bea set about being a mother, finding it more difficult than any task she'd set out to do. Her initial impulse was to spend as much time with her son as possible; she'd missed out on too many years to waste time away from him. After a week of walking him to and from the parish for his lessons, joining him in the stables after lunch, and telling him stories at night, he asked her to leave him alone before stomping out of the house.

"You're smothering the boy," Agatha said when Bea wandered into the kitchen to seek advice. "He's his own person and has lived ten years without you. The lad finds comfort in his routines, but your arrival has disrupted his safe, cozy world. Like you, he's trying his best to adapt."

"Why is it wrong to want to be with him or take an interest in what he does?"

"There's taking an interest and there's stifling him. It's been a week and you've not let the boy out of your sight. Give him some space to adjust to your presence in his life. Pushing him like this will serve to drive a wedge between you two."

"I missed out on so much of his life. I want to learn all I can about him."

"It's been less than two weeks. Slow down and get to know him. Never forget he loves you. Give him some time."

He'd been so angry when he stomped out of the house. His little face scrunched to an obstinate frown reminded her so much of Luka she ached. Before she'd had the chance to fix what was wrong, he'd thrown on his jacket and run from her. Worry, unlike anything she'd ever experienced, thrummed through her, and she walked the short distance to the kitchen door hoping to see his blue coat approaching the house. Snowy fields and waning afternoon sunlight greeted her concerned gaze.

"He'll be all right?" she asked, pressing her nose to the cool window on the exterior kitchen door.

"When he's hungry he'll find his way home. Don't you worry any. I'll send him to you when he comes back. He'll have to apologize to you for yelling. We don't tolerate disrespect in this house."

Bea took one last look out the door leading to the kitchen gardens, snatched some gingerbread, and wandered to the stairs.

"Where are you headed?"

"Maybe I'll read a book," she said, though the idea held no appeal.

"What you should do is write your sisters." Agatha waved a wooden spoon at her. Since arriving home, Agatha, Grant, and Mr. Jackson had been subtly, and in some cases not so subtly, urging her to write her sisters. She'd yet to be persuaded.

"I've taken your advice under consideration," she

said. "But I shall visit the attics today."

Grasping the railing, Bea turned and walked up the stairs, Agatha's voice a harsh slap at her back. "You can't avoid them forever!"

No, she couldn't avoid writing her sisters forever, but one more afternoon wouldn't hurt. Besides, the attic held much more possibility for enjoyment. Once above stairs, she fetched a lantern and her shawl, certain the unused space would be cold and dank. The old door creaked on its hinges as she shoved it open. No one had used it in years, yet the stairs were free of dust, and the actual attic itself was in relative repair. Someone had cleaned the floor and taken the time to wash the small window.

Setting her lantern on an old table near the window, she scanned the cluttered attic. Sheets covered most of the old furniture, bulky trunks and discarded memorabilia, but one trunk stood uncovered. It was her chest. She'd left it behind when she married, for it held old mementos and broken toys, tattered remnants of a child's former treasures. If her memory served her, though, a veritable army of lead soldiers lay nestled somewhere within the trunk's bowels. "If they exist," she said, opening the curved lid. She hoped so. Gabriel might enjoy playing with them.

The faint aroma of roses greeted her, and she stared in amazement at the dried flowers sitting on top of her preserved treasures. They had not been there when she'd packed and closed the lid on her childhood before leaving for London and her subsequent debut. Nestled next to the flowers were two unopened pieces of parchment. She did not recognize the red seal, but they were in her trunk and therefore hers to open. The light was dim so far from the lantern, so she took her letters near the window and opened the seal. Minutes later, her trembling knees gave way, and she sank to the floor clutching the letters to her chest.

Her sisters had written to her one final time. From Grant's narrative about the events following news of her death, she knew her family had held a funeral for her at Westby Estate. The dried roses had been pulled from her coffin before they buried the empty box in the family's plot. Each letter was a poignant farewell from her dear sisters.

Tears of shame burned her eyes, and she was helpless to stop their descent. She'd been a coward, alive and hiding in York while her sisters grieved. Why did she doubt they wouldn't?

"Maybe because I was a disinterested sibling for much of their adult lives." Her distance, she had reasoned, assured their safety, but it had also ensured her sisters remained strangers. Yet she held proof they had not given up on her despite her best efforts to push them away.

"They loved me." There was no doubt, for Amelia and Evelyn had each written loving tributes to her memory.

"Mother? Who are you talking to?"

She stood and wiped away the tears as Gabriel entered the attic. "To myself, Gabriel. Talking aloud helps me work through my problems."

For a little boy who was prone to bouts of extreme energy, he stood almost statue-like in front of her, his sunny face serious. "Were you crying?"

"Yes."

"Did I make you cry?" he asked, his own voice

wobbling.

For a split second she hesitated to embrace him before she ignored the voice telling her to give him some space and pulled him to her arms. "No, Gabriel. You didn't make me cry. My sisters did. They wrote some nice things about me."

"I said some not nice things about you and made you upset, didn't I?" His words were muffled against her stomach, so she stooped to hear, kneeling before him. Taking his shoulders in her hands, she said, "I was more worried than anything, but not anymore."

Tears shone in his brown eyes, and he sniffed. "I came back because I was hungry, but Grandma Agatha was gone. I looked for you all over the house, and I couldn't find you. I thought you'd gone away because I yelled at you."

"Never! I'm not going anywhere, Gabriel. I'm here to stay."

He wiped his nose on the back of his sleeve, and her heart lurched. "Good, because I don't want you to leave."

An idea formed, one she should have acted on months previous. "What if we left together?"

He wriggled and clapped his hands together. "Are we going on a trip?"

"A visit to my sisters and their husbands might be a good way to shake these winter doldrums. They live in Scotland. It's a long journey, and I'll need an intelligent, brave companion beside me."

He puffed out his chest, putting his hands on his hips. "I'm smart and brave!"

"So you are. It is a long trip, though. We might need something to occupy our time. How about we look in my trunk? There should be a score of soldiers to keep us company. Help me find them?"

Running to the chest, he rummaged through the trunk, his cry of triumph as he pulled out the first soldier music to her ears. When he'd assembled a regiment's worth of lead men and gathered them in his hands, he asked, "Play with me, Mother, please?"

She ruffled his hair, a tentative peace settling about her shoulders. "I'd love to."

Chapter 34

Stanton, March 1811

Bea and Gabriel arrived mere days after her letters arrived at her sisters' homes, but a sentry had been posted at the entranceway to Ballywith to await her arrival. Her coachman had no sooner arrived at the front door when it flew open and a blur of blue satin and red hair streaked down the stairs, an angry giant behind her yelling to slow down. The carriage door was ripped open, and green eyes scanned the plush interior, stopping when they spied her face.

Amelia scowled, her chest heaving from her hurried flight, and wagged a finger in her face. "Beatrice Josephine Westby, I swear to God if you die again and don't tell me you're alive until months later, I will rip your limbs from your body, throw them in a bonfire, and dance while the flames consume you." She pushed her fiery curls from her face, and Bea swallowed a sob. "Well? Are you going to sit there while I freeze my arse off in the cold, or are you going to make me yank you from your carriage?"

Through watery laughter, Bea jumped from the carriage and was enfolded in a fierce embrace. Bea's own arms crept around her sister's middle and peace descended. "Don't you ever do that to me again, Beatrice," Amelia whispered. "Promise me."

"I promise, never again."

When Amelia pulled away, her fierce expression and watery eyes transformed to open curiosity as she stared behind her shoulder. "Who do we have here?" She gestured to Gabriel. "He looks familiar."

Wrapping an arm around her son's shoulders, she ushered him to her sister. "This is my son, Gabriel. Gabriel, meet one of your aunts, my sister Amelia."

By this time, Amelia's husband, Tavis, had joined her side, and she clutched at his arm. "Your son? How old is he?"

"I turned ten in January," he said. "You have pretty hair."

"Thank you, Gabriel." Though still a trifle pale, she extended her hand. "Beatrice, it seems we have much to talk about, but right now I'm a little overwhelmed, and perhaps in need of some biscuits. Would you care to join me, Gabriel? A long journey makes me hungry."

"Me too! Did you know you said a bad word to my mother?" Bea stifled her choked laughter as Amelia gifted her with a withering look.

She and Gabriel walked up the stairs to the house. "I suppose I did, though sometimes it is well-deserved, nephew. Your mother knows why."

His happy chatter faded away as they entered the house, the door closing behind them.

"It seems there is more to your story than you let on in your letter," her brother-in-law said.

"Perhaps. Maybe later, after I've seen Evie and settled in, I'll be ready to tell it. Help me with our baggage?"

"Leave it on the stairs. Someone will carry it in for you. If you're not too tired, we have business to discuss." He offered his arm and escorted her up the front stairs.

"I can't imagine what." She turned and allowed the butler to remove her cloak. Already two footmen had scurried outside and were bringing her luggage indoors.

Tavis motioned for her to follow him. "A letter arrived last week addressed to you. Amelia and I have been more than a little curious." He ushered her to a cozy wood-paneled study, and offered her a seat in an oversized chair near the fire. She warmed her hands and feet, a happy sigh escaping as tingling sensation returned to both sets of extremities. Tavis, who had gone to his desk to fetch the letter, returned and sat beside her. "Amelia was of a mind to open and read it to decide if there was sensitive news you might need to know upon your arrival."

"She comes by her nosiness honestly. I'd have tried the same," she said, taking the letter in hand. The wax seal was unrecognizable. "One person knows to send me a letter here, and we did not leave on good terms."

"Would you like me to read it for you?"

"Please. I don't have the strength to do it myself." She passed back the letter, which he opened and read aloud.

" 'Dear Beatrice, My father was hung a week ago. There was a sizable bounty on his head and a generous land grant for the one to bring him to justice. I declined and suggested the Prince Regent gift it to you. After all, your compassion is what stopped you from ending his life. I've enclosed the deed to the land grant, as well as a bank draft. Both should provide for you and your child for years to come. Yours Sincerely, Thomas Wickes.' Are you well? You've gone pale."

"I'm a wealthy woman, Tavis, honored by the Prince himself, yet I'd like nothing more than to toss the money back in Thomas Wickes's face."

"An unwise decision, given you'd be insulting our sovereign and throwing away a sizable gift."

"What do you suggest I do, if not return the funds to Mr. Wickes?"

"While you were away, circumstances surrounding your father's title and line of succession have been stalled in probate. Within the last several weeks, the muddle surrounding who inherits has cleared, and your father's heir arrives in six months to assume control of the estate. After discovering you were alive, I sent some inquiries regarding your share of your husband's estate, but because you were declared dead, the annual portion you received has been terminated. This money and land deed have arrived at the perfect time, for without them you would have no home and no money to provide for your child. My business is new, and while you can live here, right now there is little money to send your son to school. It's not impossible, but it will prove to be difficult."

"Which is why you're suggesting I keep the money."

"Establish yourself in any style you please and live a happy life."

He spoke sense, and though the money added to the debt she owed Thomas Wickes, she set it aside and considered the money as payment for the years she had served the man. "Pour me a glass of whisky, Tavis. I'm a wealthy woman. It's time to celebrate."

Tavis poured her a generous tumbler filled with the amber liquid. "What should we toast?"

"The future."

****

"Your son is delightful," Amelia said. Bea smiled and burrowed further into her cloak. After luncheon, word had arrived from the dower house, where Alfred and Evie lived. Evie was awake and able to receive visitors, Amelia explained, the recent toll of childbirth having left their younger sister weak and in need of constant care, so Bea, Gabriel, Amelia, and Tavis bundled in their outerwear to walk the mile to Evie's house. Tavis and Gabriel lagged behind, his uncle having decided to educate the lad on the proper way to form a snowball.

"He's wonderful," she agreed.

"Why didn't you say you had a son? We wouldn't have judged you. Even though we were younger, Evie and I would have found a way to support you. You believe me, don't you?"

"My life since leaving home has not been easy, and I've made the best choices given the circumstances."

Her green eyes flared. "What a pretty evasion, but nowhere near an answer, Beatrice."

She sighed. "It's all I can give you now. I promise, before we leave, I'll tell you everything."

"You'd better, because after the anguish you've put us through this last year, my patience for subterfuge and dishonesty has waned."

"Me too, Amelia. Me too." They rounded a corner, and the dower house loomed on the horizon. A modest two-story home, it boasted a wide front door, large windows, and a pleasant-looking wooded area behind the home. They were halfway up the walk when the door flew open, much as it had done at Amelia's, and

Alfred rushed to meet them. Enfolding her in his arms, he said, "I knew you were too stubborn to die, Beatrice. Thank God, you're here."

"Alfred! Bring her in," her younger sister yelled from inside.

"Motherhood has not dampened Evie's commanding charm, I see. Shouldn't she be above stairs in bed?"

He released her and smiled, though it didn't reach his eyes. "Your letter took us all by surprise. She was already weak from childbirth, but the shock you weren't dead sent her into a relapse of sorts. I carried her to the front sitting room after her nap. She's tucked on the settee, waiting for you."

"At her insistence."

"Of course. Come, she will want to see you before growing too weary."

Bea followed Alfred and entered the cozy home and removed her cloak. After giving him stern orders to behave, she left Gabriel with his uncles and entered the sitting room, Amelia close behind.

Evie was surrounded by blankets, her already delicate features made even more so by her recent illness and the strain of childbirth. Dark shadows circled her eyes, and anxious expectance wreathed her mouth in small lines. Bea could see her little sister had suffered, and she had prolonged her agony by refusing to come home.

Rushing to her side, she knelt at the settee and cupped her sister's hands in her own. "Evie, I'm so sorry."

"Whatever for?"

"For causing you and Amelia to suffer."

Evie framed her face with her small hands and smiled. "Your journey must have been difficult, for your grief, even after all these months, is so strong." She studied her, much as Master Jones had done the night they had parted. "But you are stronger now, my dear. I see a lightness in your soul which was absent when last we met."

"I was lost for a long time."

Evie's hands dropped to the blankets, and she sighed, resting her head against the pillows. "And now? Have you come home to us?"

She took her sister's hand and reached behind her for Amelia, who sat in a chair near the settee. "I need to tell you what happened, but it's a long, unpleasant story."

"Even now you hesitate, despite our reassurance and love. What is your fear, Beatrice? What can be worse than the isolation and separation you've inflicted upon yourself?" Amelia asked.

Her sister was right. Fear, her constant companion, was whispering its ugly lies, convincing her to remain quiet and avoid further heartache. Already, the urge to distance herself demanded action, and she experienced an intense sorrow as she imagined her sisters' loathing when they discovered what she'd done to survive. "I would not have you turn from me in disgust."

"Instead you condemn us for an act we've yet to commit," Evie said.

Amelia squeezed her hand. "Credit us with enough sense to know our own minds. We want to be a part of your life, which includes the good and the bad parts. You don't have to be alone anymore."

Bea hung her head. They asked her to trust them,

yet she was unwilling to offer the same consideration. "Trust is a muscle I've not exercised in a while. It doesn't come naturally. How do I start?"

"Start at the beginning, whenever that is," Evie said.

Amelia tucked a stray golden curl behind Bea's ear. "We'll be here in case you falter."

There was only one beginning, one event which had defined her childhood and had shaped her into the woman she was today, and she found, despite her reluctance, she knew where it all began. "I was eleven years old, and the gypsies had come for the summer. There was a boy named Luka."

Chapter 35

York, England, June 1811

Bea and Gabriel stayed in Scotland for six weeks, until the snow had melted and spring flowers were visible around the castle. The time spent with her sisters and their families was a precious gift. Surrounded by their love and acceptance, old wounds closed and she recovered scattered pieces of herself she'd abandoned when life's disappointments had demanded she do so. Saying goodbye was harder than she'd expected, but she promised to visit again, a vow she was eager to keep.

With a renewed heart, she and Gabriel left for home. Bea wanted one last summer in her childhood home before her father's heir came to take residence at Westby Manor in September. She wanted one last summer to show her son what made this part of England so special. They arrived in York as the trees blossomed, their fragrant flowers a welcome gift as she and Gabriel found their way home. However her happiness did not mask the growing restlessness spring's arrival brought.

April turned to May, and the days grew longer. The refreshing spring weather turned warm, and by the first week of June, summer had arrived. A persistent disquiet dogged her heels, and she spent her afternoons walking across the fields, showing Gabriel her favorite childhood haunts and regaling him with tales of her wild adventures. Her son's constant presence and the peace found at her childhood home marked her days with quiet contentment, but her nights brought a surge of restless yearning. Dreams of a dark-haired warrior flitted through her subconscious, whispering the name of the boy she'd never forgotten. Each morning she awoke empty, her arms reaching for someone who'd already gone.

One lazy June morning, she awoke before the cock crowed, having passed another restless night, and snuck out of the house in time to see the sun's pink rays kiss the eastern horizon. Her slippered feet sped across the dew-laden grass, her steps quickening as she flew across the fields to the eastern woods. Instinct drove her faster across the field, and when her skirts wrapped around her legs and slowed her pace, she pulled them over her knees and ran unhindered.

Please, let them be there today. There was a reason her daily walks took her to the eastern woods and why her dreams were filled with taunting images of the man she loved. Each night since returning to York, she'd wished for him to come, and each day she'd gone to the woods and found disappointment. After months of waiting, she'd awakened and known today they'd come.

By the time she reached the edge of the woods, her sides ached and her leg muscles screamed. She doubled over and sucked in large gulps of air, straining to hear above her pounding heart, but the woods were quiet. "When will I learn? Wishes are for children and those who believe in magic." She'd left the schoolroom long ago and had never believed in magic the way her sisters did. Her conviction the gypsies had returned was nothing more than optimistic fantasy.

Laughter floated though the air, and hope beat like a thousand winged birds in her chest. Maybe magic was real after all. She navigated through the woods to the clearing beyond. Horses neighed, and the sweet smell of crushed hay tickled her nose. Colorful tents and wagons filled the clearing, and people milled about, laughing as they set up camp. She clutched a large tree trunk to steady herself, and rested her cheek against the rough bark, drinking in the familiar sight.

A spry, gray-haired woman with wild curls wrestled with a length of rope. The wind whipped through the clearing and snatched the line from her hand. She pushed her curls from her eyes and tied back her hair in a vibrant purple scarf before securing the final end of rope to a wagon. Her heart squeezed in her chest. Aba had returned with the family. The old woman had once told her she'd never travel again, much preferring the comfort of her little cottage in her advanced age than the incessant inconvenience of a nomadic life. She didn't question why Aba had broken her word and left her cozy island home, for Luka strode into the clearing. Tall, broad-shouldered, and strong, he stopped to help an elderly couple as they struggled to set up their home. He bent over to secure a pole, and his black hair gleamed in the early morning light. When he stood, the older couple laughed and slapped him on the back, causing him to smile and stoop to hug the older woman. His eyes scanned the clearing, a leader looking for others in need of assistance—and he spied her.

His entire body stiffened, and he stared at her. The

force of those warm, brown eyes flew across the clearing and spanned decades. Once again she was eleven, and he was her home.

Luka strode across the clearing in the time it took for her to raise her hand in greeting. His large hand raised to cup her cheek but dropped to hang at his side, nervous and unsure. Bea's own fingers curled, anxious to touch him after so many months apart. She had no words to describe the joy she experienced upon seeing him in their clearing, yet they were as awkward as when they'd first met. An impish smile touched her lips as she found the perfect greeting for this man she'd loved forever. Channeling her inner eleven-year-old, she said, "Aren't you going to say something? It's rude to stare. You do know that, don't you?"

Luka smiled, a slow, wicked upturn of his lips, as he caught on to her little game, and her heartbeat sped.

She cocked her head to one side, and stepped closer to the raw heat emanating from his sun-kissed body. Trailing her hand over his muscle-hardened torso, she peered at him from beneath her lashes. "Are you slow?" She placed each lingering caress with precision to aid in his comprehension.

He closed the distance between them and snaked an arm about her waist, pulling her tight against his body to better nuzzle the sensitive cords along her neck. "I am not."

"Of course you're not." She pressed soft kisses along his firm jaw. "But if you were slow, I imagine that is what you would say, hmm?" She captured his lips in a kiss, and his embrace tightened.

"Woman, you may speak to me any way you wish, for I have been and always will be yours."

"I came here today hoping yet never imagining you'd be here. Returning to England was one of the hardest things I've ever had to do. When Cosette showed me the portion of the letter you read, I broke, Luka. To hurt you in such a manner, unintentional as it was, broke me, and I couldn't stay, or even follow you."

"So I followed you. You did nothing wrong. Once again it was my foolish pride which caused you harm."

She smoothed her hands over the linen shirt covering his chest and fiddled with the ties at his neck, not ready to discuss what had happened in Paris. "How did you enter the country without being extradited?"

"I might have mentioned the approximate whereabouts of a strategic military stronghold in Paris. Before traveling here, I stopped in London and spoke to Thomas. He helped me petition the government for a pardon, so I was no longer a wanted man. We're free to come and go as we please."

"Thomas and I didn't part on the best of terms, but I'm not surprised he helped you. He believes himself to be an honorable man, though his choices have been less so."

"Add reticence to his list of faults. I had to push before he told me what he had done to you. I almost killed him."

"I did, too. He was wrong in so many ways, but as much as I wish to hate him, I pity him. He was offered a precious gift, and he warped it with his deceit and thirst for vengeance."

"My own actions were inexcusable. Despite the precious gift you gave me, I didn't trust you or us. Old fears were resurrected and I was a young man again, scared and convinced I was not enough to hold your interest. Your letter confirmed what I already believed. It was too much to credit you'd chosen me, so I ran before giving you a chance to explain."

"What changed your mind?"

"If you recall my telling you, I sulked and brooded for almost a year after leaving you ten years ago, and the same happened this time. Anyone past the age of two remembered my moody self-obsession then and flat-out refused to follow my command during this most recent bout of melancholy. One week after I arrived to find my family safe in Russia, the clan had enough of my black moods and decided to return to England. On the way to port, I stopped at Cosette's, hoping you were there. She let me know what had happened and where you were going. After leaving Paris, I became a man possessed, and pushed us hard to reach York before summer. I have an important question I want to ask you, in the same place we met, and to tell you I'm not going anywhere."

"If you're here to stay, why is your family here? Are they staying as well?"

"Fortier and Andres will lead them back to the Continent at the end of summer. They traveled with me for another reason."

"Have you asked her yet?" Aba shouted across the clearing.

Luka grimaced, pressed a quick kiss to Bea's lips, and yelled over his shoulder, "Quiet, you nosey old woman. I'm getting to it."

Gentle laughter floated on the breeze, and Aba's voice when she replied was laced with amusement. "Get to it faster. We're all waiting to hear what she says."

"When I say what?" Bea asked.

He grabbed her hand and pressed a kiss to it. "Will you marry me, Beatrice Josephine Westby? You are my soul's companion and the reason my heart beats. Will you be my partner and my wife?"

"Yes, Luka." She wrapped her arms around his neck, and their lips met in a gentle kiss. Loud cheering, punctuated by shrill whistles, surrounded them, and Bea raised her head to see Luka's family watching, their faces wreathed in joyful smiles. One young smiling face stood out, her fat brown braids bouncing as she squealed and clapped.

Bea smiled and waved. "It's Amy. How did she get here?"

"Fighting has increased in the peninsula, and Cosette worries about a resurgence of violence in Paris. She wants Amy safe, and I assured her we'd give her a loving home, if you are agreeable."

"Of course I'm in agreement," she said. Amy waved back before leaving with Aba, her cheerful voice like music carried on the summer breeze. "Mother, Mother!" Bea spun around and watched as Gabriel raced across the field to the tree where she and Luka stood. Ignoring the man beside her, her son tugged on her hands and spun her about. "Grandma Agatha said the Rom have come. Uncle Jack says they haven't come in years! Can I meet them?"

Laughing, Bea pulled her son into her arms and pressed her forehead to his, winded from their impromptu spin around the clearing. "Look behind you, and you'll see."

He twisted around, his bright eyes curious.

"Hullo," he said to Luka who had blanched and grabbed the tree for support. "I'm Gabriel Westby." He bowed, a short perfunctory bending of the waist. "Who are you?"

Luka's mouth opened and closed, but no sound emerged. His beautiful eyes, so like their son's, drank in the sight of the gangly boy, whose golden skin, impish smile, and black hair declared him none other than child of his seed.

Placing a hand on her son's shoulder, she ushered him closer to Luka, who was too overcome to do much more than clutch the tree and stare. "Gabriel, this is Luka Stefano, your father," Bea said to the boy.

"You have a lot to explain, Mr. Stefano," Gabriel said, his black eyes snapping. The boy's ire jolted Luka out of his stupor, for he released the tree and cleared his throat. "I do, but I want to spend the rest of my life making amends to you and your mother, if you'll let me."

Gabriel's hand snuck into hers as he stared at his sire. "Are you going to go away and make my mother cry again? Mother cried heaps this spring when she thought no one was around to hear her. You are not to hurt her again. I forbid it." Bea longed to intervene and smooth things over for both her men, but Luka had to find his way with their son, as she had done.

"I'm here to stay. I want to be a good husband to your mother and, with your permission, a good father to you."

"Who's that lady staring at me?" Gabriel asked, pointing to Aba, who stood near their little circle. Bea chuckled and ruffled her son's hair. His young, curious mind did not stay focused on one topic for long. Family was his current obsession, and he had pestered her for weeks about hers until she'd drawn him a detailed family tree. He'd been disappointed at the small size. With Aba here, Gabriel was soon going to discover another branch to his family tree, starting with his great-grandma.

"I'm your grandmother, boy."

He cocked his head and studied Aba. "I've got a grandma. Grandma Agatha makes me biscuits and cakes and tells the best stories. Can you do that?"

"No, but I can whittle a stick, catch fish with my bare hands, and spit farther than any man," she said.

Gabriel licked his lips, eagerness brightening his face. "Perhaps you can show me this spitting business."

"Come with me. I've a new granddaughter, too, whose spitting education is almost as lamentable as yours. I'll introduce you to some of your cousins on the way. They'll want to see you're properly educated, too." Aba offered her hand, and Gabriel fitted his own within it.

"You'll be here when I'm done?" he said over his shoulder to Luka.

"I'm not going anywhere." The boy nodded and went with Aba. They were halfway back to camp when he whispered something in the old woman's ear and sprinted back to the tree where Bea and Luka sagged against its weathered trunk. He barreled into Luka's stomach, wrapped his arms about his middle and squeezed before he turned and raced back to Aba, yelling over his shoulder as he ran, "That's so you don't forget me while I'm gone!"

Curling an arm about Bea's waist, he rested his cheek on her hair. "We have a son," he said.

She snuggled in his embrace. "He's a joy, Luka. You're going to love him."

"I already do."

Her son grew smaller in the distance, but she didn't worry. He was safe with Aba and his new sister, Amy. "Aba is going to corrupt our son."

"It's an important skill every child should have. Isn't it?" His brows furrowed. "God, I can't credit I'm a father. What a terrifying prospect!"

Her gentle laughter eased his frown.

"What's so funny?"

"Us. I'm as terrified as you."

"Doubtful. You've had months to acquaint yourself with him. I've known about his existence for less than a half hour."

"You'll be fine. We both will. We have years to figure out how to be parents, so no more distractions, Luka Stefano. Our children are currently learning the fine art of spitting, and your family have all returned to other tasks, leaving us alone."

"What do you have in mind?" he asked, his nimble fingers feathering along her spine to cup her curved bottom.

"My sisters have informed me that, with children underfoot, it is important to seek time together whenever possible. Since we are alone for the time being, you have years of kisses to make up for. I suggest you begin making amends."

"With pleasure." His slow smile when it came melted her insides and buckled her knees. With a gentle push, he settled her against the tree and slanted his mouth atop hers. The rough trunk dug into her back, but she didn't care. Luka's arms enfolded her, keeping her where she belonged.

****

They were married a week later, on summer's solstice, choosing to wed in the clearing beyond the eastern woods where they'd met as young children. She wore a simple dress of pale green, with bluebells woven in her curly locks. Gabriel, after some tense moments with his father, accepted the man was staying, made a tentative peace with him, and agreed to give her away. Amy was her attendant, the young girl dressed in a new gown of rosy pink. Her elation at being a part of the ceremony rivaled the discovery she was part of a family again. Gabriel adored his new sister and accepted her presence more readily than his father's, but these were early days. Bea fully expected both of her men to love each other as much as she loved them. After all, she was delightful.

As the sky darkened and the family prepared to celebrate the longest day of the year, Luka's family, along with Agatha, Uncle Jack, and Grant, gathered around a large bonfire. The lively strains of a country dance floated above the crackling fire. More musicians joined the lone flautist, and a steady beat accompanied the light airy tune. Beatrice grabbed Amy's hand and they danced around the fire. A small hand grasped her free one, and she smiled into her son's bright eyes; they twirled and spun around the flames. Luka grabbed onto their son, while Aba joined in next to Amy. With each addition to their dancing line, Bea's joy crested higher and higher as they danced in an unending circle of love and family. The music carried her feet around the ever-growing fire, her curls tumbling about her flushed cheeks. Flames bathed her face in light and shadow, and she closed her eyes, savoring the weight of her children's hands in hers. The simple band Luka had given her warmed her skin, and she welcomed the press of metal against her finger. Happiness bubbled within her until it burst free, and she threw back her head and laughed. After years of searching, Beatrice Westby had finally come home.

A word about the author...

Sara Ackerman is a lifetime lover of words. After years of encouraging students to write, she finally took her own advice and "sat down and did it already." She lives in southwestern Wisconsin where she was born and raised.

She loves to read all genres of books, though her true love is historical romance. Unsurprisingly, that is what she can be found reading when she is not writing. Her particular favorites include Jane Austen alternative histories.

When not found with a nose in a book or in her writing lair, Sara enjoys superheroes, believes in magic, and loves spending time with her family (but not necessarily in that order).

You can visit her at:

http://seackerman.com